# LETHBRIDGE-STEWART
## THE SCHIZOID EARTH

Based on the BBC television serials by
Mervyn Haisman & Henry Lincoln

## David A McIntee
### Foreword by Amanda Haisman

CANDY JAR BOOKS · CARDIFF
*A Russell & Frankham-Allen Series*
2015

Copyright © David A McIntee 2015

*Characters and Concepts from 'The Web of Fear'*
*© Hannah Haisman & Henry Lincoln*
*HAVOC developed by and © Andy Frankham-Allen & Shaun Russell*
*The Vault © Gary Russell*

Doctor Who is © British Broadcasting Corporation, 1963, 2015.

Editor: Shaun Russell
Deputy Editor: Andy Frankham-Allen
Cover: Nathan Hudson & Adrian Salmon
Editorial: Hayley Cox & Brian Jones
Licensed by Hannah Haisman

Published by
Candy Jar Books
Mackintosh House
136 Newport Road, Cardiff, CF24 1DJ
www.candyjarbooks.co.uk

A catalogue record of this book is available
from the British Library

ISBN: 978-0-9933221-1-2

*For Nick Courtney*
*and the memory of all those who are no longer with us but who*
*made the Brigadier such a memorable and wonderful character*

# The Man Behind The Legend

My father created a *Doctor Who* legend. There are not many who can say that.

When I was born my father and mother had their own repertory company. It was not the most comfortable welcome into the world; we lived in a small caravan which my parents had toured in for the first six months of my life. It was 16ft long by 7ft wide and had no insulation. I was told how we would wake up and the bedclothes would be stuck to the wall. Not comfortable at all.

My father had some hard thinking to do and tough decisions to make. He might have wanted to be an actor but he had a family to keep. With this in mind, he decided to get a job in life insurance, thinking initially it would be for six months until he could get himself back on his feet. It took him ten years! We had a detached house, a car, a television, and a lovely au pair called Guri, and yet my father hated the life. Luckily my mother told him that if it was making him unhappy, he had to get out of life insurance and back to the theatre. For stability my father stuck with the day job, but in the evenings he wrote. A lot of what he wrote was, naturally, rubbish, as it often is when starting out and holding down a full-time job and family, but eventually he got better and better.

*

My father had met up with an actor called Henry Soskin whilst working on *No Hiding Place*. At this time we lived in Twickenham and Henry lived in Kew; they used to meet up from time to time. It was at one of these meetings when Henry told my father about his friend Patrick Troughton who lived around the corner from him. Patrick was enjoying his time on *Doctor Who* but was less keen on the adventures in space. He didn't want to be dealing with monsters in weird planets; Patrick wanted to deal with monsters on this Earth.

My father and Henry wondered whether they could do anything about it. It started them thinking. Their first thought was to do something with the Loch Ness Monster as it was a creature that everyone knew about, yet nobody had ever conclusively proved its existence. But then they came up with the idea for the Yeti. This was put forward to the *Doctor Who* production office and they were asked to write a treatment for it, which they did. The *Doctor Who* production office liked the concept and my father and Henry were commissioned to write a six-part serial; it was the start of a great writing partnership. Henry didn't want to be credited under his real name, since he used it when acting. He preferred to write under the name of Henry Lincoln, thus keeping the acting and writing separate.

As a child, it was lovely to have my father around all the time, even though he spent most of his day tucked away in a smoke-filled study. When he started writing *Doctor Who*, I have great memories of going to the recording sessions, seeing the very wonky sets and meeting the actors. It was amazing for me to see my father's name on the credits. And now, as an adult, and a mother myself, it's wonderful to see my father's work being honoured by Candy Jar Books. I don't think that, even in his last days, my father ever realised how popular his writing was. Since his passing a number of his creations have become more popular.

My father was a lovely, friendly man, ahead of his time and with a huge personality, and we all miss him dearly. At the time he was simply doing what he loved: writing. And in so doing, he created a legacy of which we are all so very proud.

*Amanda Haisman*

T he window beside his ear splintered with a startling crack as something dented the Land Rover's door. Colonel Alistair Lethbridge-Stewart winced instinctively as the oncoming traffic flashed past the side of his head, so close that it almost felt as if it had gone through him, and that the pain would soon catch up.

In the driver's mirror, the olive-green jeep that he had sideswiped was weaving back and forth, trying to get into a good position for the man standing at the rear-mounted machine gun.

The cracks of the shots were almost lost to the rush of wind past the Land Rover, but the bullets punched through its steel skin as easily as through any tin can. Metallic clangs punched the air behind him, and the passenger seat spat chunks of leather and foam. Spider webs exploded like lightning across the rear window, and something stung Lethbridge-Stewart's ear with white heat. He stomped on the accelerator.

The crumpled door swayed open and clanked closed, making the Land Rover handle a little drunkenly. Lethbridge-Stewart pulled it shut with his left hand, but the catch didn't engage, and it fell open again, almost pulling him out.

The jeep was almost level with him on the left side, the gunner standing in the back re-cocked the machine gun as he swung the muzzle around to aim down at Lethbridge-Stewart. He stamped on the brake, downshifting violently.

Jolting forward, he saw the jeep shoot past, tearing the loose door off with a judder and a bang, and sending it tumbling across the macadam. A sharp wind stung his cheek. In front, the gunner swung around in his mount, trying not to stand in the driver's lap. Lethbridge-Stewart's hand came off the gear stick and rooted around in the glove compartment for the pistol there. His fingers wrapped around the cold metal, and he thumbed off the safety catch. Weaving slightly with the wheel in his left, he rested his hand on the glass-strewn dash, and began to fire steady shots through the jagged windscreen frame, aiming for the gunner.

Sparks flew from the back of the jeep, and from the steel back of its driver's seat, but then the gunner fell from his twisted position, blood bubbling from his thigh. He flailed around in the back of the jeep, and the driver was forced to hit the brakes. Lethbridge-Stewart wrenched the wheel, veering aside just in time to avoid running straight into the back of the jeep. He risked a glance into the mirror, but wasn't stupid enough to turn his head, and saw two more jeeps in hot pursuit, sweeping around the one that had stopped.

The pistol was empty, and Lethbridge-Stewart couldn't reload it while driving, so he dropped it into the foot well and accelerated past the jeep. He jinked the wheel to the left, his tyres almost dropping into the roadside ditch. A saloon car and a small sedan in quick succession had to straddle the centre dividing line as they hurtled past, but they at least kept the jeeps on their side of the road.

Ahead, a stone bridge crossed a narrow river, and a stout signpost promised that the Suffolk village of Deepdene was on the other side. The road was already shrinking into a single lane, and Lethbridge-Stewart stamped on the accelerator, making sure to get onto the bridge before the jeeps. He didn't want to risk one of them blocking him in on it.

The Land Rover shot across the bridge and darted around another oncoming sedan. Lethbridge-Stewart hoped the driver wouldn't hit a jeep head-on, but knew that they'd at least have to slow down to let him off the bridge. Either way, the sedan should buy him some much-needed time. The quaint brick houses and front gardens of Deepdene were approaching rapidly, and Lethbridge-Stewart began evaluating options for getting off the road he was on.

A newsagent's van tottered, top-heavy, as it tried to swerve out of his way. Metal crumpled with a deafening boom that drowned out his exclamation as the Land Rover sideswiped it. Lethbridge-Stewart squeezed his eyes shut against the sudden blizzard of glass that filled the air, and fought to stay in the seat without being flung sideways out of the vehicle. The windows hadn't been able to fold as much as the steel panel. Two more jeeps were growing in the rear-view mirror.

He kept his leg locked out, foot jammed on the gas pedal, and opened his eyes again as the Land Rover surged forward. A spray of *Radio Times* magazines, Elvis Presley staring out from them, fell across the road like cards flipped by a magician who was all thumbs. They fell out of his vision just in time for him to twist the wheel, and narrowly avoid hitting a running pedestrian. He mashed the clutch, kicking it as he gunned for the corner. The tail of the Land Rover swung wide, carrying it sideways across the pavement, and Lethbridge-Stewart floored it down another street.

He took his mind off the wave of nausea by cocking his pistol, and looked back in time to see one of the pursuing jeeps try the same trick. The jeep didn't make it; a rear tyre burst, ripped apart by the sideways drag across the macadam, and the jeep slammed side-on into the grocer's window, coming to rest among a snowstorm of shattered glass fragments. The other jeep's driver took the more sensible precaution of slowing down as it reached the corner.

That was just what Lethbridge-Stewart had hoped for. He revved the engine, barrelling directly for another hairpin turn into a narrow alley. 'If I'm lucky I could lose them here,' he murmured.

The sides of the vehicle struck sparks from the walls on either side, and then he was back in the open air, bouncing across a patch of green towards a small duck pond. A copse of trees stood on the far side, and Lethbridge-Stewart thought it an ideal place to ditch the Land Rover while he was out of eyesight of his pursuers.

A dark shape dashed his hopes by emerging from the copse, eight wheels churning the mud as it forded the pond towards him. Lethbridge-Stewart recognised it at once from Czechoslovakian news coverage as a Russian armoured car. A BTR-60 they called it in the recognition manuals.

Its turret swung round, the muzzle spat flame, and Lethbridge-Stewart found himself hauling on the wheel as gouts of earth burst upwards in his path. The world tumbled,

4

and then came crashing down upon the Land Rover's roof, the vehicle's steel skin howling and screaming as it flexed and dented.

Lethbridge-Stewart struggled to keep his eyes open, but sank anyway, lurching down into warm darkness. As the world faded, he heard a faint voice.

'He almost made it this time.'

'Yes,' another voice agreed, further away. The voice sounded lighter, perhaps even female. 'He's almost ready.'

'Almost isn't quite good enough.'

'He will be ready,' the lighter voice said. 'It's inevitable.'

If anything else was said, Lethbridge-Stewart never heard.

# CHAPTER ONE

# *Episode One*

Maurice Palmer could hear them out there. They were being as quiet as they could, not marching or talking, but the fastenings on their equipment tinkled, and the leaves and branches rustled as they moved. They were just trying to hide their numbers and direction, he supposed, not the fact that they were there at all.

He turned to Sergeant Craig, wondering what he thought they were up to, but as Palmer drew breath, Craig put a finger to his lips. The sergeant's eyes glinted, seeming to dare him to say a word, and Palmer bit his tongue. On the far side of the road, the woods sloped away from a trench filled with overgrown brambles. The mass of plants looked like rusty barbed wire, and Palmer was sure it would hurt as much if he tried to go through it.

A thunderclap shook the trees, and something exploded some way behind Palmer. He looked round and saw smoke above the railway line a couple of hundred yards beyond the road.

'Bloody artillery,' Craig muttered, as another shell arced across and hit a water tower by the railhead, toppling it.

One of the soldiers scrambled along beside him, and pointed. 'It's over there, Sarge. About forty yards.'

'Right, lad.' Craig signalled to a couple of other soldiers, directing them towards the shaking leaves from which a gout of fire had just flashed. 'Hodge, get word back to Battalion. Give them the map reference and tell them we're under artillery fire, and need more support.'

'Right, Sarge,' a voice replied quietly.

The conversation had been loud enough. A pair of what looked like stubby peg-legs tumbled through the air and thudded to the ground a few feet away and bounced towards them. Everyone flung themselves aside, instants before the stick grenades exploded. Palmer felt something gash his leg with searing heat. Shots rang out after the blasts, and a couple of the soldiers rose to their knees to return fire.

'*Hurra! Vorwärts für den Kaiser!*' The shouts were audible even over the crack of rifle fire. They came out of the woods suddenly. At least thirty men in grey-green uniforms with red piping. There were little spikes on the crowns of their leather helmets, and all were wearing gas masks. Palmer flung himself into the mud and brambles as bullets snapped overhead. He could hear Sergeant Craig and his men. For the first time in his career, he wished he had a proper weapon, rather than a satchel full of correspondence gear. At least the real soldiers could shoot back.

Another shell boomed out, with an accompanying explosion from the railhead, and suddenly a hand grabbed Palmer's collar and dragged him to his feet. He flailed his arms in an admittedly useless attempt at fighting off his assailant, but then realised it was Craig. The sturdy sergeant pushed him forward.

'Come on, lad, they're flanking us!'

Palmer ran, already imagining bullets tearing through him. There was gunfire all around, branches whipping at

7

his legs, arms, and face. He had no idea where he was going.

Two nightmare creatures with huge black bulging eyes and grotesquely stretched-out heads burst from the undergrowth, huffing and snorting. For a moment Palmer thought he must have been hit in the head and was seeing things. Then he realised that they were horses, wearing some sort of gross gas masks themselves, and that he had actually burst into the clearing where they were tied. The horses flinched and whickered as a deafening report took the wind from Palmer's lungs. He looked beyond the animals, and saw a gun carriage with a jet black howitzer on thick iron wheels like the ones on a fairground traction engine. Palmer darted to the side of the horses, and kept going.

A soldier in grey-green leaped to his feet, reaching for a Luger pistol, but Palmer was too close to stop in time, and both men tumbled to the ground. The Luger bounced into a clump of nettles, and Palmer flailed wildly at the German soldier. His wild punches somehow knocked the man's head back into the ground, and Palmer immediately straddled him, trying to secure his arms so he couldn't fight back or reach for the gun.

The soldier yelled instead. '*Der Engländer hat mich!*'

Two more German soldiers came running, but bloody blooms flowered on their chests before they could stop and work the bolts on their rifles.

Sergeant Craig and a handful of men rushed into the clearing, rifles still raised. 'Well done, lad.'

Palmer was still too stunned to think straight. He knew he had a hell of a story, but that could wait until he stopped shaking. 'What now?'

'We haven't got the gear to demolish this howitzer,'

Craig admitted. 'So let's hope Hodge made it through. Those Jerries are going to want to take this gun back.'

Palmer's heart sank; already he could hear men advancing through the trees. At least there was cover near the gun, as the Germans had set up a low wall of sandbags around it.

The British troops, and Palmer, took up position behind the sandbags, and the bullets began to fly again. Grey-green figures darted through the trees, appearing from behind the wood to fire, and then disappearing again. The man Palmer had knocked down lay nearby, his hands cuffed by one of Craig's men. Palmer glanced over and saw that he was staring intently at Craig's rifle, with a strange expression. It was almost as if the man had never seen one before, or as if he was concussed.

Craig noticed too, and paused to backhand the prisoner. 'Don't get any funny ideas,' he warned.

Grenades hurtled in, but exploded out of range, and Palmer suspected they were just trying to provoke the British to run again. They surely wouldn't want to risk blowing up their own gear.

'They'll rush us,' Craig warned. 'Get ready.'

Everyone except Palmer reloaded and re-cocked, and Palmer belatedly remembered the Luger the prisoner had dropped. He picked it up, heavy in his hand, and tried to work the mechanism. It stuck.

Then the Germans were running forward again, shooting as they came. One or two dropped, hit by British fire, but not nearly enough.

There was a whirring from overhead, and the German prisoner's eyes suddenly widened. Palmer flinched instinctively as a whirlybird swooped down. He thought it was a Westland Scout, but couldn't swear to it. The horses pulled against the ropes that kept them from wandering while, among the trees, the German soldiers looked up, confused. A couple raised their rifles uncertainly, but none got round to firing.

Sergeant Craig suddenly popped up and hurled a canister out towards the attackers. Thick red smoke began to billow from it. The helicopter immediately seemed to spin on its axis, and swooped again. Now Palmer could see that there were two machine guns mounted on its landing skids, their muzzles blazing.

A good half of the German soldiers, and both of the horses, went down, blood and mud splashing across the ditch. The Scout roared overhead, and wheeled again. This time the Germans began to drop their weapons and raise their hands.

Palmer was slightly surprised to see his trusty – and rusty – Kadett A still sitting beside the platoon's Bedford three-tonners, where he had left it. He almost fell into the driver's seat, shaking, and pulled a hip-flask from the glove compartment. Hopefully a shot of scotch would steady his nerves.

He emptied his satchel onto the passenger seat, and was relieved to see that his portable tape recorder was undamaged. He wasn't ready to listen to what was on it, not yet.

He heard more vehicles approach, and looked out to see two Land Rover ambulances and another pair of three-tonners pull up. Several Royal Military Police and provost troops, in their red-trimmed caps, dropped from the back one of the new trucks, and conferred with Craig for a moment. From the gestures Palmer saw, it wasn't that amicable a discussion. The provosts then escorted the German prisoners back to their truck.

Sergeant Craig's men were by now helping the newly arrived medics see to the dead and wounded. Palmer would have dearly loved to know what the Redcaps had said to him, but he knew that Craig wouldn't tell him. Palmer kept looking, feeling strangely ignored and forgotten, as a couple of the Redcaps walked past with enemy equipment they'd gathered up. Two more were patrolling in a low crouch, stopping again to pick up things from the ground; cartridge cases, coins, fag ends. Palmer couldn't see, but whatever they picked up, they put in a canvas bag.

He almost jumped out of his seat as something rapped the window behind his ear. It was an RMP corporal, with a medic. 'Open the door, please,' the corporal said. He was small and wiry, but had the air of someone you didn't want to muck about with. Palmer opened the door. 'Just want to make sure you're all right,' he said gruffly. 'Were you hit?'

'Uh, no, no... Thank you, Corporal. I'm just a bit... surprised.'

'First time under fire?'

'Yeah. Not a lot of firefights at Lindenalle or Parkstrasse.'

The corporal dismissed the medic with a slight twitch of the head. 'You're staying at Lindenalle, or have you got yourself a flat?'

'Lindenalle. Still looking; you know how it is.'

'I'll have someone drive you back.' The corporal beckoned to another Redcap. 'You've had a shock, you'll

11

need to be debriefed, and I can smell the whisky from here.'

'I'll be all right—'

'You want to get drunk and crash, that's your business, but not before we've got a written report out of you.' He pulled Palmer out of the car, and guided him round to the passenger side. 'Or we can just give you a ride with us.' Palmer shook his head, and got in the passenger side. The corporal nodded to the Redcap who was now in the driver's seat. 'Civilian mess number six, Tom. Make sure he's OK, and wait for the SIB to take his statement.'

He awoke with a start, his flailing arm knocking the handset from its cradle. His fingers scrabbled around for it. 'Larry Greene speaking,' he said.

'Larry? It's Maurice Palmer.' The Bermondsey twang was all but hidden by a distant metallic echo to the line.

'Maurice...? Oh, yes, of course...' Greene dropped the hint of Alan Whicker that he liked to put in his voice in professional dealings. 'I thought you'd gone off to Europe. BFBS, wasn't it?'

'British Forces Broadcasting Service, best in... well, Cologne, anyway.'

'Nice there?' Greene wasn't really interested in life in Cologne, but it would buy him a few more moments to wake up.

'Nice enough, but something happened that... I dunno, sounds like something off the telly. I dunno what made me think of telling you, but... There's nobody else who'd believe it.'

That did interest Greene. 'Why would I believe whatever it is?'

'I dunno. But you're chums with Harold Chorley, right? And he was there in London, in the Underground, right? I heard a lot of weird things about that.'

'So did I.'

'Thought so. But Chorley's pretty unreliable, and I know you sometimes work for the BBC, so you must have some clout. So I thought of you...'

Greene sighed. In for a penny. 'So, what was it?'

'Can you meet me?'

'You're back in England?'

'No. Here in Cologne.'

'Oh, of course. On my salary I can jet off to Europe at the drop of a hat, can't I?'

'No need to be like that, Larry,' Maurice protested. 'There's transport if you want it. You'd be a good guest for one of our Current Affairs slots, wouldn't you? A leading BBC broadcaster known for working well with the...'

Greene nodded to himself; that sounded fair enough, even if he'd been dumped by the BBC after trying to help Chorley. A trip would do him some good.

'If you'll come, that is,' Maurice added.

'All right. Where and when?'

Maurice had been as good as his word. A courier had brought a BEA return ticket round to Greene's flat two days later. Not a First Class seat – thanks to Chorley, his star had fallen too far for that – but Greene didn't mind. He was just relieved that he wasn't going to have to travel by ferry and SNCF and Deutsche Bahn trains. Exactly one week to the hour since Maurice had phoned, Larry Greene walked across the tarmac at Gatwick to board a gleaming white

Trident airliner that bore a thin line of royal blue along the side, and a parcel-label shaped section of Union Flag on the tailfin. They called that the 'Speedjack', Greene recalled. Greene had reported a couple of times on a government body, the Edwards Committee, which had been set up to look at the future of British transport. There was a rumour that they would come out in favour of merging BEA and BOAC into one airline, but Greene mainly just hoped that they would change that damned insignia, and its name. He also hoped that someone would engage him to report on the eventual publishing of their findings.

For now he simply enjoyed the flight, if not the lunch served aboard, and dozed off until the Trident touched down at the rain-damped *Flughafen Köln-Bonn*. In a way he was glad of the cloud cover, as he'd forgotten to bring the sunglasses he had bought on his last trip to America. He didn't even have shaded lenses to clip over his normal glasses.

Something inoffensive and jazzy was playing over the too-echoey speakers in the airport concourse into which he walked after collecting his one suitcase. Maurice was waiting for him. Greene didn't at first recognise the taller, lankier man who stepped forward with a hand extended to shake. 'Larry! You haven't changed a bit.' Maurice himself had changed a lot since they had last met; he had grown a moustache and longer hair for starters.

'You've gone native,' Greene said.

'Maybe just a bit,' Maurice admitted. His eyes flicked to either side, as if he was afraid he was being followed, which made Greene a little nervous. 'Come on, my car's outside.'

They exited the airport, and made their way to a rusting white Opel Kadett in the car park. 'I tried to persuade them to arrange a proper car,' Maurice said, 'or at least a taxi, but they said they couldn't spring for that when I had a car I could pick you up in anyway.'

'Not to worry, Maurice. I'm sure your car's fine.' *If the wheels don't fall off at the first pothole*, Greene thought.

'Yeah, well, it's not the newer model, but I've never had any problems with it.'

They made small talk as they drove into Cologne, and to a large white building on the Lindenalle.

'I've got a bunk sorted out for you,' Maurice said. 'Nothing fancy, but at least it's a private room. Or you can go to a hotel or B&B if you prefer, but the BFBS won't pick up the tab for that. If you're worried about squaddies knocking about with their hobnailed boots, you can relax. We're all civilian MOD and BFBS contractors at this mess.'

Greene nodded. 'Not worried at all.'

He followed Maurice through the warren of corridors in the building, and into a tiny cubbyhole barely big enough for the camp bed that was laid out in it. There was a shared bathroom at the end of the hall. Maurice left Greene to freshen up and change. Greene's suits were all fairly similar, lest he need to appear on camera at short notice, but for this trip he had brought a more casual jumper and tweed jacket to change into, in the hope it would put Maurice more at ease. Not that Maurice was usually anything but.

Until now, that had been the case, anyway. His voice had lost the faint edge of suppressed stress that it had had on the telephone last week, but there were more tension lines on his face than Greene remembered. It was agonising to not ask him to spill the beans yet, but Greene managed to hold off until they had eaten, in number six civilian mess, adjoining the BFBS headquarters.

Over a pint in the NAAFI bar afterward, Greene could wait no longer. 'All right, Maurice. You called me to come over here about a story. Well, here I am. So, what is it that had you so worked up?'

Maurice looked around. There were only a few people in the bar this early in the evening, and none of them were looking his way. 'We'll need to go to my quarters. There are some things you'll need to hear.'

'Then tell me them.'

'No, no, I mean tape recordings. Evidence, you might say.'

'Well then, there's no time like the present.'

To Greene's surprise there was a soldier waiting outside the door to Maurice's quarters. A stocky sergeant wearing the Yorkshire Regiment's badge on his cap. 'Larry,' Maurice said, 'Sergeant Craig.'

'Is he here to keep an eye on us?'

'To help me tell you the story,' Maurice said.

'A bit of both,' Craig corrected them. 'So, Palmer, are we doing this in here, or in the office?'

'The office.' Maurice led them past his quarters, and down into the working area of the BFBS headquarters. They turned a corner and went past a couple of glass-walled recording booths filled with mixing desks and microphones, then up another short flight of stairs. Maurice unlocked a steel door, letting them all into a cramped control room. It was fairly familiar to Greene, very much like a typical BBC control gallery, but smaller, to fit into the space available in the 19th Century building. A row of mixing desks and editing equipment overlooked the recording booths they had already passed, and there was even a TV monitor with what looked like video playback equipment.

All three squeezed into the room, and Maurice immediately began threading a tape into a recording deck. 'I was on my way to cover an exercise,' he began. 'You know, get a few cheery quotes from our lads, to intersperse with music on a show at the weekend.' Greene nodded his understanding, as Maurice continued. 'It'd go out on other BFBS stations a week or two later – in Britain, Hong Kong, wherever.' Greene had listened to some British Forces Broadcasting Service shows while living alongside the troops before.

'At first it was just a normal thing, Larry. I got some quotes, watched Sergeant Craig's set up, how they'd defend an important railhead from Soviet tanks… And then… Just listen to this.' Maurice started his tape machine playing.

'You should see some fun, today, Palmer,' Craig's voice was saying. 'We've got some Jocks set up to play the opposing force, so it should be a good little dance this evening.'

'It's to be a night exercise,' a tinnier version of Maurice's voice said on the tape.

'Well, evening into night-time, yeah. Give us a chance to get into a bit of a routine before the Jocks—' A crashing blast suddenly drowned out every voice on the tape.

'What the hell?' someone shouted. More shouts and curses followed, and the sounds of running men, and then came what were unmistakably shots.

'Those aren't Jocks,' another voice exclaimed, and then there was another explosion.

17

'We're under attack for bloody real!' Maurice's voice warbled.

There was some more shooting, and then a distant yell of '*Hurra! Vorwärts für den Kaiser!*' The tape screeched then, and gave out nothing more than a hiss. Maurice switched it off.

'The exercise was attacked, for real?' Greene asked. That was interesting to him; nothing had been reported in the news, and the scent of a cover-up was irresistible.

Maurice nodded, and took the tape off the player. He started fidgeting with it, rolling it over between his fingers. 'At first everybody thought it was Reds, but their gear was old, so then we thought they must be some kind of Nazi holdovers, right? Werewolves, or whatever they wanted to call themselves, at the end of the war.'

'But...?'

Maurice gave Craig an overly stagey nod, in response to which Craig produced a thicker reel of tape, which Greene recognised as video. Maurice took it, and began threading it into the reels below the TV monitor. 'Of course, we only broadcast radio here – they keep suggesting there might be TV transmissions someday, but it'll be years before they stump up the budget, you know? Anyway, we do have this video equipment, for extracting the audio track from TV news back home, so we can play the clips on our shows.'

'And...?'

'And that's why we're doing this here.' With that, Maurice switched on the monitor.

On the screen, a young man sat on a chair in a small room with a desk and a couple of other chairs, the sort of interrogation room familiar to Greene from a host of TV detective programmes. His trousers had a stripe down the side, and he was in his shirt-sleeves. And old grandad-style shirt, Greene noticed. A provost corporal stood by the door, a SLR slung over his shoulder, and his arms folded. The prisoner didn't seem discomforted in any way, but kept looking up at the ceiling, and at the guard on the door.

'This is one of the Jerries who attacked the exercise,' Craig said. 'We brought a group of them into the glasshouse for questioning. There'll be an SIB bloke come in in a minute.' True to Craig's word, the provost on the monitor opened the door to the interrogation room, allowing a scowling, shaven-headed officer in. The prisoner watched the guard's every move, and Craig pointed to the monitor. 'Look at him; desperate to shoot his way out, he is. Can't take his eyes off the weapon.'

'I'm no soldier or psychiatrist,' Greene said, trying to sound light, 'but I do know how to read a man on camera. It doesn't look to me like he's about to jump anyone. Looks more like he... No, it sounds stupid, but it looks more like he doesn't know what that rifle is.'

Craig snorted. 'He's a soldier, isn't he? He had a rifle too, when he was chasing us through the woods.'

'A Nazi one? He looks like he's never seen anything like our SLRs.'

Craig snorted. 'Even if he had to make do with his grandad's kit, he must have seen us around on patrol.'

'I suppose...'

'That said,' Craig allowed, grudgingly, 'this is the really weird bit.'

On the tape, the SIB officer slammed the desktop with his hand. 'How many other Nazi sympathizers were in your group?' he demanded.

The prisoner shook his head. '*Wie bitte? Was ist ein 'Nazi'?*'

'What did he just say?' Greene asked.

'Exactly what you think he said. He doesn't know what a Nazi is.' Maurice laughed. 'Where's he been for the last thirty years, eh?'

The provost on screen seemed equally doubtful. 'Probably doesn't even know what day it is, from the look of him.' He nudged the prisoner's leg with his boot, none too gently. '*Kannst du mir sagen, welcher tag heute ist*, Jerry?'

'*Der siebte oktober neunzehnhundertvierzehn.*'

Greene stiffened, unable to believe his ears. 'What the—? He says it's nineteen-bleedin-fourteen.'

Maurice and Craig exchanged glances. 'Thought that would interest you,' Maurice said quietly. 'Here's the other weird thing: All the prisoners who were taken after the attack on that exercise have disappeared.'

Greene looked at Craig. 'The army...?'

'Your guess is as good as mine, lad. Or, hopefully, better. Otherwise I don't know what the point of your mate bringing you over here was.'

Greene's mind was racing. There was a story here, but what? And where was it coming from? 'Did they all give the same story?'

'Same story, same date,' Craig said.

'And do we have a recording of any of the others?'

Maurice and Craig exchanged glances again, before Maurice replied, 'just that one.'

Greene stood, shaking his head. 'There's no story here, Maurice. You know that, I know that, and I expect the sergeant here knows it better than either of us.' He sighed

20

and reached for the door, but Craig blocked his way.

'What are you implying?' Maurice asked.

'Oh, come on. Where did this tape come from?'

'I brought it,' Craig said.

'Why? At best you're breaching the Official Secrets Act, and at worst, well, imagination is our only limit on what's worst.' Greene stepped in closer to the scowling man, feeling queasy but wanting to establish that he wouldn't be either fooled or intimidated.

'Some of those Jerries killed a couple of my lads,' Craig said calmly. 'And then talked a load of cobblers about it. I'd like to know why, but I'm not a copper, and I'm not James bleedin' Bond, so I got to thinking that a journo is the next best person to be able to poke his nose into things. And since Palmer here was actually involved, I'm not giving away any secrets to him.' Craig tapped Greene on the chest, the pressure of his fingertips was enough to push Greene back. 'Your mate here tells me you know about the Underground.'

'I wanted to tell the story, not keep it secret.'

'You wanted to be a voice who could tell what wasn't allowed to be told, didn't you? You still had to keep quiet about some of what went on. That's how it works.' Greene couldn't deny it. 'It's the same here; there's a story, and you'll be able to tell parts of it.'

'Parts? And who'll decide which parts? You? You'll forgive me if I expected the chain of command to...'

'The three of us,' Maurice interrupted. 'We'll work it out together,' he added, encouragingly.

Greene sighed. *You really believe that*, he thought. He wasn't born yesterday, but his curiosity was locked in now. 'Where are your prisoners at the moment?'

'Spandau.'

That made sense to Greene. The notorious prison that held Rudolf Hess was secure, and had plenty of room to spare for other potential Nazis in need of interrogation. 'We won't get a chance to talk to them, then.' It would take months of negotiation to even try, Greene thought. 'What happened to the weapons and equipment your attackers had?'

Craig shrugged. 'Impounded, weren't they? The rifles will be checked to see if they've been used in any other crimes, and the uniforms... Well, depends who ends up getting custody of them. They might be destroyed, or sold off to a costume supplier for the telly, or who knows what.'

'But they must still be physically stored somewhere.'

'Back at barracks. Building C, probably. Secure storage.'

'If we could get access... See the equipment for ourselves.'

'We've seen enough of it,' Craig muttered. Maurice nodded in agreement.

'I haven't. You're a forces broadcaster, Maurice, not to mention a participant in the event, and Craig was involved, so we should play the participant card. In fact, quite frankly, it reflects badly on the authorities that they haven't done so.' Greene put a hand on Maurice's shoulder, while keeping eye contact with Craig. 'You were both there, you saw what happened, and you have a duty to confirm that the materials recovered from the scene are the same ones you saw.'

'I suppose...' Craig nodded to himself. 'The best thing would be to make it part of the after-action report. They'd let Palmer and myself see the gear, I'm sure of that. You'd have to take your chances.'

'I'm sure we can work something out,' Greene said thoughtfully. 'There is a man I could think of who might be able to get to the bottom of this... Unless he's the man *at* the bottom of it, of course.'

'What, some kind of doctor? A psychiatrist, I mean.'

'A colonel in the Scots Guards, actually. Lethbridge-Stewart. He was in the thick of it in the London Event.'

'Well that's great, then! Let's get him over...'

Greene shook his head. 'The last I heard, Lethbridge-Stewart's in Tibet.'

'Tibet? What, looking for abominable snowmen?'

Greene forced a smile. 'Maybe he just wanted to get away from it all. Anyway, that's where he's gone.'

Colonel Alistair Gordon Lethbridge-Stewart picked up the phone on its first shrill ring, before it could make his headache any worse. 'Lethbridge-Stewart.'

'Colonel, Lieutenant Robertson. Switchboard has had a call from the civilian authorities about a possible device being found.'

'Device? If they mean a UXB, transfer their call to–'

'No, sir. They were insistent it wasn't simply a bomb. But they said it fell from the sky.'

'Where did it land?'

'Place called Deepdene. Right in the High Street, apparently.'

'Give me the map reference, and have a driver pick me up.'

Within half an hour, Lethbridge-Stewart was climbing out of a jeep on a quiet rural high street. It was a typical English street, with a mix of mock-Tudor and Victorian buildings. There were relatively few modern monstrosities, and he supposed the town had been lucky enough to avoid too much damage during the Blitz.

There was a bowling green, and a duck pond at either end of the street, and the usual range of Post Office, library, butchers, greengrocers, and so on. A man in overalls was painting letters on to the window of the greengrocers, and Lethbridge-Stewart noticed there was a distinct hole in the tiled roof of the newsagent and tobacconist's shop. A couple of policemen were chatting to the few bystanders, keeping them at their distance, while soldiers placed a cordon around the whole side of the street.

A sergeant, whom Lethbridge-Stewart didn't recognise, came over with a salute. 'The captain's already inside, sir.'

'Good. Any casualties reported?'

'No, sir. It went right through the kids' bedroom upstairs, but they were both at school at the time. Their parents were running the shop, but they were both at the opposite end from where it landed. They're shaken up a bit, but physically unharmed.'

'Good. Establish a CP in the pub over there, and have the witnesses put up there too. We'll need to talk with them, and I imagine they won't mind something to steady their nerves.'

'Right, sir.' The sergeant saluted again, and trotted off, beckoning a couple of soldiers to assist him.

Lethbridge-Stewart marched over to the door of the stricken shop, glancing up at the lintel and the ceiling inside as he stepped through. The place looked, he had to admit, as if a bomb had hit it, albeit without actually exploding. A thick beam of sunlight pierced the dusty air at an angle, tracing the path along which the object had fallen. The light streamed in first through a hole in the building's roof, and then the room's ceiling, providing the only real illumination, since the lightbulbs were now missing in action. Plaster dust still hung in the air, and the floor was strewn with displaced magazines and packets of snacks and miscellany.

A large hole gaped in the floor at one end of the shop, surrounded by broken pieces of shelving, small sewing kits, and postcards.

Lethbridge-Stewart looked around for the stairs down to the cellar as he passed through the room, but something caught his peripheral vision; a flash of red and a screaming face. He turned, ready to call out an order, but then saw that it was only a *Radio Times* hanging part-way off of the counter, not quite hiding the penny-trays of sweets under the glass. The face was Elvis Presley, whom Lethbridge-Stewart certainly didn't expect to ever have to order around. He felt a sudden shiver, though he couldn't say why. The star might not be to his taste in music, but was hardly likely to be enough of a threat to anyone to cause a moment's discomfort.

He picked up the magazine, momentarily curious, and looked to see what page the magazine was open at. It was just a page of Tuesday's TV schedules; the BBC on one side and ITV on the other. Neither channel showed anything of much appeal. He put it back down the way he had found it, though he wasn't sure why, since it must have fallen that way during the impact. He supposed one never knew when some forensics bod might make something useful of it.

He could hear voices from below, and followed them to

the staircase, which he found behind a heavy curtain, with a stockroom to one side. At the bottom of the stairs, the cellar was a mess of broken floorboards and smashed cardboard boxes. A couple of Royal Electrical and Mechanical Engineers – a black staff sergeant and a tall and broad-shouldered corporal – had cleared away the debris from around a flattened cylindrical metal canister.

'Captain?'

A slim woman with Intelligence Corps collar flashes, buttons, and badge on her green beret, turned. 'Colonel Lethbridge-Stewart,' she acknowledged. Her smile faded, a look of concern replacing it. 'Are you all right? Is something wrong?'

Lethbridge-Stewart rubbed his temple, which felt rather sensitive. 'Just a headache.' He didn't want to mention that the whole side of his head felt as if someone had hit it with a sledgehammer. After all, it wasn't as if he'd been injured recently.

'Shall I send for some aspirins? Or, if it's a migraine, there are some better ones in the dispensary.'

'That won't be necessary, Captain.' His tone brokered no argument. She nodded, and switched on a torch, playing it over the object that had crashed through the shop. At first glance it looked like a large bomb, such as the Tallboys carried by Lancaster bombers in the Second World War, but with the addition of stubby wings. Lethbridge-Stewart had never seen a bomb that had windows in it, however, and the torchlight revealed that a section of the nose had a seam around it, forming a doorway. 'Definitely not a bomb, then,' he said. 'I wonder who is inside.'

'Or what.' She reached out a hand towards the door

seam, but refrained from actually touching it. 'Do we dare open it here?'

'I'd rather not,' Lethbridge-Stewart admitted. 'But I wonder whether it can even be moved without demolishing the entire building to get it out.'

'If it had been a bomb...'

'The building would be demolished either way, yes.' He looked up at the smashed floor. 'Then again, Captain... I'm no structural engineer, but I have my doubts about how much of the building will stay up for long anyway.' He turned to the REME staff sergeant and asked, 'Will we need to prop this building up, or pull it down?'

'Neither, sir. None of the main supports seem to have been damaged. But we will need to uplift the floor and take down the east window to lift this... whatever it is out.'

'See to it, Staff,' Lethbridge-Stewart said with a grimace. The captain also nodded her agreement. The REME staff saluted, and beckoned to his comrade to follow him back up the stairs to the ground floor. 'Have you ever seen anything like this before, Captain?'

'I don't believe I have, and I'm sure I would have remembered. You?'

He shook his head. 'Can't say that I have. It's not quite an aircraft... no engine, no wings to glide on... And yet not a bomb either, as it has passenger space.' He frowned. 'Give me your torch.' She handed it over, and Lethbridge-Stewart approached the nose of the object. This time he did touch the metal, leaning against it so that he could direct the torch in through the glass. The glass was darkened, and it was difficult to see much detail inside. There seemed to be at least two seats inside, and there was a vaguely humanoid

27

shape in at least one of them, but even the torch beam didn't make much impact through the tint in the glass.

What did show up under the torchlight was a thick line around one side of the hatch. Lethbridge-Stewart ran the palm of his hand over it, feeling a slight ledge. 'Has anyone tried to open this?'

'No, sir. Not while I've been here.' Her hands joined his in tracing the raised line that went part way around the hatch. 'If it has been opened it must have been from the inside...' She broke off, her eyes widening. She drew her pistol, as did Lethbridge-Stewart, who switched the torch into his left hand, and rested his pistol butt on that wrist.

The torch beam played across the cellar floor, picking out the marks where boxes and crates had been dragged around. There were scuff marks everywhere, but then a slight glint caught Lethbridge-Stewart's eye.

It was a glistening droplet on the stone floor. The captain knelt and touched a fingertip to it, which came away red. 'Blood,' she confirmed. 'And not from any of the residents.'

'Did they have any pets? A dog or cat that could have been down here?'

'I don't know.'

Lethbridge-Stewart grunted, and moved on through the cellar. There were a couple more droplets of blood, the last of which was on a step at the foot of a low arched door, which laid at an angle across the lowest part of the ceiling. He pushed lightly against the door with the torch, and it lifted up easily. Outside, a narrower street stretched along behind the row of shops, filled with dustbins. 'Something injured went out this way.'

'I'll have a search made.'

'If it was a person, they can't have got far. If it was a cat or a dog, they'll find a box to hole up in, and…' A loud clang echoed behind them, making both officers jump. They darted back through the rubble-strewn cellar, arriving before the metal object at the same time as two soldiers reached the bottom of the stairs.

The hatch had fallen out from the side of the object, and a body had followed. A man in a sheepskin flying jacket was sprawled unmoving on his back, partway out of the hatch. A leather flying helmet was wrapped around his head, and a one-piece combination of oxygen mask and goggles, like an old gas mask, covered his face. He wasn't moving. Lethbridge-Stewart directed the torch into the object, and saw two simple seats, lots of padding, and only a few dials. 'No flight controls,' he murmured. 'Not that I recognise, anyway.' He looked down at the sprawled body, watching the chest for any sign of respiration.

'We'll get an expert down to make sure, Colonel.' The captain knelt beside the body, putting her gun away.

'And the other seat is empty.' Lethbridge-Stewart turned to the other soldiers. 'Arrange a search party. We're looking for another person, dressed like this. He or she is wounded and bleeding. We'll need a medical team also, and an ambulance, pronto!'

'Yes, sir,' the nearest man replied, and both ascended at the double.

Lethbridge-Stewart could hear shouts and the sound of running men as his orders were relayed. He returned his attention to the body. The captain's hand was pressed to the side of his throat, and she frowned in concentration. 'Is he alive?'

29

After a moment she looked up and shook her head. 'No pulse.'

'Then we shall certainly need an expert to tell us about this thing, since he can't.' He put away his pistol, and returned her torch. 'There's a chap I know, who might be able to help identify this thing. If I can get a hold of him.'

'Military or civilian?' She began undoing the thin straps that held the goggles and mask on to the body's face.

'Scientist. I've worked with him before. Odd sort of chap, but very useful in his own way. His name's Travers.'

The mask and goggles came away, revealing the pallid face of a middle-aged man with a thick black beard. Dried blood was crusted round his nostrils and mouth. The pallor of death was obvious to them both, but Lethbridge-Stewart was the one whose breath caught in his throat.

'Edward Travers!' he exclaimed.

# — CHAPTER TWO —

## *Seekers of Truth*

Major General Oliver Hamilton hated being dragged into the office in the wee small hours almost as much as his wife, Vera, hated being disturbed by his going. Corporal Wright was already there, with surprisingly little trace of tiredness in her green eyes. She couldn't quite hide the yawn as she greeted him, however, but he let it slide. He wouldn't have been able to do any better himself. 'What's the flap?' he asked.

She handed him a telex printout and a mug of strong sweet tea. 'This came in from BAOR.'

'Not another punch up between border patrols who can't read maps, I hope.'

'Definitely not, sir.' She left the office. He couldn't blame her; the strain must be getting to her, but it wasn't showing. He liked that.

By now Hamilton had scanned the message. 'Who...? Oh, yes, I remember now.' He sat behind his desk, and made to look out the window at Fugglestone. The hour was too early, the night still too dark, to see the village. He laid the telex on the desk and buzzed for Wright to come back in. When she reappeared, he tapped the telex. 'Find Colonel Douglas and have him round up a platoon ready to move out at dawn.'

She nodded, and disappeared out of the office again. Hamilton picked up his desk phone with a sigh. Vera might have a long wait to complain about his early rise. 'Switchboard,' he said, as soon as a signals operator came on the line. 'Put me through to RAF Brize Norton.'

The rock hissed like a huge wounded beast, throwing out ear-splitting groans and wails in its death throes. Then there was a sudden booming crack that split the air, putting the tortured leviathan out of its misery.

A white-topped swell roiled around the spreading black mass at the base of billowing clouds, as it settled into its new and independent existence. Glowing fire settled like crystallising honey in the grey-black North Atlantic waters, rocking slowly from side to side, and sending out more waves. The ocean looked as vast and eternal as it had before, caressing the rough dark stone.

Anne Travers supposed that technically they were ripples, but that word was too insignificant to fit the scale of what she was watching. Wafts of steam drifted along the ship's rail, already chilly against Anne's face. Even though the icebreaker *Amundsen* was designed to safely approach solid icebergs, and was built for the utmost possible stability against any turbulent waters that could be thrown at it, Anne still felt her skin prickle, and held on tight to the nearest stanchion.

The ship tilted by several degrees as the swell rolled under her, but it did so very slowly and steadily. Anne knew there was no danger of the ship being swamped or overturning, but knowing something and feeling it were two completely different things. She knew she was safe, but she certainly didn't feel safe. What she did feel was a pair of eyes on her, and a sense of amusement at her expense. The amusement was written all over her father's face, when she turned to see who was watching her. He wasn't even bothering to hold onto anything, she noticed, a little jealous. Stocky and grey-bearded, he looked every inch the sea-captain, apart from the glasses and Homburg hat.

She knew that Edward Travers had spent a chunk of his youth exploring the snow-capped Himalayas, and had learned very quickly that it was good sense to keep the head covered when winter was snowy and cold, or when one was in the vicinity of one of the Earth's polar caps. The skies remained clear and blue, and she was glad that no storms were filling the air from horizon to horizon with shrieking sharp particles. Her father rolled with the ship's motion, and gestured towards the new-born berg with the steaming coffee-mug he held in his left hand.

'Always a privilege to be at a birth,' he said. 'Not as meaningful as yours, of course, but I prefer to take the more glass-half-full view on such a bright day.'

She couldn't resist a chuckle. 'You're right, of course, Father. A new island... A lot of geologists are going to be very jealous of us.'

'Yes, well, that's academia for you, Anne. Wolves fighting over the nearest deer.'

'Was it as bad in your day?'

'I'd like to say no, but I rather fear I'd be lying, on nostalgic grounds. You know, the whole "when I grew up nobody locked their doors", and all that gubbins. It's all nonsense, of course...'

'How long do you think it'll be before we can look for

the crater?'

'Up to the captain and the pilot, I suppose.' They looked towards the stern of the ship, where a couple of overall-clad sailors were pulling a tarpaulin off the helicopter. More accurately, off most of what would be the helicopter – it was tied down by many cables, and the rotor blades were still stored below decks, not attached to the chopper itself.

'Well, it looks like it won't be long, Father.'

Sergeant Craig drove up to the barracks gate in an open-topped Land Rover from the motor pool. Greene sat in the passenger seat, in a simple brown suit, and Maurice lounged in the back. An MP on the gate stepped forward to check their passes. 'Right, Sergeant,' he said. 'Mr Palmer,' he nodded to Maurice. 'Doing another show about little us?'

'Better than that,' Maurice said. 'We've got TV coverage coming up.' He pointed to Greene.

The Redcap frowned for a moment, then shrugged. 'I thought you looked a bit familiar.' He reached back with one hand into his little gatehouse booth, and brought out a clipboard. 'Building C, isn't it?' Craig nodded. 'Morgan from SIB is already waiting. He'll see you right.'

'Thanks, lad,' Craig said. The Redcap pressed a button by the wire gate, which rolled open, allowing Craig to drive through. He directed the Land Rover to what looked to Greene like any other warehouse in the world. A guard was on the door, and a Redcap officer was leaning against a jeep. He was quite short, but had the air of a terrier, a fast little bugger who'd never let go once he had his teeth into something.

'Lieutenant Harrison,' he introduced himself crisply. 'I

don't know how you journalistic fellas managed to wangle this visit, but wangle it you did; mine not to reason why.' He gave a smile that said that wondering the why of things was what he did for a living. 'Shall we?' He pulled open the Building C door, and indicated that they should enter. Inside, the warehouse was subdivided into many sections and rooms, some just sectioned off with chain-link fencing, while some parts were secure porta cabins.

Harrison led them up a flight of steel stairs and unlocked one of the porta cabins, which itself was full of locked cages. Rather than animals, the cages contained cardboard boxes, metal canisters, wooden crates, paper folders, and so on. He unlocked another section of chain-link to a set of shelves containing a couple of rifle racks, and a larger wooden crate. 'Their ID and personal effects went with them to Spandau, of course,' Harrison said, 'but these are their weapons and kit.'

Greene indicated the nearest rifle, propped in its rack. 'These have been, er, unloaded, I assume?' Harrison's expression was all the answer he needed. 'May I?' Harrison nodded. Greene lifted the rifle, looking to see if there were any identifying markings on it. There were arcane marks hammered into the breach and the beginning of the barrel, but they meant nothing to him. No swastikas or hammers and sickles, or anything so obvious.

'Kar 98,' Craig said. 'Jerry's been using them for at least fifty years. From Queen Vic's day through to Hitler topping himself.'

'So they could be from anywhere in that period?'

'We'll be able to tell their dates of original manufacture and issue from the serial numbers and inspection marks stamped on the steel,' Harrison said.

'Of course there's no telling what happened to them after that,' Craig added. The sergeant had opened up the larger crate, and pulled out a folded uniform jacket by the shoulders. His brow furrowed. 'Bloody hell,' he said. 'This is definitely the same clobber the men that attacked us were wearing. Their gear's a bit old, isn't it? That's not Nazi rubbish.'

'You sure of that?' Greene asked.

'Course I'm bloody sure. Every junk shop's got a back room with some illicit SS threads for lads looking for souvenirs.' He laid the jacket down, and picked up the helmet.

Greene leaned in to examine it too, and saw that it was leather, not steel, and covered by tan canvas. 'And this thing... This looks like something from the First World War. In fact I'd say it all does.' None of them had to say what Greene was thinking; they were all thinking the same thing, having all seen the same interrogation tape.

There was a commotion at the door to the warehouse. Angry voices and running boots echoed through the building. All four men almost tripped over each other trying to get to the landing and see what was happening, but it was Greene who got the first sight of the disturbance.

A group of soldiers in full battledress, not the barrack dress worn by Harrison and the Redcap on the door, were rushing up the steel stairs. 'What the hell?' Harrison exclaimed. Before he could react any further, the leading two soldiers had grabbed him by the arms and forced him to his knees. Two more did the same with Sergeant Craig, and then Greene found himself staring down the barrel of a Sterling submachine gun.

'Two civvies,' one of the soldiers said. 'Which one of you is Larry Greene?' Greene's blood turned to ice, and, perversely, it felt like his bladder was melting. He wanted to run or fight, but his legs didn't agree with the thought. He wasn't sure whether it was best to answer or not, and it didn't help that he also wasn't sure whether or not to be offended that these squaddies didn't recognise his face from television.

Before he could make up his mind, one of the other soldiers pointed to him, the gesture made him feel uncomfortable as if the man's finger was loaded. 'Him with the Michael Caine specs. That's the one.'

The helicopter was an ex-Royal Navy Westland Whirlwind, supplied, along with the pilot – a woman named Parr – by the British establishment. When in naval service, it had been heavily winterized for operations in the Arctic Circle. It had also originally been painted yellow, for an air-sea-rescue role. Aboard the ship, however, it had been re-painted a brighter orangey-red so that it could easily be spotted in a storm, or found if crashed anywhere on the Arctic ice.

The ship's mechanics had fitted the rotor blades by now, and Anne was keen to get started. The Whirlwind was a good, solid machine, far more reliable than the smaller choppers Anne had flown in before. She actually felt confident about getting into the Whirlwind, rather than fearing that something was going to fall off in mid-air, not that she was keen on chopper flight as a rule. Susan Parr seemed thorough in her pre-flight inspection, but still found time to wave a greeting to Anne as she and her father boarded, along with a couple of technicians.

'Ready to go?'

'Yes indeed. Will it be a long trip?'

Parr shook her head, before pulling her helmet over her cropped blonde hair. 'Ten, maybe fifteen minutes, tops. There's a slight headwind, but that just means we'll be a little faster on the way back.'

'There's nothing wrong with that, if the galley has dinner ready.'

'Can't disagree with you there, Doctor. Anyway, you're in command, so as soon as you're ready, it's your show.'

And so it was. She was working on behalf of her Vault paymasters, of course, and by extension the Ministry of Technology, but this was her show. And she had something to prove, not least to the mysterious General who ran the Vault. Mostly, the Vault had provided the team she would command, but she had insisted on the assistance of her father, pulling him from his plans to return to Tibet.

'We've just got some measuring equipment to load,' Anne said, 'and then we will be good to go.'

'Good. We're all checked out and fit to fly.' Parr patted the side of the chopper, then stepped up onto the big port side wheel mount, and pulled the cockpit door open. She strapped in and busied herself with the pre-flight instrument checks, while Anne made sure the equipment loaded by a technician was properly secured, and that her father was also safely strapped into his seat in the high-ceilinged passenger compartment. A moment later, Parr leaned out to look down the short staircase that separated the cockpit from the passengers. Anne was putting a helmet on, so that she could hear and be heard over the engine noise when they were in flight, and gave Parr a thumbs-up.

Parr returned the thumbs-up, and started the engines. Once Anne had buckled herself into her seat, she gestured upwards with her hand. 'Take us up, please,' she said to Parr. 'We're ready, Susan.'

'Up, up, and away,' Parr said cheerfully, working her magic on the throttle, pitch and collective controls. The Whirlwind rose smoothly into the bright sky, and leaned sideways to fall away from the ship.

It was only a short distance to the main part of the new island, which already rose tens of feet above the frigid ocean. Within the promised ten minutes or so, Parr was looking for a landing spot.

The upper surface of the island was at least half a mile across at its widest point, and looked to be a uniform field of charcoal ash. Anne couldn't tell by eye whether the surface was solid ice or deep and soft snow. Neither could Parr, who admitted as much to her.

'It's most likely a thin layer of broken rock and ash, like gravel,' Anne told the pilot. 'Four or five centimetres, perhaps.'

'Two or three inches, in real money?' Parr said.

Anne nodded. She was sure from her studies and Vault briefing on the new island that this was the most likely surface, but not being able to trust mere eyes on the matter made caution wise. She also knew from experience that everyone aboard had exactly the same thoughts. 'Well, let's see for ourselves, shall we?'

Parr guided the Whirlwind low over the surface, the rotor wash sending a mist of sooty ash out in a huge circle around it. The visible surface of the island looked unchanged, however, and so she eased the chopper down until its tyres touched down. Nothing gave way, and the bulky two-storey chopper gently settled. Once it was landed, Anne pulled the big side door aside, letting in a stabbing breeze. She took off her helmet, and dropped cautiously to the surface. She kicked at it with one boot, then walked around the chopper, stamping occasionally.

'Gravel and ash over basalt, Father,' she called back. 'As solid as anything, and nice and cool too.'

'That's a relief,' her father grunted. 'Would have been damned awkward if it was still hot tar.' He climbed down from the helicopter. 'Then let's get to work.'

Greene had been shoved into the back of a truck with two of the soldiers, and the canvas flap at the back tied closed, sealing them in with no view of where they were going. Neither soldier pointed their guns at him, which was something to be thankful for. They also didn't object when he sat on the bench on one side, as far from them as possible. They sat on either side of the tailgate, which meant he was leaning against the cab, so he supposed that they couldn't have an objection to his being as far from a means of escape as possible.

On the bright side, leaning against the cab meant he could reduce how sickly he'd have felt from trying to sit sideways to the direction of travel for the whole journey. He had even managed to doze off, without falling from the bench.

Eventually the truck stopped, and the tarpaulin was pulled back from the tailgate. The two soldiers jumped down, and beckoned him to come out. Greene was surprised to find an officer waiting for him; a lieutenant colonel, if he remembered the pips on army uniforms correctly.

'That's him,' the colonel said to one of the soldiers. 'Good work, Finch.' He stepped forward to offer a hand to help Greene down from the truck.

Greene took it, and looked around. The truck was parked on the dispersal area of an airfield, and he recognised the buildings in the distance as those of the *Flughafen Köln-Bonn*, at which he had so recently arrived under much more pleasant circumstances. The aircraft before him, however, was not a jet airliner, but an Argosy; a machine with four propellers, a shortened bulbous fuselage, and a twin-boom tail, all in RAF Support Command colours.

'Lieutenant Colonel Douglas,' the officer introduced himself. 'If you'll come with me, Mister Greene.' He led Greene towards the Argosy. As they approached, Greene could see that the cargo doors between the tail booms were open. 'I'm sorry we had to be so… persuasive about bringing you out here.'

'Persuasive? You kidnapped me!'

Douglas didn't say anything, but led him into the Argosy's cargo bay. The bay was empty, apart from a couple of folding chairs, a rough table with some papers and glasses on it, and a general. Greene recognised him from occasional news pieces as Oliver Hamilton, and Hamilton offered a hand to shake. Greene was tempted not to take it, but did so after a moment's hesitation.

Hamilton nodded to Douglas. 'That'll be all, Colonel.' Douglas saluted, and left. Hamilton indicated one of the chairs, and uncorked a bottle of Johnny Walker. 'I'm sorry about the, shall we say, unorthodox method of securing your

41

co-operation.' He offered no other explanation for it, and Greene didn't really mind, as he was in no mood to accept whatever it would have been. 'I hope the whisky doesn't insult you by implying I subscribe to the cliché that all journalists – or writers – are alcoholics. In my opinion it's just the most civilized way to conduct a conversation.'

Greene downed his glass in one, and grimaced at the bite. 'Now look here,' he began. 'I'm insulted by this... abduction. I have always had the utmost respect for our armed forces...'

'I know.' Hamilton sat opposite him, and tapped a thick manila folder on the rickety table. 'I've read your file, and about your involvement with Harold Chorley.'

'Then you should know that I have always co-operated with...'

Hamilton poured him another whisky. 'Don't bother, and I won't bother counting the number of breaches of the OSA your exploits this week involve. Or at least could be construed as.'

Greene savoured the second drink for longer than the first, thinking. There was some truth to that; he had bent, if not broken, the sacred rule. Of course, he had never actually signed the Act, but Chorley had, so by association... Greene decided not to push his luck. 'Is that what this is about? I crossed a line in search of a story? In search of the truth?'

'It could be. But it doesn't have to be.' Hamilton smiled faintly, though he didn't seem that practiced at it. 'As a matter of fact, you might not be done breaching that Act.'

Now Greene was highly suspicious. Was the general planning to frame him for something? 'I've never set out to break a law.'

42

'What did you set out to do?'

'Find the truth in a story.'

'According to your telephone records, you were looking for Colonel Lethbridge-Stewart.'

Greene's smile managed a sort of guilty amusement. 'He is someone who might be useful to talk to.'

'About the attack on that exercise?'

'Maurice isn't given to making up nonsense, and I'm sure Sergeant Craig isn't either. I thought Colonel Lethbridge-Stewart might be able to help me, yes.'

'Except that he's in Tibet.'

'So I heard.'

Hamilton looked at Greene for a long moment. 'Then you need to listen some more.'

Greene wasn't sure whether he was thrilled or frightened, or which he should be, but it certainly felt like Hamilton was trying to warn him off. Perhaps he was too close to something. 'Is this one of those "stop nosing around" warnings you see on television?'

Hamilton laughed. 'Far from it. This is one of those "we'd be very interested to see what you learn" speeches. Or would be, were I foolish enough to say such a thing.'

Greene's journalistic instincts tingled. 'Something's wrong, isn't it?'

'There's always something wrong somewhere, and there's always something right somewhere.'

'Are you suggesting that I need to listen to someone who is right, rather than someone who is wrong? In which case, the colonel is not in Tibet.'

'Let's just say that, just as we have sources unavailable to civilians, so a man in your profession may well have sources equally unavailable to us.'

Dammit, the man was reeling him in like a fish. He knew just how to gain Greene's journalistic interest. He was, Greene thought, wasted as a soldier; he'd make a bloody good TV interviewer. 'To do what?'

Hamilton's smile faded. 'To find Colonel Lethbridge-Stewart.'

There was a light but biting wind blowing volcanic grit in their faces as they trudged across the barren island. 'My money's still on a crashed plane,' one of the technicians said.

'Always a possibility,' Anne's father agreed. 'Especially if one was flying above the initial eruption that birthed the island. The volume of smoke and steam would have been more than enough to blind any pilot.'

'And reduce the air density under his wings,' Anne added. She was carrying a portable magnetometer, and kept an eye on the needle of its gauge. 'The readings look interesting,' she added. 'There's definitely a huge metallic mass a mile or so to the north.'

'That's not our crater, surely?' her father asked.

'No, that's just over this ridge.' Anne pointed to her left, and walked briskly up the dark slope. Her father and the two technicians followed, and in a matter of minutes they were all standing on the rim of a crater about forty yards across, and ten deep. 'It doesn't look volcanic,' Anne said, 'and there's something metallic in the centre.'

'A meteorite, most likely, in *my* opinion,' her father said, with a challenging glare at the technician who had predicted a plane crash.

Anne turned, trying not to let the technician see her amusement. As it was, she could see the Whirlwind from the lip of the crater, and even make out Susan Parr walking around it. She turned her attention back to the interior of the crater.

'The temperature isn't any higher in there,' the second technician said.

'Then let's not waste any time,' her father said eagerly. He set off down into the crater. Anne struggled to keep up, despite his age. Soon, the four of them were standing on flat ground again. Anne knelt in the gravel, and cleared a small patch with her hand. 'Look at this, Father, I was right. There is something metal here.' As the others gathered round, they saw that she had uncovered a patch of dark metal. Anne's eyes widened. 'Oh, this has to be some kind of joke...'

Her father looked at her, his expression mixing excitement and concern. 'What is it, Anne?'

She put down the magnetometer, and used both hands to scoop the broken rock and ash away from more metal. She directed the others to step away. There was a raised curve bulging upwards, and she cleared the gravel away from it. 'I don't believe I'm saying this, but see if you can find the edges.'

Encumbered by his thick coat, her father was the first to do as she said. His gloved hands followed the other side of the raised curve. Smoked glass reflected the sky back at them.

All four of them redoubled their efforts. Within half an hour, they had exposed enough of the metal to see that it was a large flattened cylinder, with stubby wings, but no engines.

'An unexploded bomb!' Anne exclaimed.

She and the technicians scrambled away from it, but her father stood where he was. 'No, Anne, no… Oh, it's about the right size for a Tallboy, but look at these glass panels, and a hatch… Whatever it is, it isn't simply a bomb.' He harrumphed, fixing her with a glare. 'This was clearly meant to transport a person, or persons. I wonder who was in it?'

'Or,' Anne said ominously, 'who *is* in it?'

# — CHAPTER THREE —

# *Chronological Disorder*

Lethbridge-Stewart winced slightly as he emerged back into daylight outside the newsagent's. A Land Rover ambulance had arrived, and stretcher-bearers passed him on their way down to the cellar. Just along the street, on the corner, a man in overalls was still painting lettering onto the greengrocer's window. The window looked somehow cleaner than those of the other shops, and Lethbridge-Stewart had the distinct impression that it was new.

On impulse, he walked along to the shop. 'Excuse me,' he began. 'New window?'

The man – a tall and stout bearded man with a weather-beaten face – paused in his work. 'Yes, Colonel. That it is.'

Momentarily surprised by the recognition of his rank, something most civilians didn't manage, despite the pips on his shoulder, Lethbridge-Stewart nodded towards the newsagent's. 'Was the damage by any chance related to the damage over there?'

'The whatever-it-was that fell on their roof?' The greengrocer shook his head. 'That just happened early this morning. I had the window replaced last week. Just got round to painting it today, is all. Had to wait till all the putty had cured, and whatnot.'

'Oh, I see.' Lethbridge-Stewart turned to go, then

hesitated. 'Was the window broken before, then?'

The man's hesitation was barely noticeable. 'It was time for a new one,' he said with a smile. He looked momentarily uncertain, then added, 'all that dust and oil raised from the road, you know? And the vibrations from lorries going past. Mark my words, the others will have to change them soon too.'

Lethbridge-Stewart glanced at what looked to him like a street full of perfectly serviceable shop windows. 'I'm sure you're right,' he agreed, out of politeness. At either end of Deepdene's main shopping street, and on the far side of the bowling green and duck pond, he could see pairs of soldiers moving in a search pattern, looking for whoever – if anyone – had fled the crashed capsule. Behind him, the stretcher-bearers were loading a covered body into the ambulance. He jogged over to the nearest pair. 'Any luck so far?'

'Nothing yet, sir,' one of them replied. 'Captain Kyle has set up a perimeter based on how far an injured person is likely to have got, but...'

'Personally, you think it was a cat or dog?' Both soldiers nodded. 'So do I, to be honest, but let's be thorough, just in case.'

'Yes, sir,' they said, and he exchanged brisk salutes with them, before returning to the village pub.

Entering he found a typical rural public house, all rough whitewashed stone walls, and thick black Tudor-style wooden beams. The furniture was dark polished wood, and the gaunt grey-haired barman was washing glasses behind the bar. From his age, Lethbridge-Stewart presumed him to be the landlord at least, if not proprietor.

'Upstairs, sir,' the old man said, before Lethbridge-

Stewart could speak. 'Private meeting room's first on the right; your lads have set up in there.'

Lethbridge-Stewart thanked him in passing, and ascended to the smaller wood-panelled meeting room. It had an ash-stained dark red carpet, and a couple of longer wooden tables that could be used for dining. Lethbridge-Stewart suspected they were as often used for gambling, and he had no problem with that. Now the tables had been moved to the edges of the room, with a set of radio equipment and several telephones arrayed along one of them, and maps laid out on the other. A signals corporal was manning the radio gear, while another soldier was marking points on a large-scale map of the village.

Captain Kyle was seated at the shortest table, which had been pressed into service as an office desk. 'That's right,' she was saying into the phone, 'from the moment he arrives. I'll be taking a look myself, yes. They should be on their way already.'

As Lethbridge-Stewart stepped across to examine the map, another soldier came into the room and started pinning photographs of the fallen object to a board. 'Junction of High Street and Cromwell Lane secure,' the signalman said. 'No sign of wounded, man nor beast.' The soldier on map duty acknowledged this with a grunt, and marked off an area on his map.

'No luck so far, Captain Kyle?'

She rose from behind the shortest table, which had been pressed into service as a central desk. 'Nothing so far on whatever escaped from the newsagent's cellar. A REME unit should be here within half an hour, to extract the... Capsule, shall we call it?' He nodded; it was as good a word

49

as any. 'To extract the capsule from the shop, for transport back to the compound.'

Lethbridge-Stewart took the seat behind the desk, and thought for a moment. 'Yes, that's a thought; where best for it to go.'

'The important thing will be to get it to a secure facility, before the arguments start over whether it belongs to the army or the RAF.'

'Secure, but where it can't do any harm either.'

'You mean if it explodes? It had passengers, not an explosive payload.'

'And what if there's a hidden compartment? A man with a gun, a camera, or a bomb, could cause a lot of trouble in the compound.'

'I'll make sure it's put in a suitable section, where it can be secured in, as well as others locked out.'

'Good.'

'Sir, you said something earlier, about an expert whom you thought could help.'

'Yes... Professor Edward Travers.'

'But when you spoke that name, it sounded more like an exclamation.'

Lethbridge-Stewart nodded. 'The dead man in that... capsule, if that's what you want to call it, was Professor Travers. At least, I thought it was, though the light was bad. Except...'

'Except?'

'Except that he was – he *looked* – younger than when I last saw him. Much less grey in his beard, fewer lines around his eyes...'

'Some men are vain like that. But, as you say, the light

was bad, and even a torch can make a face look odd, with the brightness of the bulb.' Lethbridge-Stewart was about to disagree, but she was being clearly professional, and she was usually right about things, in the short time he'd been working with her.

'I suppose I—'

Suddenly the R/T squawked. 'Forward CP, radar control. Two unknowns have entered the no-fly zone, vectoring to your position. Repeat; Two unknown—'

Lethbridge-Stewart could hear them already; the drone of engines. Not jet engines, but old style propellers. Kyle grabbed the R/T microphone. 'Air defences?'

'Heat-seekers can't lock on!'

'Because they're not jets,' Lethbridge-Stewart snapped. 'Where's RAF cover?'

'Three and a half minutes to fighter intercept, sir,' the voice came back. That was when the first explosion rocked the village and all the room's windows shattered into a blizzard of glass flakes.

Thunder rumbled over Berlin like the echo of distant artillery, which seemed appropriate to Greene, but still sent a shiver down his spine. He sat in a folding jump-seat in the back of a large Daimler, facing Hamilton and Douglas on the back seat, as the car hissed through the rain-slick streets of the Western Zone.

Greene braced himself against the partition that separated him from the driver as the car turned. He twisted his neck around, and saw that they were approaching a castle-like building of red and pink bricks. The red arched gateway in which the car paused for the checking of papers was of solid red brick, with crenelated towers at either end. Greene recognised it at once, of course.

'Why Spandau?' he asked. 'The word among the troops is that it's pretty much a centre for Soviet espionage in West Germany.'

Hamilton nodded. 'It's also more secure than any other prison in Germany. And, as it happens, our month in charge just started. The Russian spies can all take their holidays while we have the use of the place.'

'Are we likely to run into Rudolf Hess?' The former leading Nazi was the prison's sole official prisoner, and Greene knew he'd be a liar if he said that an interview with him wouldn't be a major coup.

'He's in hospital with a perforated ulcer,' Douglas said, 'rather conveniently for us. We've sealed off the whole second floor of the British Military Hospital for him, and he's got a whole company of troops to keep him where he is. Which means we can keep our mystery men under wraps for a good couple of weeks.'

'And then?'

'And then they'll have to be moved, I suppose. Not my department.'

In a few minutes, Greene and the officers had been passed through several checkpoints manned by Redcaps, and were finally shown into the prison's garden where the warden, accompanied by a Special Investigations Division Major, greeted them. Both men looked askance at Greene, but didn't ask anything about him.

'Best to meet here,' the warden said. 'Less chance of red bugs.' Greene looked around, and saw that the flower beds were quite well tended. The warden saw his glance, and smiled faintly. 'The old bugger has got slightly less lazy in recent years. Boredom, probably, being the only prisoner.'

'How have things gone with the... new arrivals?' Hamilton asked the major.

'We've been liaising with the German police, trying to track down who these men are, and the results have been... Well, a bit of a mixture, to say the least.' He put a box file on the desk, and opened it. Inside were a number of folders, which he started passing across to Hamilton. Each one, the general noted, had a photograph pinned to a fingerprint sheet as its top page. 'German fingerprint records match with all of the names that the prisoners used to identify themselves.'

'Then it shouldn't be too hard to work out how they relate.'

'Not hard at all. In fact it's all there on their cover sheets: they all belonged to the same army unit.'

'*Wehrmacht*, SS, or *Bundeswehr*?' Douglas asked.

The major hesitated. 'That's the... odd bit.'

'Odd?'

'*Deutsches Heer*. The Imperial German Army.'

'You must be joking!' Greene couldn't help himself, though he knew he should just keep quiet and listen. 'They haven't been called that since Kaiser Bill's day.'

'I'm not joking. The prisoners might be, but I'm not, and I doubt the *Bundeswehr* archives are.' The major turned back to Hamilton. 'I suppose they could have been briefed on the names to use, matching ones already in the records.'

'Could be... But getting the fingerprints to match... I suppose they could have been swapped, but what would be the point? They're not going to fool anyone if they're trying to pass themselves off as men in their seventies.' He let out a long sigh, trying to think through the problem. 'Let me guess: That unit of the *Heer* disappeared in 1914. Or were at least reported missing.'

The major shook his head. 'If only it were so simple. At least three survived the war, which makes it very odd that they still think they're in 1914. It gets worse, too.'

'It can't possibly get worse,' Hamilton said.

The major nodded to the warden, who turned and beckoned to one of the provost guards who were waiting discreetly by the door to the prison chapel. The guard emerged, gently leading an old man, whom Greene supposed was the German equivalent of a Chelsea Pensioner.

'Gentlemen, may I introduce you to Heinrich Kursten.' They all exchanged handshakes and pleasantries.

He seemed like an affable chap to Greene. 'Are you a relative of...?'

The major drew him, Hamilton, and Douglas aside, and opened a manila file for them all to see. 'And so is this.'

Hamilton looked from the file photo of a dead young soldier in First World War uniform to the man leaning on the gnarled cane. 'You're not serious?'

'I'm perfectly serious. These two men are one and the same. Except that clearly one of them survived, and one didn't.'

'Grandfather and grandson?'

'Their fingerprints match exactly.'

Hamilton and Douglas exchanged glances. 'I think it's time we spoke to your temporary guests.'

'Yes, sir.'

Greene stepped forward to accompany them, but Douglas blocked his path. 'Sorry, old man. Official Secrets and so forth.' He nodded towards the old man. 'But there's nothing to stop you chatting with another civilian visitor, is there?' To reinforce the warning, the provost officer took Douglas's place blocking Greene's way as the officers moved off.

Greene looked from the old man to the provost. 'Is there somewhere we could speak privately?'

'Nobody's using the chapel at the moment, sir,' the provost replied, nodding towards the door.

'Thank you,' Greene said drily, and stepped back to the old man. '*Herr* Kursten,' he began, 'my name is Greene – Larry Greene – and I wondered if I might have a few words with you?'

'You are an interrogator?'

'No, as a matter of fact, I'm a journalist. I work for the BBC.' Among others, he added silently. 'I'm researching a story that's, well, still ongoing, and hoped you could help shed some background light.'

Heinrich chuckled. 'I'm afraid I'm retired now, *Herr* Greene, but... All right. It may pass the time. About what do you wish to ask me?'

Greene wasn't really sure, but was happy to go along with the first thing that came out of his mouth. 'I'd like to hear about your experiences in the First World War.'

Lethbridge-Stewart stumbled downstairs as another explosion thundered somewhere outside. A plane roared overhead, and Lethbridge-Stewart drew his pistol just in case, though he knew he would never be able to damage an aircraft with it. The plane was larger than a fighter, with two engines. The underside was painted black, and the tall tailfin above a glass turret showed a distinctive green and brown pattern.

'Wellington!' he exclaimed.

The Wellington bomber tilted, joining a second one to wheel around above the fields beyond the town. Their bomb bay doors were open, and he could see the bombs fall. The ground shook, even at this distance, and flame and smoke burst skywards from somewhere on the far side of the town's rooftops.

Soldiers waved their arms, ushering the fleeing townspeople away from the side of town nearest the bombs. A couple of soldiers raised their rifles and let off shots at the arcing planes. 'Cease fire!' Kyle shouted, behind him. 'You're just wasting ammunition!'

'Cease fire!' Lethbridge-Stewart echoed, for exactly the same reason. They wouldn't hit anything at that altitude, and wouldn't have done any damage in any case. 'Get Bren guns to the crossroads, and on the flattest roofs you can find!' He turned to Kyle. 'What's in that direction, Captain? What are they attacking?'

'Plastics factory, sir.'

Something flashed across the sky and one of the bombers simply exploded. As the smoke and debris lingered, the whine of a jet engine split the air, and this time he saw the glint of a rocket an instant before it blew the whole tail section off the second bomber. The suddenly shortened plane tipped forward and dropped like a stone as a pair of swept-wing silver jet fighters flew overhead. A final explosion punctuated the bomber's impact with a gentle hillside.

The interior of Spandau's chapel was meticulously well-kept. Greene didn't know whether to be surprised or not; he wasn't an expert on either churches or military prisons. It was quiet, though, and Heinrich seemed comfortable sitting on one of the pews.

Greene unpacked his tape recorder, and set it up on the pew between them, balancing the microphone on a little wire bipod. He wondered how many other microphones he was speaking into without knowing it.

'I have to admit,' he said, just to make conversation, 'I never thought I'd find myself conducting an interview in here. Hoped, some days, but obviously...'

'You want to interview Hess. Not an old soldier from the First War.'

'Well, no. But as a matter of fact, it's not just Hess; not today.' He put on his best smile.

'So, what can I tell the BBC about my experience in what they, I believe, like to call the Great War? As if there is such a thing.'

'Well, let's start at the beginning. When did you join the army?'

'1914. I was a volunteer, like many of us at the time. They said the war would be over by Christmas. Did they tell the Tommies that also?'

'Yes.' *And the second time around*, Greene thought. 'Did you fight near Cologne?'

The old man nodded. 'Actually my first battle was there. In October of 1914. I was with an artillery company.'

'With a horse-drawn howitzer?'

'Yes, that's right.' Heinrich smiled. 'I liked the horses. They were named Willy and Otto, after the Kaiser and Bismarck. I used to feed them extra apples as a treat when no one was looking. In fact, that was why I volunteered for the Army: so I could choose to go into the artillery and look after the horses. The battles were less pleasant.'

'I understand.' Greene forced himself to relax a little, knowing it would help the old soldier to relax also. 'Did anything... unusual happen to you during that battle? The first one, at Cologne.'

Heinrich's eyes looked into the distance. 'Nothing is usual in battle. It is... random savagery, however well planned by the generals.'

Greene saw a moment's doubt in Heinrich's eye. Then it cleared, and Heinrich said, 'So I see.' Greene wasn't sure whether he liked that or not.

He composed himself, and cleared his throat. 'What I meant by "unusual" is... something that no-one could explain. Something outside the battle, perhaps. Just something that didn't fit.'

Heinrich shook his head. 'Not exactly, but...'

'Go on.'

'Something happened to the sky.'

'The sky?'

'There was... a shadow. I don't know how to put it in words, even in German, and with English there is no hope! It was as if there was something above us, casting a shadow, like a huge thundercloud. The air around us was dark, but there was nothing to cast that shadow. No clouds or anything. But the shadow was there, and the air was dark.

At the time, I thought it was something to do with the guns – the smoke from the muzzles perhaps, but nothing like it happened at any other battle. Nothing quite like it. It was as if we were in the shadow of something that wasn't there. And there were sounds, of course, but there were many odd sounds on that day, but that is normal in an artillery company, when there are guns firing, and shells falling all around the countryside.'

'Falling…' Greene's instincts tingled. It wasn't much, but he just knew it was important. He continued the interview for another half hour or so, and thought there was a good human interest magazine article in the man's story. There were a lot of military magazines out there, and he was confident one would take it.

When Hamilton and Douglas returned to the garden, they looked rather dour to Greene's eyes, and he wondered whether they had heard anything interesting from their chats. 'Any luck?' he asked. 'Luck that isn't top secret, I mean.'

'They just talked about something in the sky,' Douglas said. 'Something they couldn't really describe. And how about you?'

'I think I need to make a phone call.'

'Who to?'

'Maurice.'

The next day, the late afternoon sun shone through broken cloud, and Maurice's old white Kadett bounced along the road next to the railway line west of Cologne for the first time since the short battle. Eventually Maurice pulled up at a wide lay-by on a ridge, and he and Greene exited the car. Greene had brought along a notebook and camera, just in case. He was no photo-journalist, but he wanted to be sure that if he needed any lasting documentation of anything, he could get it, however amateurishly.

He pointed across to the overgrown ground before the tree-line. 'Well, Larry. There's the stage.'

'This is where the... episode occurred.'

'The attack, you mean. Yeah.' Maurice led Greene towards the trees. Aside from a few scorched patches, and some clumps of churned earth here and there, nothing of the strife showed. 'You see that clearing? That's where they had their howitzer and horses.' Four trees had been cut down, the trunks all pointing toward the railway line, and Maurice frowned. 'These weren't cut down when I was here...'

'The army probably had to chop them to get the German howitzer out.'

'I suppose so. But if we had to cut down the trees to get the howitzer out of the woods, how did they get it *in*?'

Greene thought about it for a moment. 'By helicopter?' He knew that was impossible, as Sergeant Craig's platoon would have noticed. 'Or maybe it was put there the night before.'

'Maybe. But they had horses to draw the carriage, so did they lower them on a rope from a whirlybird as well?'

'Search me.' Greene surveyed the battle site. 'It looks like there's a lot of damage over here.'

'There *was* a battle, Larry.'

'Not that sort of damage.' Greene pointed up at the highest branches. 'It looks like something fell through the trees somewhere over there. Well, I say fell, but I suppose I mean lowered; you might be right about that helicopter bringing the big gun in.'

They proceeded deeper into the woods, stepping over rough ground and rotted boles. Greene stepped between two slim trees, and looked round behind him. If a chopper had dropped off the gun over this way, it still must have been pulled at least a couple of hundred yards through solid tree trunks, without damaging, or even touching them. It was obvious that whatever had damaged the treetops had come down through the branches; they were clearly broken in that direction, rather than upwards. He and Maurice angled towards the centre of the damaged area. Ahead, a couple of trees had been felled, but not neatly cut down. The trunks were shattered and split, and reminded Greene of newsreels from the war, and footage of trees hit by shellfire.

He could feel more soil underfoot, having been cast in chunks atop the underbrush. There was a slight rise ahead of him, and Greene stepped up, bracing a hand against a tree to catch his breath. Now he saw the source of the displaced earth: a crater, as if from a large-calibre shell. It was about six feet deep and twenty feet across. Looking up and back, he could see that the path of broken branches led straight to the crater from somewhere above. The soil had dried out, but he could see that the path was still fresh.

'Bloody hell, Larry. What happened here?'

'I don't know, but whatever it was, it was quite recent. In the last week or two, I suppose.'

'Do you think it happened at the same time as… as the attack?'

Greene spread his hands helplessly. 'I'm a journalist, not

61

a… whatever sort of person works out such things. But I'll tell you what, Maurice; I think it'd be an awful coincidence if wasn't something to do with what happened to you and that platoon.'

'Instinct?'

'Well, can you tell me you don't feel the same thing?' Maurice didn't reply. 'It looks like a shell crater or something. Did the exercise fire any shells into the trees? Either before the attack, or in reply?'

'No. There was no artillery on our side.'

Something gleamed dully at the bottom of the crater. At first Greene thought it might be something like a water mains pipe, but then he noticed a curve of smoked glass, and what might be part of a very short – or torn off – wing. 'What's that at the bottom?' Greene's feet were carrying him into the centre of the crater before his mind could tell them not to.

'Larry, stop! It looks like an unexploded bomb to me!'

It did somewhat resemble a bomb, Greene had to admit, but for the glass and the door. 'Left over from the war? Not a chance. I think it's a plane.'

'A plane? A little private job, you mean?' Greene nodded. 'Where are its wings?'

'Looks like they've been torn off.' Greene approached it cautiously, just in case it still was some sort of unexploded bomb after all. 'Are you coming? Douglas should be arriving soon.'

'I think I'll wait here,' Maurice replied.

Slightly envying him, Greene looked over the object half-buried in the crater. It was definitely some sort of vehicle, with a windscreen, hatch, and portholes, but he stayed a couple of feet away. After a moment, he returned to Maurice. 'I don't know how, but... the old man was right.'

The long flatbed lorry that arrived at the layby later was escorted by a pair of lightweight Ferret armoured scout cars, one of which had a small enclosed gun turret mounted on it. The other was simply crammed full of heavily-armed soldiers in full battledress.

While the troops jumped from their vehicles under their sergeant's orders, three men in khaki overalls emerged from the lorry cab, and consulted a map. After a moment, they set off into the woods at the double, escorted by a trio of armed soldiers.

A roar from over the treetops heralded the arrival of a pair of helicopters. An armed Westland Scout settled into a watchful flight pattern over the woods, while a larger Wessex descended to hover over the shredded gap in the leaf canopy.

Greene shielded his eyes with his hand against the rotor wash from the Wessex above, partly to protect his eyes from dirt and debris blown around, and partly to stop his glasses being blown clean off.

Two of the men in overalls worked quickly to uncover the capsule or fuselage from the earth in its crater, while the third guided a thick set of cables down from the chopper's winch to just a few inches right above the capsule.

Between them, they attached a harness of thick straps, then waved thumbs-up to Douglas. Douglas spoke briefly into his R/T, and the Wessex's engines audibly spun up a little faster. Slowly and carefully, the crashed whatever the hell it was, ascended. As the helicopter rose, the winch cables tightened, pulling the craft up a little further, until it was just above the treetops. The chopper rotated, and crept towards the clearing at the end of the roadway, where the lorry and armoured cars were waiting. The craft swung woozily below the chopper.

The men in the overalls ran back to their vehicle a lot faster than they had left it for the crater. When they got there, they scrambled up on to the back of the lorry, snatching up straps and buckles. The chopper lowered the capsule on to the back of the lorry, and the men secured it.

'Take a good look,' Douglas said. 'It's the last time you'll see it.' He gave little smile. 'Last time I'll see it too, most likely.'

'Where will it be taken?' Greene asked, purely out of habit; he wasn't quite stupid enough to actually expect an answer.

'FTD and DI55 will probably fight over it,' Douglas replied, to his surprise. 'Oh, by the way. Rumour has it there's an air traffic controller at Manston who's disgracefully loose-lipped after a few drinks. I suspect I should find him...'

'Listenable?'

'A good working contact. Just remember, Mr Greene, you are doing a little job for us.'

## — CHAPTER FOUR —

# *Air, Land and Sea*

Travers straightened up from where he knelt to examine the capsule, and groaned. Mist was beginning to form in the crater where the icy breeze from the sea met the warmth still radiating off the rocks from the tectonic heat below. Anne leaned forward to help him up.

'Quite fascinating, wouldn't you say, eh?'

'Very,' Anne agreed. 'It must have landed very recently. It certainly wasn't uncovered by the volcanic activity. The question isn't so much can we open it, as should we?'

'There must be a door handle inside, so if any occupants survived, they'd have opened it themselves. Unless they're dogs, or monkeys. The Russians and Americans have both used animals as passengers in test flights.'

'Or unless they're injured, in which case we ought to open it. If we can.'

'That's a point,' Travers admitted. He scratched at his beard, and shuffled his shoulders around inside his coat. 'Anne? What's the name of our pilot again?'

'Suzy Parr.'

'Good, good. Come along, then.' He started back towards the helicopter. 'Miss Parr,' he called out, as soon as he was sure he was within earshot. She waved, and came forward to meet him and Anne. 'Miss Parr,' Travers said quickly. 'Can you get on your radio and call the ship to send over a medical team and an engineer with some cutting equipment?'

To her credit, Parr didn't ask why; she simply swung herself back up into the cockpit of the Whirlwind, and switched to the ship's frequency. She spoke on the radio for a couple of minutes, then dropped back down. 'Doctor Collins is coming over on a launch, with some first aiders and engineer's mate. They should be over in ten minutes.'

'Splendid! Now come on. While we wait, there's something I'd like you to see.'

Wreckage was scattered over hundreds of yards of wheat field, the air filled with the stink of hot metal and fuel. The distinctive geodesic pattern of thin supports in the fuselage interior was unmistakable, even though the tail section was missing, and the nose turret and cockpit had been mashed into the earth. Lethbridge-Stewart had been right about the bombers being Vickers Wellingtons, and that troubled him more than the actual bombing.

'A penny for your thoughts?' Captain Kyle asked, as she stepped from the jeep to join him. They were a safe distance from the larger pieces of debris, and a truckload of soldiers had drawn up behind them.

'I was just wondering why such old aircraft, and why Deepdene? It must be at least a quarter of a century since a Wellington went on a bombing sortie, and why would the RAF bomb an English village anyway?'

'I wish I knew. Somehow I don't imagine the pilots will be in any condition to tell us.'

'I doubt it too.' He frowned in thought, 'Or would they?

They must have identification on board, and flight plans. If we can find them, then at the very least we can see where they came from, and the name of their CO.'

'Who hopefully can tell us something,' Kyle agreed grimly. She turned to watch soldiers emerge from a truck that had pulled up near the jeep. The men were beginning to sift through the wreckage. They wouldn't be expecting to find survivors, Lethbridge-Stewart knew, though an ambulance was on its way just in case. It would probably only be needed if the wreckage had landed on a farmer, he thought.

He felt a hand on his arm. 'Are you all right, Alistair?' she asked, very softly.

'Yes, S—' He hesitated, and frowned. 'Sorry, Marianne. That's odd... I was going to say something, but I'm not sure what.'

'It sounded like it was going to be "sir". Chance would be a fine thing.'

'Not if you were seconded to the Navy. Captain there is at least equal to colonel here, isn't it?'

'And the captain of a ship is called sir by all, regardless of posted rank,' she added.

'Well, we are a joint services establishment,' Lethbridge-Stewart said, deadpan. 'It would only take a move of your office across the corridor.'

'Tempting, but I much prefer the view from the office window I have.' She cleared her throat, nodded towards the approaching soldiers, and spoke in a more normal tone. 'Orders, Colonel?'

'First thing to do is make sure that whatever that object is, it's taken to the Establishment and put under secure guard

67

for examination.' Kyle nodded. 'The RAF will want to collect and examine this wreckage, so we should let them do so, but... I think it should also be brought back to the Establishment.'

'Do you think these really are RAF aircraft?'

'I can't imagine why the RAF would set out to bomb in the vicinity of an English village. Can you, Captain?' He noted her expression, and allowed a small and grim smile. 'Before your time, I'm afraid. I'm sure the RAF will be as keen as we are to know who owns them today.' He pointed to several spots around the area. 'Post guards to patrol a perimeter to make sure the wreckage is undisturbed until a recovery crew can arrive.'

'What is that thing?' Parr sounded as much impressed as puzzled, and Anne couldn't blame her. Whatever the thing was, it was extremely well made, and yet somehow ageless; neither futuristic nor simply modern. 'It's not just any old plane, is it?'

'We're not sure what it is. Not yet, anyway.' Anne paused a moment. 'What's your impression of it?'

Parr looked it over. It had no engine, and no sign of a mount for one, but its short winglets were clearly meant to generate lift, and control its flight. There was a very tough glass windscreen and portholes, but darkened beyond the point where a pilot could, in her opinion, usefully see out. It was clearly designed to carry two or three people. 'Some sort of experimental lifting body?' she suggested at last. 'Something like the American X-1?'

'Chuck Yeager's supersonic testbed, you mean? It's not dissimilar, is it?'

'A little wider, to accommodate the additional seats, but otherwise, it's fairly similar. The extra seats might be for scientists or technicians observing the test from inside. Is there anyone inside?'

'We don't know,' Anne's father admitted. 'We can't open it, even if we were sure we should, and nobody has opened it from the inside. That is why I had you call for medical staff and an engineer with cutting gear.'

'Speaking of which,' Anne said. 'I think I hear their boat approaching.' Everyone paused to listen; there was indeed the sound of a boat engine chugging towards them from somewhere below and to the northeast.

'They must be using the oldest boat they've got,' Parr said, as they stepped back out of the crater. The engine fell silent, and there was a sudden rush of booted feet on ash. Anne looked out to sea and saw, not one of the *Amundsen*'s launches, but a squat looking ship with a surprisingly rounded bow, painted in eye-wateringly jagged black, white and grey lines. On the beach at the foot of the slope, a wooden boat with a large outboard motor was leaning to one side.

Before she could turn to her father and ask whether he recognised anything about the other ship, half a dozen men in heavy blue coats and flattened steel helmets from decades previous had ran up and lifted rifles in their direction.

'*Hände hoch!*' the nearest man was shouting.

Confused, everyone could only raise their hands.

The convoy rumbled past a yellow sign edged in red, warning that the area beyond was prohibited, along with dire warnings of the penalties meted out to trespassers. The road turned and ran parallel to a double layer of high chain-link fence and concrete posts, with barbed wire coiled along the top, and downward-slanting spikes around the top of the posts. Small square plaques bearing a lightning bolt symbol were spaced along the fence at regular intervals.

In a few minutes, the road arrived at a gap in the fences. Hardened blockhouses and an observation tower flanked the gates, and armed soldiers were on alert as they approached. Lethbridge-Stewart stopped at the main sign by the gate: *Joint Warfare Establishment. Ministry Of Defence Property.* Beyond, other signs directed visitors to where they should report, and posted speed limits for vehicles once inside the fence.

A sergeant came over and saluted. They showed him their papers, and he nodded. 'Building H has been prepared to receive your cargo, as ordered.'

'Very good, Sergeant,' Lethbridge-Stewart said, and nodded to Kyle to drive on.

'*Hände hoch*! Hands up!' The men with rifles spread out a little, but kept their weapons trained on the scientists and their pilot. Travers' heart raced and he couldn't catch his breath for a moment. Then he noticed that the rifles were Lee-Enfield .303 calibre, and standard British armed forces issue until only a few years ago. The helmets were old style British military ones too. 'What!' he exclaimed. 'How dare you!'

The sailor who had spoken shuffled slightly. 'Wait a minute... You're English?'

Travers glared. 'Yes. Professor Edward Travers, if the name means anything to you, and I am indeed English. So is my daughter, my pilot, and everyone else in this expedition. Apart from the ones who are Scots, Welsh, or Irish, obviously. And our ship is Norwegian registered, that I'll grant you.'

'What are you doing in this area?'

'Conducting a scientific survey of this newly-risen island.' He squinted at the leading sailor's sleeve. 'Lieutenant.'

'Your survey's over; you'll have to return to port.'

'Whatever for?'

'This is a restricted shipping zone. There have been reports of U-Boat activity in the area.'

'U-Boats?' Anne couldn't help but laugh. The sailors gave her an odd look, but at least they had lowered their rifles.

'I know we're quite far from the Baltic, but Donitz's boats will attack British shipping wherever they can.' The lieutenant paused, observing their expressions. 'It can't be that confusing, Professor; you must have noticed there's a war on.'

'The war, yes...' Travers frowned then cleared his throat and put a tentative hand on the lieutenant's shoulder, leading a couple of steps aside. 'Perhaps, before we go any further, we should both report in to the Admiralty. I rather suspect, given our meeting like this, that they'll have something to say to both of us.'

The lieutenant nodded slowly. Another engine sound had made itself known by now, and a couple of the armed naval ratings turned to see a rubber fast launch beach itself. They looked to their lieutenant as several men in thick parkas jumped out. Most of them were emblazoned with a

Red Cross symbol. 'Sir?'

'They're medics?' the lieutenant asked Travers.

'And one engineer. We found something interesting nearby, and there may be injured men inside.'

'All right, Bosun. Let them through.'

Travers sighed with relief, and said, 'Can you tell me, Lieutenant – and, yes, I know it's a silly question – but what do you think the date is?'

The man was clearly bemused, but shrugged and said, 'November 2nd, 1939.'

'November 1939?' Anne exclaimed. 'But that's impossible, that's nearly thirty years ago.' The armed sailors looked startled, glancing at each other for reassurance, no doubt thinking she was insane.

Travers leaned closer to his daughter's ear. 'Impossible? Remember we've met someone before – three people, actually – who hadn't aged a day in almost forty years.'

'Almost thirty-five, Father,' Anne whispered back.

'Is it?' The sharp nod from his daughter convinced him. 'Yes, well, even I have my off days. Point is, Anne, we've seen it's not impossible.'

'Yes, but they claimed to have a time machine,' she said quietly, so no one else could hear.

'Yes. And they certainly didn't have those fitted to Flower Class corvettes during the war.' He indicated the ship she had noticed first. It was about the same size as their own survey ship, but it was clearly built for a very different purpose. The pairs and quads of guns angled upwards at several points around her decks. 'Oh my. I didn't think there were any left.'

'Didn't I read something, some rumour, about an

American experiment with time travel on a ship during the war?' Ann asked. 'In Philadelphia, I think.'

'There were rumours, but much later in the war, not in '39.'

'Then what—?'

'How should I know, Anne?' Travers scratched at his beard. 'I'll tell you one thing, though. That ship is the *second* mystery vessel we've seen today, after the capsule thing, and I don't believe in that much coincidence. Oh, no, not in the slightest.'

'You think they're connected?'

'Think? No, not really. But *feel*, yes! And now we should think about how and why.'

Greene had managed to sleep quite well on the plane on the flight back from Germany, but he still felt tired and drained by the time a black cab dropped him off at home. Perhaps it was the prospect of a bit of nagging from Caroline, about being away on stories so much.

Fortunately she was in a good mood, just glad to see him back. They had dinner and watched TV before bed, and in the morning he finally felt truly awake. He filed a couple of minor stories with some magazines that he knew would take them – such as the interview with Heinrich Kursten – and then had a relaxing lunch. Caroline was going to be babysitting her sister's kids for the night, so Greene knew he would have no problems about being out for another night at a bar.

It wouldn't be a matter of drinking for pleasure, however, but meeting up with the military air traffic controller at RAF Manston. Hamilton and Douglas had said he might have an idea of where Colonel Lethbridge-Stewart went. Manston was only a ninety-minute drive or so, which meant he could pop down and back in one evening. He'd best not drink much if he was driving back, but that didn't matter as he wanted to loosen the air traffic chap's tongue rather than his own. He wanted to be alert for whatever the man might let slip.

Thanks to the hints given to him, it didn't take him long to spot the right person in the village pub off-base. Even in civvies, the service personnel in the pub were obvious by their bearing and their haircuts. The one he was looking for, he'd been told, was a prematurely-balding fella with an early paunch and a fondness, if not a talent, for the dartboard.

He wasn't at the dartboard when Greene arrived, but he recognised the man anyway. He was looking uncomfortable in a corner seat in the snug, while a couple of fitter looking men, who also had the air of servicemen, were chatting to him with rather unpleasant smiles. Greene supposed there were fewer Queen's Regulations to worry about in a civilian pub.

Nobody seemed to recognise Greene, which rather made his heart sink, but he reminded himself that in this case the anonymity was a definite advantage. His opportunity came when several local young ladies came in, diverting the attention of the others in the company of his target.

Greene had already prepared another pint of stout – and whisky chaser – for Flight Sergeant Collins, and a Virgin Mary for himself, and now he swiftly took a seat next to Collins. The man barely registered his presence, until Greene slid the pint across the table. 'The usual?'

'Er, yeah.' Collins compared it to his near-empty glass,

and nodded. 'Thanks, mate.'

'Thought those chaps would never go,' Greene said, 'and I'd be standing all night.'

'It's always pretty busy in here. At least since *The Crown* was turned into a fancy coffee and wine bar.'

'Which nobody can afford to drink in anyway.'

'Right. Apart from officers, of course. Silver lining for the landlord here, though.' Greene nodded, letting the guy ease himself into talking to him.

It was a quiet night, and General Hamilton found it strangely relaxing to get some of the backlog of paperwork done, when he wasn't being interrupted. Of course, as soon as the thought had crossed his mind, Sally Wright knocked on the door. 'Enter,' Hamilton called.

Her face was still slightly drawn, and he regretted not being able to give her any news about her Alistair, but he was also proud to see that she was professional enough not to ask if there was any. 'Call from the Admiralty, sir. Hargreaves.'

Hamilton looked up in surprise. 'What on earth does the Navy need with the likes of us?' He picked up the phone and pressed a blue button on the edge. 'Hargreaves? This is General Hamilton. What can I do for you?'

At the other end of the line, Hargreaves cleared his throat before speaking. 'A little birdie tells me that you've been having some interesting days in Germany of late. Talking to some soldiers who were under the impression that they were still fighting the Great War.'

'That sounds rather far-fetched.'

'As far-fetched as a Flower Class corvette disappearing

in 1939 and reappearing this week – with all the original, and somewhat confused, crew aboard?'

Hamilton had no answer to that. He did have a duty, however, and reached for a notepad and pen. 'What details can you give me?'

It hadn't taken that much effort for Greene to keep Collins talking, but it had taken a lot of effort to not get bored with details of the job. In a way, however, that made it easier for him to come up with the right phrasing to lead the conversation to the subject he wanted to get on to. Letting out that he had some connection with the British Forces Broadcasting System, and was in cahoots with a general – hints, without any actual lying – had also eased the way.

It occurred to Greene that he might in fact make a good spy, or at least a good spy story spinner. Fleming was dead now, and there was no reason to leave all the fun to Deighton and Le Carre.

'You must dispatch aircraft to all manner of different places,' he was saying, once the bar was a little quieter, and Collins a little more relaxed. 'Exotic locales across the world.'

'Absolutely. Not holiday destinations, mind, but lots of places. Can't tell you where, though, as I'm sure you understand.'

'Of course, I won't press.'

'Heh, the Press won't press; that's a good one.'

'I don't care whether they go to Timbuktu or Tibet...'

'Well, there you're in luck. There's no law against me saying we've never done either of those, actually.'

'Really?'

'Well, not from this station, anyway. Funny you should

mention Tibet, though – there was talk of doing a flight to there a few weeks back, but nothing ever came of it.'

'Nothing?'

'Orders get changed all the time, situations in the world change. I think I remember them having a plane ready, actually, but it never took off. Last minute order change, I expect. Or passengers or cargo never showed up.'

'Does that happen a lot?'

'Not so late that the plane's waiting on the tarmac... But I'd be a liar if I said "never".'

'I'd swear this island wasn't here yesterday morning,' Lieutenant Thompson said. He was standing on the foredeck of the *Amundsen*, sampling some modern coffee, while his Corvette lay alongside. Anne was staring at the other ship, fascinated.

Travers grunted. 'I can assure you it was – but it wasn't here a fortnight ago. We've watched it grow, you see. It's part of a geological project.'

'Does it have a military application?'

'Undersea volcanic activity? Of course it does. Imagine if a group of ships for a convoy were meeting up and an island suddenly grew under them? Or the temperature from undersea lava to boil the water and reduce its buoyancy?'

'Not to mention the changes needed to charts,' Anne added.

'All right, I get the idea, Prof.'

Travers cleared his throat with a harrumph. 'If you don't mind, Lieutenant, we – I mean my daughter and myself – would like to ask you something.'

'I can't give answers on operational matters. Not before

clearing things with the Admiralty first, anyway.'

'That's all right. All we wanted to ask was what you last remember doing, or happening, before you saw this island or our ship?'

'The ship's meteorologist and I were having a somewhat heated discussion. He had assured us of fine weather, but the sky... Well it was just solid black. Never seen such a thunderhead.' He nodded to the new island. 'But if that's a volcano's baby, then I suppose much of the confusion is explained. Smoke and ash and what have you, eh?' Thompson didn't sound convinced.

Travers coughed. 'Perhaps, perhaps. Did you, by any chance, follow some of that smoke and ashes here?'

'No, actually. We were just battening down the hatches, ready for the storm that our met bod insists was non-existent.'

'And then you saw the island?'

'Yes. Well, after the noise. There was a long whistle, like an incoming shell passing over, but no splash, no explosion.'

Travers exchanged a glance with Anne. 'I think we know what might have made that sound.' He hesitated. 'I also have something of a favour to ask you.' Thompson looked attentive. 'I should like to examine your radar tapes.'

'I'm not sure that's something I can allow.'

'Dammit, man, who do you think helped develop the thing? I probably understand your radar set better than your own operator does.'

'That's as may be, Professor, but—'

'If you have any doubts, signal the Admiralty again. Tell Hargreaves there what I've asked. I'll go along with whatever he happens to decide.'

*

An hour later, Anne and her father sat at a console with a monitor set amongst a lot of controls. 'Quite takes me back,' her father admitted. The radar screen looked very different than the ones Anne had seen on their ship. Instead of a circular screen with a rotating arm that swept round and highlighted little illuminated blobs, and making a pinging sound, this display was a square screen, with constantly-scrolling jagged peaks and troughs. Somehow it all fitted in with the tiny, cramped and soaked interior of the Corvette. She wondered how anyone could have lived or fought in such a thing. Yet here Thompson and his men were.

Her father shook his head. 'I haven't seen a set like this is twenty years.'

'And it was a decade old then?'

'Hmm, well, yes, yes it was.' He squinted over the top of his glasses. 'Would you wind it forward, Anne? No, backwards, but slowly.' Anne raised an eyebrow, but turned the dial to rewind the display. 'Yes, there's the little blighter,' her father said with satisfaction. 'Well don't stop! Keep rewinding.'

Thompson, leaning over their shoulders, planted a finger on the screen. 'Look there. What's that?' Under his nail, the pixels flashed into existence, on and off in a loop from one second to the next.

Travers put his nose to the screen. 'Something falling from the sky. The capsule, I feel sure... But whatever the capsule is, it didn't come from space.'

'It just appears there... out of nowhere! But that's impossible.'

'Course it is!' Travers agreed, 'which means it didn't, of course. It appeared out of somewhere. Somewhere we just can't see.'

'What altitude is that?' Anne asked.

'Oh, about eight thousand feet,' Thompson said.

Travers tapped Anne on the shoulder. 'Do we have the radar tapes from the *Amundsen* as well?'

'Yes, Father. As a matter of fact I brought some printouts with us.' She opened a leather briefcase that had been slung over her shoulder, and pulled out a thick sheaf of papers.

Travers snatched them at once, and began ruffling through them. 'Excellent! Excellent!' He flicked excitedly at a piece of paper with one fingernail. 'There, the same thing. Eight thousand feet.'

'And out of nowhere,' Anne said.

'That we can see.'

'So, if it didn't come from outer space, then… what's at eight thousand feet?'

'An aeroplane?' Thompson suggested.

'Invisible to radar?' Anne asked.

'Why not?' Travers demanded. 'You can't deny it's a dream that every air force has.'

Thompson shivered visibly. 'Or a nightmare, that the other side develops one first.'

'You don't need to worry about that,' Travers muttered. 'What worries me is that this same object, whatever it is, seems to have fallen last night, thirty years or so ago.'

'Twice?'

'No. Just the once. It's clearly quite recently—' He broke off as Susan Parr came into the radar room, escorted by one of the Corvette's ratings. 'Professor, Lieutenant. I'm sorry to interrupt, but you and Anne are required.'

'Required?!' Travers spluttered. 'By whom?'

'According to Admiral Hargreaves, I've to take off with you for home within the hour. You're to report at the Joint Warfare Establishment. He said you'd know who—'

Anne and her father exchanged a look. 'The London Event,' Anne whispered.

Her father nodded. 'What have we stumbled across?'

When the phone rang, Kyle had answered and gone to report to duty first. Someone needed clearance through the gate, having recently arrived from London. Lethbridge-Stewart also rose and left their quarters, taking a walk across the Establishment's central concourse, where an RSM was yelling at some marching privates – and down a slip road to a nondescript hangar-like building.

Inside, under proper lighting, the object was a flattened cylinder, slightly wider at the rear than the nose. It had a couple of pairs of compact fins at the tail, and short flared wings barely worthy of the name. A crack had split the almost-black glass on the port side, nearest the nose. The hatch, which had already fallen off in the newsagent's cellar, had now been laid on a gleaming trolley for examination.

'What are you, I wonder?' Lethbridge-Stewart murmured to himself. 'Chinese, American, or Soviet?'

The door was opened by a guard, and a bluff and burly red-headed man came in with Captain Kyle. 'You're in charge here, I presume,' he began, making eye contact with Lethbridge-Stewart, but not offering a hand to shake.

'I am, Mister...?'

'Doctor. Doctor John Mackay.'

'A pleasure to meet you,' Lethbridge-Stewart said. 'I hope the Ministry briefed you about our... find.'

'They did. But if you don't mind me saying so, you seem a little surprised about something.'

'Nothing personal, Doctor,' Lethbridge-Stewart said reassuringly. 'I had just been hoping I could still have had the assistance of the late Professor Travers. He was in that capsule, or whatever it is.'

Mackay smiled and nodded. 'Worked with this Travers chap before, I suppose?'

'A few months ago, yes.'

'Can't say I've heard of the fella, but if he did a good job, then the best of luck to him, and I'll try to match up.'

Lethbridge-Stewart liked the man immediately. There was a sense of honesty and getting on with it there. 'I'm sure you'll do us proud, Doctor.'

Mackay turned to the capsule, looking at it intently. 'So this is the beastie you're looking to unravel. Intriguing.' Without taking his eyes off the capsule, he went on. 'Funny you should mention a Professor Travers. I knew a Travers once.'

'It's a small world.'

'Edward Travers. Not a professor, mind you.'

'It may be a small world, but that shrinks it further...' Lethbridge-Stewart halted as his brain caught up with his ears. 'Edward was the professor's first name.'

'Really? Aye, well, it's not so unusual a name, though.'

Lethbridge-Stewart turned Mackay around with a hand on the shoulder. 'Who was the Edward Travers you knew?'

'Fella I was at university with. We had a shared interest in anthropology.'

Lethbridge-Stewart felt a shiver. Someone walking over his grave, perhaps. Certainly over someone's grave. 'Did you, by any chance, make an expedition to Tibet?'

Mackay nodded dourly. 'We did, in 1935. We had this daft idea that we could make our names by finding a damn abominable snowman, and bringing it back to put on display, like King bloody Kong at the pictures. Walters, well, he insisted on coming along to prove us wrong. He and Edward had never got on, so I ended up having to try to keep the peace between them.' He shook his head. 'Walters... He's bloody lucky he got... Well, never mind, that's all past now.'

'I need to know what happened. I can see the memory must be uncomfortable for you, but I feel it's very important. And, as it happens, potentially a security issue.'

'Everything's a security issue to you people,' Mackay grumbled. 'But, we'd only been above the snow line for a couple of days, when... Well, our expedition didn't end the way we'd planned. Not the way Edward or I had planned anyway. Walters, well, I don't like to cast aspersions that cost legal fees.'

'What happened? An animal attack, or...?'

'There was an avalanche. Travers... Edward, was buried alive. I was lucky enough – if luck is the right word – to land in the branches of a tree when the force of the snow carried me off a ledge. Edward and the tent went over a few yards away from it, and... Well, it took the local Sherpas a week to find his body.'

'And this other man, Walters?'

'It was his shots that caused the avalanche. He said he was hunting a hare for our dinner, but I never believed that. He knew it was an avalanche area.'

'Did Travers's body have any bullet wounds in it?'

'No, Walters wasn't that stupid. He always kept claiming it was an accident, but... Shooting in a known avalanche area? As I said, he wasn't that stupid.'

'What happened to Walters?'

'Had a short but bright career in the Ministry of Agriculture, then retired to India. And there he can stay, in the Black Hole of Calcutta for all I care.'

'It sounds like you care something.'

'Aye, but my arms are only this long. They won't reach to a neck in India.'

# CHAPTER FIVE

# *Post Mortem*

'What the hell am I doing?' Larry Greene breathed. He was crouched behind a fuel bowser on a concrete dispersal apron between two runways at RAF Manston. Twenty yards or so away, a pair of armed RAF Regiment whitecaps were strolling along the runway's edge, accompanied by an Alsatian dog on a leash.

He was more bothered about the possibility of the dog catching a hint of an unfamiliar scent from him than the guards looking round; it was still pretty dark, so he doubted they'd see him in his charcoal two-piece suit anyway.

He was pretty sure his good graces with the military, in the shape of Hamilton and Douglas, didn't extend to sneaking on to military airfields, but something had got a grip on him that was making him giddy by his standards – and reckless. He suspected it might be overindulgence in the pub, getting details out of Flight Sergeant Collins. Give the man his due, he wasn't stinting on getting his rounds in.

The aircraft that Lethbridge-Stewart had been intended to fly out on was a Vickers VC-10, an airliner used by the military with minimal tweaks as a troop transport. As far as Collins knew, the plane had still never taken off on another flight, and remained on site in a maintenance hangar.

Greene had decided that he wanted to see it. He wasn't

even sure why, other than that he had what the American detectives on TV called a hunch. He couldn't quite imagine that some strange conspiracy had set out to kidnap the colonel, but at the same time he couldn't keep the thought entirely out of his mind – or the thought of what a scoop it would make. Such a scoop would get him at least a half hour special on ITV, and probably in colour too. Chorley would not be impressed, but that's what one got for burning one's bridges.

So here Greene was, having slipped away from the limits of the official BFBS visitor's pass, and looking for that maintenance hangar.

There were aircraft and helicopter engine noises all the time, but one particular sound was growing ever louder, and Greene thought it sounded almost as if it were about to come down on top of him. He looked up, and saw a huge plane with four propellers, which *was* dropping alarmingly towards him.

Seeing a plane as large as a Hercules land close-up was surprisingly impressive. Its tyres screeched and billowed smoke as it braked hard on the runway. Even slowing, the mass of it and the prop wash from its engines combined to almost pull him from his hiding place.

In a few moments, however, it had slowed to a crawl, and began to turn on to the dispersal apron where, Greene supposed, it would be either loaded or unloaded.

A small group of specialist vehicles appeared almost immediately. A sort of tractor pulling a set of boarding stairs led the way, followed by a flatbed truck. The fuel bowser in whose shadow Greene was hiding suddenly started up, and he almost yelped, realising that he'd never make a real secret agent if a truck driver could walk up and start the engine without his noticing.

Greene darted into the doorway of a small bunker – a sign on the door said it led to drainage tunnels – as the fuel bowser headed towards the Hercules as well.

A number of armed Whitecaps – RAF police – were running towards the vicinity, and Greene began to be convinced that he had pushed his luck too far by coming here.

As the sweat trickled down his back, however, the Whitecaps slowed to a halt, and they formed up around the boarding stairs, helping move them to a passenger door just behind the cockpit. Greene let out a shuddering breath, and watched one of the Whitecaps step forward and open the door. Greene got an even bigger shock when the passengers emerged from the plane

He recognised the bearded old man and the pretty girl at once: Professor Edward Travers and his daughter, Doctor Anne Travers. The very same people Chorley had sent him to 'interview' a few weeks ago. Had they been drafted in to try and find Lethbridge-Stewart as well?

The sound of a helicopter engine was growing louder, and seemed to be approaching from behind him. Greene ducked deeper into the shadows, and looked back and up. A Westland Wessex was descending towards the area. His heart skipped a beat, and he started backing off slowly, not wanting the movement to draw the Whitecaps' attention and confirm his position.

The Wessex's wheels settled onto the ground at the same time as the Travers' stepped off the mobile staircase. At the rear of the Hercules, the flatbed truck was backing into position to meet the ramp that was being lowered, but Greene was more interested in the Travers'. Whitecaps escorted them across the tarmac, and for a moment, the urge to step forward and ask them was strong, but common sense survival instinct took over. Greene stayed where he was, and watched as a tired-looking Edward Travers was helped into the chopper by his daughter. She followed him aboard, and the Whitecaps stepped aside and began to disperse. The whine of the Wessex's engines grew again, and it lifted off, heading west.

Greene's mind was racing, from one potential scoop to the next, when his eyes fell upon the flatbed truck by chance. Several men were moving a tarp-covered object from the Hercules' rear ramp onto the truck. The object was concealed, but he knew from the size and shape exactly what it was. That explained a lot, he thought; the Travers' were just the sort of people who ought to be looking at the capsule he and Maurice had found.

Now he slightly regretted not just boldly stepping out and talking to them. They were probably working for Hamilton as well, after all.

He sighed, and returned to his original objective for all this cloak and dagger nonsense. The sooner he found the maintenance hangar, the sooner he could get back to an area where he was at least allowed to be without risk of being shot, and the sooner he could get a good stiff drink in the pub.

Colonel Lethbridge-Stewart had left Mackay to supervise assembling a small working group of qualified and security-vetted mechanics and engineers from the Joint Warfare

Establishment's crews. There were people from the Army, Navy, and Air Force for him to choose from, so Lethbridge-Stewart knew that Mackay would have no difficulty finding someone qualified to help him check over the capsule.

Captain Kyle fell into step with him as he strolled out of the hangar building, and turned in the direction of the main headquarters building. 'Do you think he'll be able to make anything of the capsule?' she asked.

'I don't know, I never met the man before. But he seems competent enough, so I suppose we have to trust that the top brass know what they're doing by choosing to send him. Has the RAF recovery team picked up the wreckage of their Wellingtons yet?'

Kyle gave him a momentarily puzzled look, then shrugged. 'They've begun forensic examination of the crash sites, so it shouldn't be long before they're able to move the pieces.'

'Do we know where they'll take them?'

She hesitated, then said, 'They originally wanted to analyse the pieces at Farnborough, but I took the liberty of arranging for orders to be issued to bring the wreckage here.'

Lethbridge-Stewart was surprised but pleased. 'Good thinking. I don't believe in coincidence, Captain, and two sets of anomalous aeroplanes dropping around the same village...'

'Believe me, Colonel, I know exactly what you mean.' They both smiled. 'You still seem tired; didn't you sleep well?'

'Moderately, Captain. Moderately.'

'Bad dreams again?'

'Yes...' He didn't need to ask how she knew he had bad

dreams. The 'again' explained it all.

'Do you remember what it was?'

'You ask a lot of questions.'

'Sorry.' She tapped her Intelligence Corps insignia. 'Force of habit; ask questions, don't give answers.'

'Quite. To be perfectly honest, I'm not sure I remember anyway. I was... going somewhere. Tibet.'

'Tibet? Why Tibet?'

'I don't really know. It just felt like a natural place to say. Somewhere cold and remote, overlooking the world.'

'Looking for the abominable snowman?' she asked cheerfully.

He felt his expression freeze, and heard something in his head; neither a memory nor an imagined sound, but something in between. A distant howling roar, echoing in the confined darkness.

'I wish I knew. It was just a dream, after all. Now, let's see what the MO has made of the late Professor Travers.'

'Hey, what are you doing here?'

Greene started, and swallowed hard. The game was up. He was walking between two huge pale green hangars, looking for a signpost in something resembling civilian English rather than acronymic military jargon. He turned to see a man in a jumpsuit, with a sergeant's stripes on the sleeves, approaching.

'Who are you anyway?' the man added.

Greene was tempted to make up a lie – claim to be Travers, perhaps – but if the game was up then it was up. 'Larry Greene,' he said weakly. 'I'm visiting on behalf of the BFBS, on a story.'

'And you have a pass that says so?'

Greene handed it over meekly, awaiting the inevitable. However, the man simply looked at it, shrugged, and said, 'Well, you're a bit lost, aren't you?'

'I was looking for the main maintenance hangar,' Greene admitted. 'See the everyday work of the base, that sort of thing.'

To his surprise, the sergeant didn't question this; after all, his pass was genuine. 'Oh, then you're not too lost. It's round that corner. I was just heading back there myself. C'mon, I'll take you there.'

'Thanks,' Greene tried to sound cheery rather than simply relieved. He fell into step with the sergeant. 'I was beginning to think I'd end up wandering forever, like a castle ghost.'

'Don't worry about it. Someone would have stumbled across you and set you right. Or thrown you in the glasshouse.'

'As long as they didn't just shoot me.'

The sergeant laughed. 'There isn't a war on, you know. Not unless I've missed something on the morning news. And if I have, we'll all be glowing in the dark before they can form up a firing squad.'

By now they had turned the corner, and faced a wide steel-roofed concrete building with huge green-painted steel doors the size of tennis courts. The doors were slightly open in the centre, to allow some air in for the workers inside, and the sergeant led Greene to that gap. When they got there, Greene was astonished to see that the gap was several feet wide. Enough for them to walk through side by side.

The hangar interior was like a mini airfield in its own

right. Several vehicles such as jeeps and forklifts were dotted around, and there were a couple of helicopters and small training aircraft tied down, with hatch covers and inspection panels open. Men in overalls were strolling around, poking into exposed engines and the like.

The largest object in the hangar, taking up perhaps almost half of it, was an airliner with a high T-shaped tail, and four engines under it, well behind the wings. Though an airliner familiar to Greene from airports, this one was painted in a typical RAF light grey.

'Funny,' Greene said, 'you never quite realise how big these things are, unless you work on them every day, I suppose.'

'Still pretty impressive, some of them,' the sergeant said.

Greene noted the aircraft's serial number, painted on the side. It was the same one that Lethbridge-Stewart should have left in. He nodded towards it. 'What actually is wrong with this aircraft? If you don't mind me asking. Or is it just in for a regular MOT?'

'O-rings in the fuel pumps have corroded. The engines conked out last time it was meant to fly out. Which is probably just as well, or they'd have leaked hundred-octane juice all over the pistons, and whoof!' He made an upwards-rushing gesture with both hands.

'I get the picture,' Greene said with a shiver. 'Actually, a man I've worked with, Colonel Lethbridge-Stewart,' he lied, 'was meant to be on that flight.'

'Fella with a moustache?'

Greene nodded. 'He didn't head home, so if the plane couldn't take off...'

The sergeant shook his head. 'He hitched a lift on a

Dominie being sent out to Cyprus. That took off about twenty minutes after this one came in to the shop.'

Greene suppressed the urge to grin and shout with delight. Now all he needed to do was follow that aircraft, and doubtless Collins had dispatched it also. The man *had* sent Lethbridge-Stewart on his way after all; he just hadn't actually known it.

This, Greene knew, was one of those situations where, as Hamilton had said back in Germany, he had access to resources that the military perhaps didn't. The RAF – and the other Air Forces around, for that matter – weren't the only organisations able to track planes on radar. Civilian airports, airlines, meteorology departments, and transportation safety authorities all had their access to radar tracks.

He would go home, rack himself up a pot of black coffee and a set of telephone numbers, and start dialling.

It had been an exhausting journey for Anne Travers, and she worried that it must have been worse for her father. Parr had flown them to Reykjavik in Iceland, where a jet transport had been waiting to fly them to RAF Manston. Now they had been bustled onto another helicopter and were swooping over Old Sarum in Wiltshire.

Soon they were descending towards a sprawling complex of utilitarian buildings, hangars, and concrete plazas, all surrounded by a perimeter of tall fencing, and with gun and missile emplacements scattered around at regular intervals.

Men in fatigue uniforms were busy with mysterious tasks all around, and a small handful were marching towards a painted H on the ground. Anne quickly realised this was a welcoming committee for her father and her, as the helicopter was descending towards the same spot. When they landed, an older man in RAF uniform ducked low to come forward and open the door for her.

'Doctor and Professor Travers?'

'I'm Doctor Travers,' Anne said, debarking and enjoying the chance to stretch her legs. She turned to help her father out of the helicopter, as he was moving much more stiffly and slowly. 'This is my father, Professor Edward Travers.'

The RAF man smiled. 'I've heard a lot about you both, and it's an honour.' He extended a hand to shake. 'Air Vice Marshal le Cheminant, commandant here. Welcome to the Joint Warfare Establishment. You should find that we have everything here you might need for the examination of the... objects.'

'I suppose so,' her father said. 'If ever our Icelandic sample gets here.'

'It's being transferred by road,' le Cheminant said. 'The Establishment doesn't have a long enough runway to fly it in on a transport aircraft, and Whitehall didn't want to attract random eyes by dangling it from a helicopter.'

Lethbridge-Stewart and Kyle walked into the post mortem room adjoining the infirmary's morgue just as the chief medical officer was covering up the dark bearded features of Professor Travers with a sheet, which covered both the cadaver and gurney on which it lay. Doctor Beswick was a striking but unsmiling woman, and nodded as they came in.

An orderly was wiping down the steel table with disinfectant strong enough to make both officers gag and try to breathe only through their mouths – and then as little as possible – while another was waiting to wheel the gurney back into the morgue for storage.

Doctor Beswick came over, saluting. 'Well, the autopsy's complete on your friend Travers.'

'I wouldn't say he was my friend, exactly,' Lethbridge-Stewart said. 'Still, it's a pity. What did you find?'

'Cause of death wasn't impact damage. It was asphyxiation. There must not have been enough air in the capsule for however long its journey took. At least it was probably relatively peaceful.'

'And definitely no sign of disease, or nuclear, chemical or biological contamination?'

'None. Although there was an unusual amount of carbon and related particles in his hair and on the skin. Probably in the clothes too, but they're being analysed separately.'

Lethbridge-Stewart frowned. 'Carbon? Is that significant?'

'Perhaps, perhaps not. Essentially it means he was in the vicinity of a large fire shortly before entering the capsule. But the fire wasn't in his transport, and neither was it – through smoke inhalation or the like – the cause of his asphyxia. If it had been, I'd have found it in the lungs, but there was nothing like that.' Beswick hesitated. 'This man, Travers... You said you'd worked with him before?'

'Yes, there was... an emergency. The... the London Event.'

'One of those things you can't talk about?'

'Top secret, I'm afraid. I know I couldn't talk about it even if...' He didn't want to say 'even if I remembered it', because then they might think he was losing it. 'Well, I suppose I have some paperwork to do.'

'Speaking of which,' Beswick said hurriedly, passing him a clipboard. 'This is the full post mortem report. Nothing particularly noteworthy, but if you can countersign it, as commandant, then it'll speed up release of the body for a funeral.'

Lethbridge-Stewart nodded and took the clipboard. 'He has a niece or – no, a daughter, I think. And a son. They'll have to be notified.' He signed his name under Beswick's, then stopped before dating it. 'That can't be right...'

'Sir?'

'You've dated the wrong year. 1959. That is a five, isn't it?' Beswick and Kyle looked at each other, Beswick blushing slightly. Kyle gave her an almost imperceptible shake of the head – almost, but not quite, and Lethbridge-Stewart wondered what it meant – and took the clipboard herself.

'I'll get some correction fluid,' Kyle said briskly. 'It'll save re-writing the whole report.'

Lethbridge-Stewart nodded, distractedly. 'Yes...' How, he wondered, could one write down a year a decade out of date? He could understand hitting the wrong key on a typed report, or putting the previous year on something signed and dated in early January, but for some reason this niggled at him.

Kyle stepped closer. 'Alistair? Are you all right?'

'Low blood sugar, perhaps,' Beswick said. 'As CMO I prescribe an early lunch. Joel's head chef at the Officer's Mess today, and you know how good he is.'

'That sounds like a good idea, Colonel,' Kyle said firmly. 'I'll meet you there, and we can discuss what to do when the RAF recovery team brings in their spoils.'

Lethbridge-Stewart pulled himself upright with a sharp nod. 'You're quite right, both of you. I'll do that. Carry on.' They exchanged salutes, and Lethbridge-Stewart left the morgue.

When the colonel had gone, Kyle said, 'While I'm here, Doctor, I'd just like a little chat.'

'If it's about the year—'

'Never mind that. You were careless, and should be more attentive to such inevitable minor difficulties, but it's not what I wanted to talk about.'

'What's troubling you, then, Captain?'

'Bad dreams.'

'You too? I thought it was Colonel Lethbridge-Stewart who—'

'It's his bad dreams that trouble me, Doctor.'

'Ah, I see.' Beswick shrugged. 'They do bear monitoring, I'll grant you that.'

'They seem to be becoming a little more frequent, and wide-ranging.'

'Yes, I'd noted as much in the reports.'

'What does it mean?'

'The irritating thing is that it means one of two possibilities. One, that the treatment regimen is working, and the memories are working their way into his unconscious mind. In which case, with any luck they will also soon become available to the conscious mind. Alternatively, it could mean that his treatment is breaking down somewhat.'

Kyle thought for a moment. 'Do you think we should

modify his dosage?'

'Not yet; not without knowing which of those things is happening. Otherwise we risk causing exactly the opposite of the desired effect.'

Caroline was still out when Greene got home, which meant he was free to do his telephone research.

It had taken about an hour and a half, and he'd had to weed out two other potential incidents that weren't related to the aircraft he was interested in, but Greene had heard enough from a Lufthansa traffic controller and a contact in the *Deutscher Wetterdienst* in Offenbach – the German Met Office – to be confident that a radar contact lost over Germany matched the Dominie's flight plan and timings pretty exactly.

He had kept a couple of maps from his trip to Germany, and got them out, unfolding them across the coffee table in his living room. He wasn't that great at map reading and orienteering, but he had a vague idea of the region that had been discussed, and was able to pick a range to circle on a contour map of Germany.

The Officer's Mess was as neat and well-presented as any top-flight London restaurant, and was largely empty as Lethbridge-Stewart entered. A couple of RAF officers and a naval lieutenant were the only other diners as yet, and were outnumbered by the stewards serving them. The seating at private tables was lush and dark, fashionably edged in chrome, and he laid his cap on one table before going to the wood and leather panelled bar to claim a coffee. It was a bit early in the day for anything stronger, and he could use the awakening.

Returning to the table to await the steward bringing his coffee and a menu, he noticed a familiar face looking out at him from the magazine rack mounted on a pillar. Elvis Presley again, grinning out at him from a *Radio Times*. For some reason he felt drawn to pick up the magazine, thinking they surely hadn't used the same picture again after only, what, a couple of weeks?

He opened the magazine at his table, and felt momentarily slapped in the face by it. There was little of interest to him on either channel, but he was sure BBC2 would have something, if he could just find it. Bizarrely, there didn't seem to be a column for BBC2 on any page.

He frowned, closing the magazine as he gave an absent thanks to the steward delivering his coffee. Then his eyes caught the date on the cover, and slid across to the year.

1959.

'It can't be,' he murmured. Even dentists' waiting rooms had more recent magazines than this. And yet it was the same issue that had been on the shelves at the newsagent's in Deepdene. They surely couldn't have had a *Radio Times* sitting unsold for a decade.

He was distracted from the matter by an RAF wing commander coming in and beckoning to the two other officers who were dining. He didn't seem to have noticed Lethbridge-Stewart. 'Lunch time is over, folks. The remains of those unidentified bomber types have arrived. We'll need to unload them in Building Seven.'

Lethbridge-Stewart rose and approached the wing commander. 'They're Wellingtons,' he said. 'Not unknown.'

The other man looked startled. 'Wellingtons?' He

nodded hurriedly. 'As you say, Colonel. The report I was given was lacking.'

'Understandable,' Lethbridge-Stewart said. 'Carry on, then.' He watched them go, and then snatched up his cap from the table, drained his coffee in one gulp, and hurried out of the mess.

He went down a flight of stairs to the small library and archive that the different service branches shared at the Establishment. Aside from works of military doctrine, it mostly contained manuals from all the services, so that cross-training was easier, and so that members of one service seconded to working with another could prepare themselves for what to expect.

At this hour nobody was in the library, so he stepped inside and closed the door behind him. On some instinct – he couldn't really have said why – he locked the door as well.

What Lethbridge-Stewart wanted, however, was duplicated among all the services. The heavy back folders were easiest to find in the Air Ministry's section. The army and Navy's folders were current and up to date, but he wanted the most comprehensive volume, and found it among the RAF's documentation. He took the heavy folder over to the nearest table, switched on the reading lamp, and – again on that strange instinct – went back and turned off the main lights in the room.

He sat down at the table and opened the thick black folder. It was filled with silhouettes of different aircraft, as a recognition manual for observers, anti-aircraft gunners, and other pilots. He flicked through, looking first to see if anything matched the shape of the capsule that had been recovered from Deepdene. He knew it was a long shot, but he also believed in being thorough.

There were a couple of experimental craft but none of the three or four depicted in the recognition manual resembled the one they had recovered.

The Wellington bombers had awakened something in him too; nostalgia, perhaps. He flicked back through the manual chronologically, looking for recognition sheets for the Second World War era.

Oddly, there didn't appear to be any. At least, there were very few that he recognised, which surprised him, as his father had been a bomber pilot during the war. He could find pages claiming to be from 1939-'40, but they were still filled with biplanes. No Spitfire, no Hurricane... And no Wellingtons or Wellesleys.

From his pocket, Lethbridge-Stewart took out a lined notebook that he had picked up at the bombers' crash site. It was an aircraft logbook, whose neat lines and columns listed mostly training flights, and one or two air raids on France and Germany. The last entry was dated November 1939, yet the paper was fresh and white, uncoloured by age. It did smell slightly smoky, however, having survived the destruction wrought by a fighter jet's rockets.

After a moment's thought, he picked up the telephone and pressed the switches for a secure outside line. 'I need a line to the Air Ministry. Archive, please.' After a moment the call clicked through. 'Hello, Air Ministry Archive? This is Colonel Lethbridge-Stewart, Joint Warfare Establishment. I'm wondering if you can track down the records of an aircraft for me.'

The voice on the other end of the line was female and

pleasant. 'If they're not classified, sir, then we can.'

'I'm looking for the service record of a Vickers Wellington bomber.' He gave her the aircraft registry number and names of the crew from the logbook. 'It certainly flew in '39, and I'd like to know what happened to it after that.'

'What sort of bomber?' the WAAF at the archive asked.

'Vickers Wellington. Before your time, I suspect, but the records should be there.'

'Right you are, sir.

'And can you send any findings to Chelsea Barracks? I'll come and view them there.'

'That should be possible, sir.'

'Excellent, thank you.' He replaced the phone on the receiver, then thought for a moment. '1959, no Wellingtons, and... Travers.' He looked at his watch. Kyle should be at the Officer's Mess by now, and Doctor Beswick would have other duties, so he might have an opportunity to visit the morgue alone.

He moved carefully through the central complex, pausing now and again to avoid bumping in to anyone he might have to talk to. In a few minutes, he was watching Beswick leave for lunch in the company of her brother, who was a bio-warfare bod of some kind at the Establishment.

Nobody was around the doorway to the morgue, so he had no trouble stepping inside and closing the door behind him, before turning the light on. There were several files on the desk in one corner, but only one clipboard, and that had the information he sought. All the dates on it read 1959 – a decade ago. To his surprise there was not just one body listed as having been brought in from Deepdene, but two. One was named as a Private George Nichols, the other as simply 'unknown male'.

Though he planned to examine the corpse from the capsule, the presence of a dead soldier piqued his interest. He was always concerned when a man under his command became a casualty, and thought it was odd that one had been killed without his even knowing about it. He took the folder through into the morgue proper, where a grid of sixteen thick square steel doors faced him from the opposite wall. A series of glass doors were set into the wall on the left, and filled with shelves of bottles and jars. Lethbridge-Stewart didn't want to think about what might be in them. A couple of gurneys for transporting bodies were parked to the right.

Private Nichols' body was stored in freezer number eight, and Lethbridge-Stewart wheeled one of the gurneys over and positioned it under the door marked '8'. He opened it and slid out the drawer on which the occupant lay. The drawer dipped at the end, but the gurney took the weight.

Lethbridge-Stewart didn't recognise the young man lying on the steel. He didn't like looking upon the dead at the best of times, but a cadaver that had been frozen to protect it from decay seemed somehow more unnatural than most, like clay with a strange grey pallor. The man on the steel had a number of cuts and scratches on his face, and a deep gash in his forehead. Lethbridge-Stewart didn't think it looked like a fatal wound, but he knew that bumps on the head could be deceptively serious.

There was a stain on the sheet covering the body, over its legs. There he found several wounds in the man's left thigh. He was no doctor or forensics expert, but he had seen enough action to know that a bullet or two in the vicinity of the femoral artery would kill a man by blood loss quite quickly.

Something made him blink, and in the fraction of a second that it took, he thought he saw a man fall, in the back of a vehicle. His hand felt heavy, just for a heartbeat or two, as if there was a pistol in it. He dismissed the thought; it was easy enough to imagine having caused such a wound, but he had never seen this man before. More importantly, he wasn't one of the occupants of the capsule, so Lethbridge-Stewart slid him back into the drawer, and then bent to open number fourteen.

This face he recognised, almost at least. The eyes were closed, and the glasses that he remembered Professor Travers wearing were not on, but the face was familiar enough, though now cleansed of the blood that had been on it when he fell from the capsule. It was the same nose, the same mouth, and mostly the same beard. There was no grey in the beard, however. It was a little shorter than Lethbridge-Stewart remembered, and completely black.

Hesitating for only a moment, he parted the hairs of the beard with his fingertips, looking for signs of dye – or lack of it nearer the roots. There was none, but the touch of it on his fingertips made him recoil in a different way than he expected. The bristles felt strange, not at all like those of his own moustache. In fact they didn't feel like real hair at all. Neither, he realised, did the skin feel quite like that of a corpse either. Then he noticed what at first looked like a cut at the corner of the cadaver's jaw, and up the side of the neck. It didn't quite look like a wound, as it was too bloodless, and neither was it near either of the incisions made during the post mortem examination.

In spite of himself, he reached out to probe the strange wound, and saw it peel back and rise up, away from the neck. Without thinking, he grabbed it between finger and thumb, and realised at once what it was. Astonished, he pulled on the latex, and the cadaver's whole face peeled away.

The real face, under the latex mask, was that of a total stranger.

# CHAPTER SIX

# *End of the World, As You Know It*

Lethbridge-Stewart returned to his office. His presence there wouldn't be suspicious, so long as nobody had seen him snooping around in the morgue. He checked his watch, opened his desk drawer and rooted around the stationery supplies for a spare ammo clip for his pistol, before settling on a round brass object. It was a simple compass, but it was all he needed.

On second thought, he took the spare clips as well, and unlocked the box containing his service pistol. He strapped it on, and pocketed the clips before leaving. He returned to the Officer's Mess, where Kyle was waiting; he was moderately amused to note that she had picked the same table as he had earlier, though she had tucked her Intelligence Corps beret under a shoulder-flap – exposing her American-style crew-cut – rather than putting it on the table.

'I thought I'd missed you,' she said.

'Call of nature between courses, I'm afraid. Happens to the best of us.'

'Oh, I wondered if some emergency had arisen. Or if something was bothering you.'

'Not at all; no reason why anything should.'

'Your acquaintance's post mortem?'

'I've seen worse.' She simply nodded, and seemed willing to drop the subject. 'Have you eaten already?' Lethbridge-Stewart asked.

'No, but I ordered for both of us. The usual.'

'Good. I'd like to get going as soon as possible after lunch.'

Kyle looked up, her head tilted, eyes widening slightly. 'Going? I thought you'd want to inspect the bomber wreckage. The Wellingtons.'

For a moment he relaxed, hearing her say the name, though it ran through his mind that he had mentioned it to her first.

'I will do, but first I want to look at some files the Air Ministry is sending over to Chelsea Barracks for me. I'll have to pop along and collect them there.'

Kyle's eyes widened more. 'London? Now?'

He was momentarily disappointed at her reaction. 'No time like the present, Captain.'

She shrugged, and smiled. 'I'll see to transport, then.' She rose, and beckoned to a steward. 'A special coffee, please; I'll be back in a moment.' The steward nodded, and Kyle carried on towards the phones by the door.

A moment later, Lethbridge-Stewart felt the steward's presence at his shoulder, and leaned aside a little to let him put Kyle's coffee on the table. Instead, to his shock, he felt a firm hand grip his shoulder. He started to rise, started to swear, but there was a sharp stinging sensation at the side of his neck and everything just went away.

Standing by the phones in their little alcove near the mess door, Marianne Kyle sighed, and dialled the internal

107

number for Doctor Beswick.

'I was just about to call you, Captain,' Beswick said when she answered. 'There's a problem with the dead man from the capsule.'

'Don't be obtuse. What sort of problem? I'm assuming he hasn't risen as a vampire or anything so ridiculous.'

'He doesn't exist.'

'Doesn't exist? What do you mean by that?'

'I sent off his fingerprints, dental x-rays, a photograph to all the usual relevant records offices. They all came back negative.'

'Negative? But he was assigned as a civilian liaison to a military operation only a few months ago.'

'I know.'

'Colonel Lethbridge-Stewart mentioned a phrase; the "London Event". What could it have been?'

'You're the one with the high security clearance. If anything happened in London recently that I don't know about, you will.'

'As it happens, I can't think of anything.'

'Here's a weird thought. Could this "London Event" be something in the future? I mean, something planned to happen, and this man is one of Lethbridge-Stewart's contacts in the plot.'

Kyle didn't answer for a long moment. 'We can rule nothing out. Circulate the prints, photographs, and dental records to external security agencies, and allied governments, in case any of them can identify him. The name must be false.'

'Doctor Mackay did mention having known an Edward Travers who died back in the '30s. Maybe they took his name?'

'Another identity stolen from the long-dead.'

'And turning up in the vicinity of Colonel Lethbridge-Stewart. Don't try to tell me that's a coincidence. He's clearly a contact.'

'Lethbridge-Stewart was as surprised as anyone when that man fell out of the capsule,' Kyle pointed out.

Beswick scoffed from the other end of the line. 'So he's a good actor! Don't you understand – this also means he must know what this capsule is, and where it came from. Everything else is misdirection, or at least good programming.'

'Well, we'll soon see. I called for you to prepare a treatment. He wants to go to London, and, all things considered, we might get the best result if he does.'

'And does the director—?'

'He gave carte blanche, remember? He knows what he's doing.'

'It's your funeral,' Beswick said sceptically.

'Not for a very long time,' Kyle promised.

Corporal Wright saw Greene to a seat in the anteroom outside General Hamilton's office. 'Would you like some tea or coffee?'

'Coffee please, white with sugar.'

She nodded, and pressed a button on the intercom on her desk. Wright ordered the coffee and looked back to Greene. 'It'll just be a moment; the mess staff here are really good.'

True to her word, a steward brought in a tray with coffee and some biscuits and extra sugar a minute later. Just after that, Colonel Douglas came in, and Wright directed him through to the office beyond. He nodded to Greene as he passed. A few moments later, Wright's intercom buzzed, and Hamilton's voice said, 'You can send in Mr Greene, Corporal.'

Once inside, Greene shook hands with Hamilton and Douglas, and then Hamilton showed him to a seat. 'Your phone call was very mysterious,' the general said. 'Have you found something about Colonel Lethbridge-Stewart's current whereabouts?'

'I believe so. Actually, I'm surprised you didn't find out yourselves, but I think inter-service communications is where there's a lack, of sorts.'

'Between the army and RAF, I presume?'

Greene nodded. 'Lethbridge-Stewart's plane never took off, due to a mechanical fault with some fuel pumps. I can't say I understand the engineering myself. In any case, I found out that the colonel instead boarded another aircraft – a Hawker Siddeley 125, which the RAF insist on calling a Dominie – for Cyprus. Presumably he intended to catch another flight there. However, the Dominie never made it to Cyprus.'

Hamilton sat bolt upright. 'Flight number?' he snapped. 'WX4747.'

Hamilton glanced at Douglas. 'Did it arrive?'

'There's been no mention of Lethbridge-Stewart from Akrotiri, sir.'

Greene shook his head, and spread out a map of Germany and the Baltic, on which a circle had been scrawled in red pen. 'I made a few calls to some contacts at Lufthansa and the DWD, the German Met Office. They both reported – off the record – losing an aircraft on radar tracking in this area a couple of hours after Lethbridge-Stewart's scheduled take-off. If the timings and flight plan are correct – and I believe they are, though I haven't checked every take-off in Europe for that night – then this is almost certainly that Dominie.'

Hamilton glanced towards his office door with a frown, to Greene's puzzlement. 'Crashed in a storm?' he asked quietly.

Greene nodded solemnly. 'All right. Douglas, shake the RAF out of their beds, and get me air traffic radar records for the whole flight plan of WX4747. Let's try and confirm whether or not it matches up to this aircraft loss.' The general turned back to Greene. 'Good work, Mr Greene.'

'I'm not sure it feels like it.' Greene hesitated. 'There is another way to confirm whether that's really the colonel's plane. Find the wreckage.'

There was a deep booming roar, answered by a second and a third. Gunfire blasted jarringly, muzzle flashes and glowing robotic eyes providing the only illumination in the tunnel. 'Bullets can't stop them!' someone yelled, and Lethbridge-Stewart was surprised to realise that it was his own voice.

He fired four or five shots from his pistol at the hellish unnatural lights that passed for eyes. A vicious roar answered, and a forearm like a steel girder wrapped in wool smashed into his gut, driving all the air from his lungs, and hurling him so far down the tunnel that he thought he'd never land. His spine and ribs hit something flat, and he stopped moving although the tunnel did not.

Except that it wasn't a tunnel, and the curved concrete sections lining the walls were actually just aluminium and fiberglass. The savage beast before him barely fit in the aircraft, the top of its head brushing the ceiling, and its jagged claws tore at the seats.

The world lurched around Lethbridge-Stewart, the lighting in the floor and ceiling flashed on and off. Something slammed into him, crushing him, and razor sharp claws dug agonisingly into his shoulders as they spun him around to face huge round eyes set into matted fur.

They shook him; the eyes resolved into thick round glasses, the fur into a beard. 'Professor Travers?' Lethbridge-Stewart gripped the man's shoulders with his own hands. 'Are you Edward Travers?'

'I am the London Event,' Travers said, from somewhere far away. 'You are the London Event.'

'What is—?'

A hand spun him around, to face a pretty girl in a corporal's uniform. She was standing in an office that listed at a weird angle, all the furniture beginning to slide. She was familiar – didn't Travers have a daughter? Anne Travers, he recalled, but the name didn't seem to fit. Beyond her, a general was strapping on a parachute.

'For you, the war is over,' the blonde woman said pleasantly, and the voice touched something in him.

'Sally,' he remembered. 'Sally, wait...' Without warning, two men in Chinese army uniforms rushed in from either side of him, grabbing his arms and hauling him roughly backwards. He struggled against them with all his might, but their grip was like solid steel. 'No, dammit! Sally wasn't there—!'

Lethbridge-Stewart was awake, heart thumping, trying to catch his breath. His head bumped against the side window.

'Sorry,' Kyle said from the driver's seat. 'Potholes are getting worse around here, I swear.'

Momentarily confused, he looked out and saw the familiar streets of the City of Westminster sliding smoothly past. There seemed to be no other traffic, and he didn't notice any pedestrians either. He shivered in spite of himself. It was a dead London, he thought, and the phrase gave him a chill. He half expected there to be fog rolling around the corners, but it was a bright and crisp day. 'Damned quiet.'

'This early on a Sunday morning? I should think so,' Kyle said. 'Probably just as well; it makes the drive a lot easier.'

'Sunday morning?' He tried to remember getting up, or getting in the staff car, and couldn't. He remembered wanting to go to London, to view some files from Air Ministry, but other than that the last thing he remembered was having dinner. He didn't even remember going to bed, though obviously he must have done.

'I can't think how I managed to walk to the car.'

'You didn't. I carried you over my shoulder,' she deadpanned. He couldn't help but chuckle slightly – she was wiry, but so petite that the idea was ridiculous. 'You didn't seem very awake, and you fell asleep again before I even got the engine started. Lack of coffee, probably. Or one too many of Doctor Beswick's sleeping tablets.'

Along the side of the river he could see a long, crenelated red brick building, which he recognised immediately; Chelsea Barracks had always been quite distinctive, especially before—

Especially before what?

'Are you all right?' Kyle asked.

In truth, Lethbridge-Stewart wasn't sure. 'Yes, I just suddenly... Is something different about the barracks?'

'Different?'

'I thought there were tower blocks... Or there *were* going to be tower blocks.' He frowned and winced, as if a headache was brewing behind his brow.

'I believe there's been talk of it, and designs drawn up. You must have seen them at some point when they were circulated.'

'Yes, yes, that must be it.'

She pulled the car to a halt in a small enclosed parking area. 'Anyway, here we are. Chelsea Barracks as ordered.'

He got out of the car – a Humber Super Snipe – and yawned and stretched. The expanse of Victorian red brick stretched to either side, and its solidity and history were reassuring, but Lethbridge-Stewart couldn't shake the feeling that something was wrong. Even on a crisp Sunday morning, with nobody around, London *felt* filled and alive. You knew people were sleeping or getting breakfast, readying themselves for later, even if you couldn't see them. Today, here, he didn't feel that

He put the feeling out of his mind; he was here on duty, and had things to do. As always, it was best to get on with them. 'Right, Captain,' he said briskly, 'let's see what the RAF have for us on our rogue Wellingtons, shall we?'

'What are we looking for?' the RAF helicopter pilot asked. Greene, Douglas, and Maurice Palmer – drafted in by

Greene as an interpreter in case one was needed – were gathered around an oil drum near his chopper in a cordoned-off era of the airport at Brunswick, southwest of Hamburg. A tired and worn-looking Greene – still in a camera-ready suit, but with unphotogenic bags under his eyes – had spread his map across the top of the drum.

'I don't know for sure,' he admitted, 'but probably wreckage. Hopefully nothing.'

The pilot nodded. He looked at the map with a grimace, and a querying look at Douglas. 'You do know the circle you've marked covers a chunk of East Germany as well?'

'I'm no navigator, but I was afraid that might be the case,' Greene admitted.

Douglas cleared his throat. 'We are aware of that situation, yes. But under no circumstances are we to cross into DDR airspace – or even give them a reasonable excuse to claim that we have.'

An RAF captain stepped forward to greet him with a handshake. Lethbridge-Stewart didn't recognise him. 'A pleasure to meet you; I just wish it was under happier circumstances.'

They were in the entrance to Chelsea Barracks, and various members of the different Guards regiments were pottering around. 'Happier?' Lethbridge-Stewart asked.

'You asked about some records in the archives; the records of some Wellington bomber ops, wasn't it?'

'Yes.'

'Perhaps,' Kyle suggested, 'we can carry the conversation on in private?' She looked at Lethbridge-Stewart, and added, 'Your office is still available while you're on secondment at the Establishment.'

He nodded, and she led the way up a flight of wide, sweeping stairs, to the first floor. The office was spartan, by Victorian standards. Wooden walls, with a few bookcases filled with military histories and doctrine, a large bay window behind the desk, a row of filing cabinets against the one wall, and a couple of portraits of men and women that Lethbridge-Stewart didn't recognise.

In fact, he didn't recognise any of it, even if it was supposed to be his office.

'Now,' the RAF Captain said. 'I'm afraid I have some bad news.'

'You couldn't find the records?' Lethbridge-Stewart suggested.

'I say, how on Earth did you—?'

'To be honest, Captain – Captains – I didn't really expect you to. It's an odd thing, and I can't explain it, but I seem to be the only person in the British military today who remembers the Wellington.'

'That's ridiculous, Colonel,' Kyle said. 'Designed by Barnes Wallis, isn't that so?'

He looked at her, confused. She was right, of course, and he nodded, but he had been so sure that nobody seemed to know about something so obviously a matter of military record that her agreement threw him from his train of thought. What was going on?

'We think someone has been stealing valuable and secret material from the Air Ministry archive,' the RAF captain said. 'Your request sparked quite a tizzy when it turned out that the records were just gone.'

'I see...'

116

'I've decided to assign a liaison to look into this with you.' He opened the door and said, 'Come in please, Lieutenant.'

A young officer with thick black hair, and wearing Parachute Regiment battledress uniform and beret, rather than office garb, came in, escorted by a corporal in shirt-sleeves. 'Lieutenant Knight, this is Colonel Lethbridge-Stewart, with whom you'll be looking at the Wellington bombers that...'

'Little Spence?' Lethbridge-Stewart had gone pale, and Kyle looked from one man to the other. Something lit up in her eyes, and he saw her face fall. 'But you're dead! I saw—'

And then it came back. The London Event: Robotic Yeti in the Underground, poisonous mists in the streets, and too many men dying under his command in fierce battles.

'All right, what's really going on here?'

'What do you mean?'

'Ben "Little Spence" Knight was killed in the London Event, so you can't be him. And Chelsea Barracks has had rather appalling tower blocks as accommodation for the Guards since '62. I remember Profumo introducing them. So who are you, and where are we really?'

'Lieutenant Ben Knight. And I've no idea where this "Little Spence" thing came from. But we're—'

An arm threw itself around Lethbridge-Stewart's neck. He reacted instinctively, grabbing the arm and hauling on it, hurling the corporal forward. He crashed into the lunging Knight, and both men went down in a tangle.

Lethbridge-Stewart leapt to the door and pulled it open. 'Come on, Captain. We have to...' He stopped as he saw two armed Redcaps appear in the corridor outside, both raising submachine guns. He slammed the door closed and shoved Kyle aside in case a spray of bullets was about to come through it. He also drew his pistol, threatening Knight and the other man with it as they rose. 'Kyle, we're leaving.'

'No,' she said. 'I'm sorry – this wasn't how I wanted our collaboration to end, but no.' She drew a compact pistol, and pointed it at Lethbridge-Stewart.

'What are you—?' Lethbridge-Stewart shook his head sadly. 'Of course. You'd have to be part of it too, whatever it is.'

The door slammed open under the impact of a Redcap boot, and the two Redcaps came in, covering both Lethbridge-Stewart and Kyle. They were momentarily confused, giving Lethbridge-Stewart an instant to leap for the big bay window. The Redcaps raised their weapons, but Kyle darted in front of them, shouting 'No! Hold!'

Knight's arms couldn't reach the colonel, as he planted a foot on the seat of the desk chair, fired a couple of rounds through the window, and then hurled himself at it. He brought his arms up to protect his face, so his elbows hit the cracked glass first, and he went clean through it in an explosion of shattered fragments.

Lethbridge-Stewart fell, but only ten or twelve feet. Thankfully his legs seemed to have remembered the basics that Colonel Pemberton of the Paras had once shown him; he landed with legs together and knees bent, and dropped and rolled across a few feet of the car park.

An alarm started up inside as he picked himself up, dripping glass shards, and ran for the gate. A single guard was emerging from the narrow gatehouse door, looking confused and unsure of himself. Lethbridge-Stewart's fist lashed out, a solid right cross taking the younger man across the side of the jaw and knocking him down. Lethbridge-Stewart's knuckles protested with a blaze of pain, but he ignored them, satisfied that the other man was feeling worse.

He kept running, ducking out of the gate and into the first alley he came to. He had to put as much distance as possible between himself and the barracks. He had to stay out of sight, knowing that there would already be soldiers and police flooding into the streets.

Kyle ran to the smashed window, lowering her pistol, her mind racing. 'Call out the provosts. I want checkpoints on the London perimeter gates, and if we can get a helo on station, so much the better.'

Lieutenant Knight caught his breath with a 'Yes, ma'am'. He started to salute, and she slapped his hand with a curt 'Go'. He ran out, followed by the two Redcaps.

The RAF captain joined her at the window. 'What now?'

'Now if he survives, we know he's ready, don't we?'

'And if he doesn't?'

Kyle didn't want to think about it. 'Then we've wasted a lot of time and effort on an abortive project, and the director will not be best pleased.' She crossed to the desk, picked up the phone, and then pressed a button for the switchboard. 'This is Captain Kyle. I need a secure and scrambled line to Chelsea Barracks. Yes, I know what I said. I want to be put through to Major Lethbridge-Stewart. It's a matter of the highest urgency.'

The roar of the Wessex's engines were deafening even inside

the chopper. They had been flying south along the border with East Germany for an hour or so, barely skirting the edge of Soviet Bloc airspace. Once or twice they had spotted a Soviet made MiL helicopter a couple of miles east of them, keeping an eye on them, but it had made no overt hostile moves, and Douglas was making sure their own pilot didn't tempt them.

As a result, Greene and Maurice found themselves being the main ground observers, scanning the treetops and fields for any disturbances. It wasn't surprising, then, that Greene saw it first; a glint of metal, a smudge of charred wood, some scars gouged into the earth below broken branches. Greene couldn't believe his eyes at first, even though it was basically what he'd been looking for. He'd been hoping he was wrong, and wished he still was.

'Can't tell what sort of plane it was,' the pilot said, 'but it definitely was one.'

'Can you land nearby, so we can examine it?'

'Maybe further upslope. You know we'll have to report this?'

'Which is exactly my intent, don't worry.'

The chopper landed a short distance away, and they all walked to the site that Greene had spotted. Fresh growth was bright across the woodland path, a green scar cut by sweeping metal. Sticks and leaves crunched underfoot, and Greene felt an odd pleasure in the day, as if he were a boy on a nature walk, or going for a picnic.

Colonel Douglas broke the moment by pointing and calling, 'There it is!' All four men jogged over the twenty feet of streaked and battered sheet of metal that lay canted against a fallen tree. It was clearly a broken wing from an aircraft, and the right size for a Dominie. 'Nothing to link it to Lethbridge-Stewart's aircraft, though.'

'There'll be part numbers that can be checked,' the helicopter pilot said. Douglas simply nodded.

Following the trail of fresh growth, they soon came upon the flattened and scattered remnants of a jet engine, some couple of hundred yards away, and a piece of tailfin a short way beyond that. They gathered around the crumpled engine housing, which seemed very out of place in a quiet forest, and Douglas and Maurice turned over a steel panel that had come to rest with the interior surface upwards. Once turned, the aircraft number was exposed for all to see: WX4747.

Greene had been hoping, really, that it would be a completely different number, or that there would be none. They all looked at each other.

'I'm sorry, Colonel,' the chopper pilot said. Greene and Maurice echoed the sentiment.

'There don't seem to be enough... remains, for a whole plane,' Maurice said tentatively.

'It'll take experts to be sure,' the chopper pilot said, 'but we're probably looking at a mid-air collision. If something took the wing and one engine off at high altitude and high speed, the lighter parts will have come down closer to the incident site, and the main body, with the other engine still going, could have come down twenty or thirty miles away.'

'Which, depending on its course, could mean well inside East Germany,' Douglas said gloomily.

'If it was a mid-air collision,' Maurice said slowly, 'where are the parts of the other... whatever? We didn't see anything else from the air.'

121

'Depends what part hit our plane. Or what it was.'

'Could it have been a missile?' Greene asked reluctantly.

'Could have been, but only an expert can tell you, and I'm not an expert.'

Lethbridge-Stewart had discarded his cap and jacket since they were too obviously recognisable; the word would be out by now to look out for a man in a British Army officer's uniform. He just wished he could change his appearance further, to blend in with... well, with the pedestrians he expected to run into sooner or later.

He still hadn't seen any early morning wanderers, and even for a Sunday at the crack of dawn, this was unusual. Not as unusual, mind you, as being able to see from the top landing of a fire escape the tips of both Tower Bridge and St Paul's. He had climbed up to better observe the pattern of searchers looking for him both on foot and in Land Rovers and jeeps.

The strangeness of the view made his head swim, and he descended again, wishing he'd swiped some aspirin from Doctor Beswick before all this happened.

As if the thought of his erstwhile comrades had summoned them, he heard a vehicle approach, and ducked behind a parked lorry, hoping against hope that it would be a civilian car. It was a jeep full of armed men, of course. It zoomed past, and turned a corner to the west.

Lethbridge-Stewart waited a few moments, and, while he did so, checked his compass and watch. When he was sure the jeep wasn't just turning to come back, he stood and started walking cautiously south.

The echo of his footsteps in the street didn't sound quite

right, though he couldn't put his finger on how or why; he wasn't a physicist or sound engineer, whatever the proper word for that sort of job was.

Ahead, he spotted a small café that was open and whose window bore a sign for breakfasts. He wasn't sure how long the drive to London had been, but he felt famished, and coffee and breakfast seemed like a good practical move. He walked briskly along, and stuck out a palm to push the door open with a smart 'Good morning'.

His arm jarred, and suddenly the pavement was lurching under him. He might have taken quite a crack to the back and tailbone if he hadn't instinctively slapped out his other hand to cushion his fall, and then rolled with it. He picked himself up, shocked, and reached out again to pat the door. Not only didn't it open, but it wasn't even a real door. It was just plexi-glass with a photograph behind it, and so was the huge window showing people enjoying coffee and croissants.

'What the hell...?' He tapped the walls, and found that they weren't real stone, but concrete at best. An apparent wooden frontage nearby turned out to be painted canvas.

No wonder the city didn't have its usual feeling of mass and solidity. It was like being on a film set; but how, and why? He spun back and forth to look around. 'More to the point,' he muttered to himself, 'where?'

'Hey!' the shout came from a soldier at a nearby junction. He raised his rifle and fired, but Lethbridge-Stewart dove behind a parked car, rolled, and darted through a narrow alley. Footsteps and shots followed, and he kept low as he ran down the centre of the alley. Instinct told him to dodge and weave, and hug the alley walls, but experience had taught him that high-velocity rounds tended to skip along the walls in such places.

He could feel his heart hammering against his ribs as he ran, bounding down a flight of steps towards a Tube station. He hurled himself the last few steps head-first, rolling painfully across the shoulders and bumping up against a closed door. The pursuing footsteps ran past above.

He listened carefully for any sound of their return, or stragglers following to catch him out, and caught his breath. He had so many questions, but knew they would have to wait; immediate survival came first, then any analysis of the situation. He looked at the door against which he had landed, and found that it wasn't any sort of Tube station entrance he was familiar with. Instead it was a simple, if solid, wooden door with a bolt on it.

He opened it, and saw that it led to a sloping grey-and-green-painted corridor. Both curious, and thinking that nobody would be looking for him down in some tunnel, he slipped through and closed the door after him.

The corridor wasn't long, but had a few turns in it, before opening into a large concrete-floored garage space. A couple of ramps about twenty and forty yards along led up to steel roller doors, and there were a couple of trucks and jeeps parked here and there between the thick concrete pillars.

He looked around once more to make sure he was actually alone, and then moved to one of the steel roller doors. He couldn't see an opening mechanism, and so moved on to the next. In between, however, he found a small cubbyhole with a number of controls. From here he could also see a couple of other doors that led to parts unknown, but resembled the one through which he had entered the garage.

Taking his best guess at the control for operating the roller door, he pressed a button. Immediately, an alarm blared. Lethbridge-Stewart cursed, and started experimenting with more controls. Suddenly, a nearby double-door burst open, and two soldiers ran into the garage, submachine guns raised. They loosed short bursts towards the cubbyhole, and Lethbridge-Stewart knew he had no choice but to return fire so that they'd have to keep their heads down and couldn't aim.

He darted across the concrete, firing roughly in their direction as he went, and hurled himself into the seat of a jeep. The instant he stopped shooting, the two soldiers popped up and started firing again. One ran towards the jeep, while the other fired, forcing Lethbridge-Stewart to stay flat across the seats. He daren't move himself, but started the jeep's engine nonetheless, and slammed the heel of his hand down on the accelerator pedal.

The jeep lurched forward, taking the approaching soldier completely by surprise; he tumbled across the floor with shattered knees.

The other man had stopped firing to reload, but a pistol was quicker to reload than a submachine gun, and Lethbridge-Stewart was waiting for him to pop up again. He shot him twice in the chest. Scooping the first man's submachine gun from the floor, Lethbridge-Stewart sat up in the driver's seat and drove towards one of the garage's steel roller doors, which was now beginning to open.

Several soldiers ducked under the rising door, already shooting. Lethbridge-Stewart ducked behind the dash and floored the accelerator. The jeep bounced and shuddered under multiple blows, and then shot forward into the twilight, leaving several groaning bodies on the ground behind it.

He was not, however, on the outskirts of London. The ramp exited onto a long sloping road at the base of a low cliff, and spread out before him were the lights of the village of Deepdene.

# CHAPTER SEVEN

# *Time Out*

'He's escaped,' Knight reported back to Kyle. The room they were in was filled with maps of London and the Home Counties, a row of TV screens mounted against one wall, all showing views of different London landmarks. The spaces around them were all deserted, apart from the occasional patrolling soldier or jeep blurring past one side of a screen.

'Colonel Lethbridge-Stewart is out of London Bounds entirely, and has killed several men.'

Kyle nodded; she hadn't expected anything different. 'Then he'll try to return to England.'

'He'll have a long journey ahead of him.' Knight grimaced. 'I've got all the major transport centres in the vicinity – civilian and military – alerted to spot him and bring him in.'

'Alive.'

'That's still the preference, yes,' Knight admitted with reluctance. 'But by no means a hard and fast necessity.'

Kyle turned slowly. She was slightly built, and several inches shorter than Knight, but he couldn't help stepping back. 'That is most definitely a necessity. This unit has invested a lot of time and effort – as well as funds – into this project, and neither the director nor myself are willing to

see it all flushed down the drain for a moment's revenge.'
She paused, then offered, 'No matter how understandable
the provocation.' Knight stayed silent, clearly
uncomfortable, but at least not arguing the point. She
softened her expression. 'Do you imagine for a moment that
I'm all right about the deaths of our men?'

'No, of course not.'

'These things happen. Whether by enemy action or
friendly fire, we put ourselves in situations that are
dangerous, and sometimes...'

'Well, at least we know he's hostile.'

Anger flashed through her again, and she saw him wince.
'No we do not. We can presume that, but right now all we
know is that he has defended himself.'

'And now you're defending him? With all due respect,
Ma'am, perhaps you're letting your close association colour
your—'

'I only allow professionalism to colour my opinions,
Knight. By being professional, and by recognising it in
others. Can you tell me you wouldn't have done exactly the
same thing if you were in Colonel Lethbridge-Stewart's
place?'

'After his... conditioning? I have no idea. But I suppose
I couldn't rule it out.'

'Exactly.'

Lethbridge-Stewart's stolen jeep bounced painfully across
the field where he had previously examined the wreckage
of the Wellington bomber. The scorch marks were still
visible in the grass between patches of churned-up earth. If
his sense of direction was right, he had just emerged from

under the complex that Kyle had said was some sort of old factory.

A figure in what was either a coverall or jumpsuit leaped for safety as he passed, protecting his face with raised hands. Lethbridge-Stewart momentarily thought it was a soldier in fatigues, but then realised he had been too young for that; it had been a pallid teenage boy.

It wouldn't take long for other vehicles to follow him, and he wanted to get out of sight, ideally somewhere that a jeep or Land Rover couldn't go. There was a tree-line off to the left, and he spun the wheel and gunned the engine. In the rear-view mirror he saw two vehicles hurtle along the road he had taken out of the faux London. Fortunately they were already peeling away from his direction, towards Deepdene. The field he had entered dipped, they probably wouldn't see him from their route.

He was just about convinced that he was right about that when a helicopter swept over his jeep, so low that he swerved aside by instinct. The chopper spun around and came in again. He ducked in the driving seat and jerked the wheel hard around. The jeep fishtailed, rear wheels digging into the earth and kicking up dirt just as the chopper-mounted machine gun opened fire. A line of earthy eruptions burst past the jeep, and Lethbridge-Stewart floored the accelerator.

Desperate to not hit a tree head on, he guided the jeep towards the woods, and aimed for a gap between the trunks that looked wide enough for the vehicle. A couple of strands of wire, making up a fence to separate the field from the woods, snapped with loud twangs as the jeep hurtled through and into shelter. Above him, wood and leaves exploded into splinters under more gunfire.

Lethbridge-Stewart stamped on the brakes as soon as he was under tree-cover, and jumped out. He zig-zagged deeper into the undergrowth as a storm of heavy calibre lead ripped a couple of saplings to pieces before peppering the jeep. Two of its tyres exploded loudly.

He didn't go far before stopping and pressing himself against the trunk of a solid oak tree, with a thick branch over his head. The chaps in the helo would expect him to run away from the jeep, he supposed. As he anticipated, the next stream of gunfire poured blindly towards the thicker part of the woods, where an observer above would logically expect a fleeing man to run.

The leaves above thrashed as the helicopter swooped low overhead. They'd be looking for gaps in the foliage, and for movement; he didn't intend to give them either. Sooner or later they'd have to move off, and then his troubles would really begin; the longer he was hiding out here, the more troops the enemy could deploy on foot to search for him. This area of woodland wasn't that large, and it wasn't going to be that difficult for them to establish a perimeter around it.

He decided to use the time to examine the weapons he had taken during his escape. The pistol was a Browning automatic, or at least a copy thereof, which was a fairly universal weapon, standard around the world for several decades. The submachine gun wasn't a British standard issue Sterling, and had a circular magazine. At first glance during his escape he had thought it was a Thompson, like something out of a gangster movie, but now he saw it was a Russian PPSH, or something very similar to that type of

Second World War weapon.

That made him feel less guilty about shooting men in British uniforms. Soviet weapons, a fake London and English town for getting infiltrators used to British ways, and all those little inconsistencies in people's knowledge of British military gear. He wasn't sure exactly where he was, but he knew it must be east of the Iron Curtain.

At some point he would have to analyse how he had got here, but for now he had to plan a journey back to the West, and that meant finding out where he really was.

The helicopter was still swinging back and forth above, however, which meant he wasn't going anywhere quite yet.

The red phone furthest away from the row of TV screens buzzed, and Kyle lifted it immediately. 'Yes, Director?'

'Since there's clearly no good news forthcoming today, I'll settle for your concise report on the situation.'

'The subject designated Colonel Lethbridge-Stewart is out of London Bounds. His current mental state is unknown, but his practical abilities are on good form.'

'Not to the extent of avoiding recapture for long, I hope.'

'Actually his methods have been well analysed; we can predict his movements without difficulty.'

'Then the question becomes do we want him dead or alive?'

Kyle closed her eyes for a moment. Was the director testing her? Or actually seeking her opinion? 'There's a wealth of information and opportunity locked in his head, but he could also be as much of a threat. Major Lethbridge-Stewart is on his way here—'

'Ah, I see. Very well, we'll let him decide how to

proceed. Make sure he keeps me informed.'

'Yes, sir.' The line went dead, and she hung up. The other officers in the room looked to her, and she knew they were curious about what had been said in the half of the conversation they couldn't hear. It wasn't her place – or her mood – to tell them, so instead she began issuing orders. 'Get me the fastest car we have so that I can return to the Establishment. When Major Lethbridge-Stewart arrives in our airspace, have him join me in Central there.'

Men in battledress were approaching, but they looked like conscripts, and not very attentive to their job.

Colonel Lethbridge-Stewart had concealed himself quite well in the thick fork of a tree, and none of them had so much as looked up above their eye level. They were all more interested in prodding at bushes and thickets of undergrowth. He had worried this new position had made him visible to a sharp-eyed observer in the helicopter up here, but it had moved off to patrol the perimeter of the woods – and doubtless to co-ordinate the men on foot – which meant he was relatively safe for the moment.

Through the trees, he could actually see parts of Deepdene, including an expanse of tarpaulin inexpertly and ineffectively spread across what was left of the newsagent's roof.

He wondered momentarily if a passenger from the capsule had gone to ground there. Then he couldn't help wondering whether he had known the answer at some point, whether the drugs or whatever they had used on him had scrambled his memories.

\*

Kyle's first stop was at the infirmary. She snapped her fingers at an orderly to get him to tell her where Doctor Beswick was. She was in the dispensary, a steel-lined room filled with containers and blister packs of pills and tablets, adjoining Beswick's pharmacology lab. Kyle marched in without preamble. 'Henrietta, what do we have available in tranquilising weapons?'

Beswick looked up from a form of some kind, surprised. 'You mean dart guns?'

'I mean any and all weaponry that will render a target unconscious for capture and interrogation.'

Beswick smiled faintly. 'Preferably without damaging valuable specimens?'

'Exactly.'

'We do have dart guns, but the dosage is unreliable with such a thing. I mean, there's a careful relationship between an individual's body mass and the amount of a specific compound needed to have a particular effect. Obviously with a syringe or an oral dose, that amount can easily be administered. With a rifle dart one has to generalise, which means there's a fair chance that, while one person or animal may be knocked out by one, another could either be unaffected, or killed.'

Kyle scowled, disappointed, but not stupid. 'And darting an apparently unaffected subject a second time would be more likely to kill them by overdose?'

'Almost guaranteed,' Beswick agreed. 'It's not like you see in films.'

'Area effect weapons?'

'Gas?' Beswick nodded. 'Can be risky in enclosed spaces – any gaseous agent can build up to over-dosage levels – but in open ground you ought to be able to use the likes of tear gas effectively.'

'I want something that would cause sluggishness, drowsiness,' Kyle said. 'If that was possible it would be enough.'

'Indoor or outdoor use?'

'Woodlands.'

'Ah.' Beswick nodded. 'Fentanyl-delta. Make sure that any operators or troops windward of the applications have respirators; anyone and anything else in the vicinity will doze off in minutes. Don't use it indoors, though; there would be fatalities, and you could have achieved that with cheaper and faster-acting compounds.'

'Can you have Fentanyl-delta prepared for use by aerial delivery?'

'Aerosol spray or grenades?'

'Grenade type.'

Beswick thought for a moment, then nodded. 'You'll need a munitions specialist to drain and refill tear gas canisters, but I can have enough Fentanyl ready for you in half an hour.'

'Excellent. It can go out with the second helo sortie,' Kyle added, murmuring half to herself.

Lethbridge-Stewart had been edging his way slowly and carefully towards the Deepdene side of the woods, and more of the village was becoming visible. He momentarily wondered how many residents might be looking this way, their attention drawn by the military activity around, but then he reminded himself that there must only be staff and trainees, not residents; if he was lucky they would all have been drafted in to help with the search.

He had let quite a number of soldiers pass underneath his original hiding spot. It wasn't usually wise to let armed enemies past oneself, and risk being surrounded, but there was an exception to every rule, and he was happy to let them have their backs to him. In time, he slid down from his elevated position as quietly as he could, and crept through the woods towards the village.

The searchers, now beyond and behind him, were taking no such care, and he could hear them thrashing about like a herd of elephants. The sound of the helicopter was also on the far side of the woods.

Lethbridge-Stewart was grateful for the fact that everybody was wearing the same type of uniform – at least once he was sure he'd been spotted by a relatively distant searcher, who then simply waved. He had waved back, and the soldier had carried on moving further away. That had given him the idea that acquiring a battledress tunic and helmet might make such passing glances easier to shrug off. He would have to make sure, however, that whoever he took the items from wouldn't be found quickly; otherwise the value of the change would be lost.

He listened carefully to the sounds of movement around him, focussing on what sounded most likely to be a single searcher closer to him than to any other soldiers. He crept sideways, keeping wood and foliage between himself and the source of the sounds, until he was able to crouch behind some brambles and ivy, and peer around a fallen tree at a burly soldier with a rifle, pausing to take a drink out of a hip-flask.

Lethbridge-Stewart reflected that the man deserved a

reprimand and some re-training but, as it was, the man's laziness and unprofessionalism worked to his advantage. He darted up and threw an arm around the man's neck in a carotid choke hold. The guard was unconscious in the time it took Lethbridge-Stewart to drag him back into a pool of shadow roofed over by the brambles and ivy, and lower him to the ground.

Quickly he took the soldier's jacket, helmet, rifle, and ammunition. He stuffed a handkerchief into the soldier's mouth, and tied his hands with his bootlaces. The guard was waking up already as Lethbridge-Stewart doubled back towards Deepdene, but he wouldn't be able to raise an alarm.

Lieutenant Knight's jeep rolled to a halt at a dusty crossroads, from which he could see both one side of Deepdene, and a fair chunk of the perimeter of the woods. The helicopter drifted lazily past overhead. His driver handed him an R/T handset, and adjusted the controls on the transmitter, which sat in the rear of the jeep. 'Control, am in position, over.'

'Stand by.'

'Roger.' He switched to a different frequency. 'Knight to Dragonfly; sit-rep?'

'No target movement,' the reply came back from the helicopter, muffled by the sound of its engines. 'He must have gone to ground.'

'That's not in his profile,' Knight said. 'More likely he's blending in with our men. How's your fuel?'

'Bingo fuel.' Knight knew that meant they were down to the reserves that would allow them to reach base and refuel.

'Understood.' Already Knight could hear a more distant

buzzing, and scanned the sky. A speck resolved itself into a second helicopter, approaching from the direction of the Joint Warfare Establishment. The R/T buzzed, and he answered.

'This is Control.' This time he recognised the voice – it was Kyle. 'Feed wind speed and direction to Dragonfly Two. Signal for respirators to be deployed.'

'Roger. Wilco.'

Over the woods, a different helicopter was approaching, while the original was disappearing into the distance. Lethbridge-Stewart smiled in satisfaction, and pulled his stolen helmet down to cover his eyes. He walked briskly along a trampled path, carrying his rifle at port arms; he wanted to look just like one of the other soldiers, if anyone glanced his way.

He moved at their speed, in their stance, and found himself almost relaxing into the walk. Overhead, even the sound of the helicopter criss-crossing the sky above wasn't particularly disturbing. He could have time to plan his next move – perhaps acquire another vehicle or, better still, a map of the real region.

As he walked, he was vaguely aware of a mist rising, which at first didn't bother him, until he thought about the time of day. It was well into afternoon, and a mist such as this was surely more of a morning phenomenon. Uncertain, he began to angle his course away from the most noticeable areas of mist.

Up ahead, there was a pair of soldiers apparently discussing which fork in the path to take. He wasn't too concerned about being recognised as their quarry – no alarm had yet been raised over the missing man – but then he saw something that did worry him: they were wearing gas masks. Suddenly he realised why he was so relaxed – the mist had to be some kind of soporific gas, dropped from the helicopter. He needed a gas mask, and quickly.

He rushed forward, swinging the butt of his rifle into the side of the nearest man's head. The soldier dropped like a stone, but his comrade already had a pistol in his hand. Lethbridge-Stewart batted his hand out of line with the rifle, and jabbed the man in the gut. He doubled over, but the pistol went off, sending two rounds into the earth. This was exactly what Lethbridge-Stewart didn't want; now soldiers would be converging on this spot, and fast. He clubbed the man again, wincing at the crudity of it, and tore the gas mask from his face.

Lethbridge-Stewart darted into the thicker undergrowth, trying to fit the gas mask over his own head as he moved. He had to drop the rifle to do it, and it was still a struggle. He fumbled with the straps at the back while moving. His foot suddenly caught in a fallen branch, and he tumbled into the undergrowth. The fall saved his life, as a shot rang out, and a bullet snapped overhead.

'Cease fire!' a muffled voice shouted. 'Fire only when fired upon.'

Now at least he knew that someone wanted him alive. He got to his feet slowly, all too aware that the mist – which he now noticed had an odd, sweet scent – was beginning to thicken in his vicinity. Worse, still, the noise he was making hadn't just alerted the enemy, it had covered their movements; a burly body crashed into him, bearing him to the ground again.

He struggled, but the soldier's knee was jammed down on his chest, keeping him down. He punched for the groin, but a hand swatted his fist away too easily. More rustling footsteps approached, and the mask was pulled out of his hand. Someone grabbed the back of his collar, and hauled him around, shoving his face towards a coalescing cloud that seeped between the twigs and leaves.

His eyes stung, and the world was spinning around him as it faded into nothing but grey fog, both inside and outside his head.

Kyle picked up the phone on the first ring. 'Yes?'

'Knight here. Colonel Lethbridge-Stewart is in custody.'

'And it's about time. Is he conscious?'

'No.'

Probably for the best, Kyle thought. Both for him and them. Now there was time to think. 'Bring him to the infirmary's secure wing. Doctor Beswick will be waiting.'

'Yes, sir.' She hung up. Now she could turn her attention to other duties, and catch up with some of the many jobs and situations that needed seeing to. She picked up a sketch of the Deepdene capsule and sighed. That was probably going to be the next most important job to both the director and herself, and she really would have preferred Colonel Lethbridge-Stewart's co-operation and assistance. Still, needs must, she reflected.

When she entered the warehouse-like space that had been so recently given to Doctor Mackay, she was surprised by how much had changed. For one thing, the familiar shape of the capsule was no longer there. Instead, the bulky tweed-jacketed Scot was prowling amidst a giant jigsaw puzzle of metal. Every single piece of the capsule seemed to have been separated from every other piece, and laid out carefully on the floor. Little labels were next to each piece, from the solid door to the tiniest screw, and it was surprisingly easy to follow which bits connected to which. In essence, he had turned the capsule into a two-dimensional grid of parts, and now the mechanics and technicians she had assigned to him were studying components in microscopic detail.

They had plenty of equipment with which to do so; two walls were now lined with microscopes, spectrometers, and other measuring and analytical devices.

'I must say,' she began, impressed, 'you've made quite remarkable – and rapid – progress.'

Mackay nodded. 'Fortunately for us all the mechanical means of holding metal and wiring and avionics together are globally similar. Even non-standard fittings and equipment like we have there.'

'Non-standard?'

'Aye; such things were standardised across the globe over twenty years ago, for the sake of aviation safety, but this… Well it's—'

'Different.'

'Individualistic might be a better word, but yes.'

'Why would anyone use such non-standard… equipment?'

'Depends who did it, I suppose. A country might do it to keep a secret, or an individual inventor might do it for reasons of vanity – so everyone would know that it was his work.'

She nodded, understanding, and walked slowly along

the lines of the disassembled capsule. 'So this is, as you say, individualistic. Not completely… alien.' She could feel his sceptical eyes on her, and turned. 'There are such things as space capsules.'

'There are, but they have to be more airtight and pressurised than this. It wasn't built by Martians, if that's what you – or your superiors – were thinking.'

'We weren't thinking that, no. Not with a dead man inside.'

'Good. This material is all terrestrial,' Mackay said. 'In fact, downright local; metallurgically speaking, it's German.'

'Could it be a part of a terrestrial space programme? A lifting body, perhaps?'

'Maybe, but those are designed for speed, protection from atmospheric friction, and so on. I think it's more likely to be a sort of escape capsule.'

'For a plane?'

'It'd have to be a very large plane. And then there's the question of why not simply use parachutes? They're lighter, use less fuel to carry up, and take up a lot less storage space than one of these capsules. You could store chutes for two dozen in the space that this capsule takes up.'

'Some people just aren't comfortable relying on a rucksack and a sheet to save them.'

'True. But I can't help feeling there's more to it than that. There's either a practical or cultural reason behind such a decision.' He shrugged. 'Anyway, coming back to the non-standard parts. A nation might do it for secrecy, I said, and there's another interesting thing about all this that makes me think that way. Some of the parts had numbers – serial numbers – and company names and logos.'

'Then we can find out who made—'

'I thought of that. I've had a couple of secretaries on phones all day, checking the files. None of the companies' names we've found mentioned on the parts exist.'

'Dummy companies, to hide their origin?'

'Perhaps. But some of them *did* exist, albeit decades ago. There are a couple of 19th Century steelworks that are listed among the makers, even though they were closed down in the early 1900s.' He shrugged. 'There's something else too; languages.' He stepped to a particular line of pieces, and lifted a small metal plate with a dial of some kind set into it. 'Look at this,' he said handing it to her. 'This plate is German, but I don't recognise these other lines.'

'Cyrillic. It's Russian, surely.'

'No, it isn't. At least, the alphabet might be, almost, but the words aren't.'

'All right, well then it's most likely still Eastern European, surely?'

'That would seem logical.'

'Then it shouldn't take long to identify.' She handed it back to Mackay. 'Wire a photograph of it to Foreign Affairs. Someone will recognise it.'

In a very similar hangar, Edward and Anne Travers were having their cake and eating it. The pieces of a capsule had been dismantled and laid across the floor for individual examination, but they could also look across at the second, still-intact capsule that had followed them back from the new Icelandic island, courtesy of the Royal Navy.

'What are we looking at here, Father? Time travel? Both capsules were found in the vicinity of men out of their time, after all.'

'How? Oh, that such a thing may be possible is certainly within the bounds of some of the latest scientific theories, but the technological requirements, well... I'm not sure I could even begin to speculate on how such a thing could be made to work. And I've met a man who...'

'A man we shouldn't be talking about openly,' Anne said in a whisper, looking around them.

'Anyway, he's not here. But in any case, there was hardly such a technology in 1914, was there? Or 1939. And you couldn't fit a German artillery crew with horses, or a Flower Class corvette into one of these, could you? Three men, maybe four, strapped in and—'

'If we're talking about time travel, then whatever time machine is involved doesn't have to have come from 1914. It could have come from a thousand years in the future, and gone there before coming here.'

'Doesn't have to have been a time machine,' Travers said. 'Scientifically, space and time are one, according to Einstein. Bend one and you bend the other. And that happens naturally, with black holes and such like.'

'So, what sort of natural event causes something like that?'

'Gravity, or the speed of light. Get close enough to the speed of light, or so says Einstein, and he knew what he was talking about, and time slows down. Gravity also warps space and time.'

'So if there was enough gravity—?'

'Oh, can't be anything to do with gravity, Anne. Not here. Not in 1914 either, for that matter. The sort of gravitational mass needed to affect time to that extent would crush the Earth – the whole solar system, in fact – like an eggshell.'

'And they didn't fly here under their own power either.'

'No.' Travers walked over to the intact capsule, which was mounted on a blue steel frame normally used for holding up jet fighters for maintenance work, and ran his fingertips along the underside. 'Dropped from an aeroplane, I shouldn't wonder. Like Chuck Yeager. Except not American.'

Anne picked up a panel with a dial set into it. 'Definitely not American. A mix of German and, I presume from the Cyrillic, Russian.'

'It's not Russian. Serbian.'

'Serbian? Are you sure?'

'Same alphabet, different language. Just as English, French, German, and so on, all use the Roman alphabet. A lot of East European languages use the Cyrillic alphabet, regardless of how different the languages are.'

Footsteps heralded the arrival of the commandant, le Cheminant, who brought a familiar companion. 'General Hamilton,' Travers said. He didn't put out a hand to shake, but accepted Hamilton's. 'Got another puzzler, eh?'

'Several, as it happens. It's nice to see you again, Professor.' He turned to Anne. 'Miss Travers. Thankfully nobody's shooting at anyone this time.'

'I heard there was some shooting when the first of these was found,' Anne commented.

'Point taken,' Hamilton said. 'So, any thoughts on these as yet?'

'Plenty,' Travers snapped huffily. 'Thinking is what I do too much of, probably.' He coughed, to cover up a pause to gather his thoughts. 'Well, at least it's not from outer space, and it hasn't gone there either. It's clearly designed for aerial flight, but has no engines. I should think these capsules are some kind of escape craft. It's the only explanation that makes a damn bit of sense, d'you see?'

Le Cheminant turned to Hamilton, and said, 'Professor Travers makes a good point. Anyone can see it's a descent vehicle of some kind.'

Hamilton nodded. 'Then there should be radar tracks—'

'There are,' Anne said. 'We confirmed that in Iceland. Was there nothing for the German capsule?'

'It came down in a high traffic area,' Le Cheminant said. 'Something so small would be hard to distinguish.'

'Can I see the radar tapes for the area on these dates?' Travers asked.

'Of course.'

Le Cheminant escorted Travers and his daughter to a secure complex taking up the whole top floor of the central building. It was filled with radar equipment and air traffic control stations, with huge windows giving a 360 degree view around the Joint Warfare Establishment, all the way to Old Sarum nearby. The room was like an airport control tower, for a complex with no runways, but a lot of air traffic.

Several armed guards were on duty on the stairs and outside the doors, and even Hamilton and le Cheminant had to show their passes for admission.

Le Cheminant sent an RAF technician for copies of the requested tapes, and showed the Travers' to a console they could use.

'Must say, I wish we had these displays back in '40,'

Travers admitted. 'Much easier to read.' He squinted over the top of his glasses as the technician installed the radar records into the console for review. 'These are the tapes for the Cologne area?'

Le Cheminant nodded. 'In the forty-eight hours before the... incident that led to the discovery of the capsule, yes.'

Travers peered at the screen with its rotating band of light, while Anne operated the controls. She was tentative at first, but she was her father's daughter, he was proud to see, and quickly got the hang of it. It didn't take long for her to find a section of radar records that interested both of them.

'Look, there,' Travers said suddenly, tracing his finger around with the rotation of the beam, and tapping it where the glowing spot that interested him appeared – and it was just one blob among many on the screen. 'This one just appears there... out of nowhere, like the Icelandic capsule on radar.'

'I see it,' Anne said, fascinated. 'There, the same altitude too. Eight thousand feet. So, if they don't come from outer space, then... what's at eight thousand feet?'

'An aeroplane, I told you already. Only thing that makes sense.'

'Invisible to radar?' Anne asked.

'Why not?' Hamilton said. 'You can't deny it's a dream that every air force has.'

Le Cheminant winced. 'Or a nightmare, that the other side develops one first.'

Travers rapped his knuckles on the desk part of the console. 'An aeroplane, dammit! What's the point of bringing me all the way to Wiltshire if you're not going to listen? A vehicle invisible to radar would require special materials capable of absorbing electromagnetic waves, and these capsules don't contain anything like that. Just simple German metals.'

'So we're back to an escape capsule of some kind?' Anne said. 'For a plane?'

'A large one.'

Le Cheminant frowned, and glanced at Hamilton. 'One of those always-on-station high level bombers? That kind of thing?'

'Exactly.'

'Not a passenger jet, I suppose. No lifeboats for them.'

'Shouldn't think so for a moment,' Travers grumbled. 'This thing can carry, what, two or three people? You'd need a hundred of them for all the passengers on a Jumbo. And the Jumbo would never get them all off the ground. No, this must be for someone special on a plane, not mere mortals like us.'

'A national leader, like the US President?' Hamilton suggested. 'Or members of a cabinet. Could something like Air Force One carry something like this?'

'It could, but it doesn't. I think this is more likely to be for the saviour of some practical VIP. A strategic planner, perhaps, or someone with the launch codes or battle plans.'

Anne tapped the screen, on which she had now frozen the moment of the capsule's first appearance on radar. 'What intrigues me is that both of these first appear at exactly the same altitude. What's so special about eight thousand feet?'

'Specifically? There are only fourteen mountains higher than that,' Travers said, a little wistfully. 'Though I doubt these capsules fell from a mountain.'

Hamilton raised an eyebrow at him. 'I should be remiss if I didn't ask which of the fourteen is closest to us.'

'Technically, Nanga Parbat, and that's in Pakistan. But it's the one closest to Europe.'

'They're all in the Himalayas, I suppose.'

Travers nodded. 'Pretty much. They're all in Nepal, China, and Pakistan.' His nod slowed, and he met Hamilton's eyes. 'Odd coincidence, that. The Himalayas again. Never shake them off.'

'Is there anything in the atmosphere special to that height?'

This time it was le Cheminant who answered. 'Not really. It's still well within the troposphere, the lowermost layer of the atmosphere. Cumulonimbus, stratoform, and stratocumulus clouds all start forming from just below that altitude to considerably over it.'

While they spoke, Anne experimented with the recording, running it faster and slower, and looking at recordings from different radar stations covering the Cologne area on the right day, which had all been brought to the console. 'Father, I think I've found something! Look! When you look at the descent of the capsule from different radar receivers, you can see that it doesn't come straight down, neither does it navigate. This is a ballistic trajectory, not a simple descent.'

Travers looked, switching between displays. 'You're right, Anne!'

Hamilton and le Cheminant both reached for telephones almost immediately. 'Can you work out where the other end of the ballistic arc would be? The source of it?' Hamilton asked.

'It should be simple enough.' Travers started scribbling some figures on a notepad. 'Bring me the largest scale map of Europe we have.' Anne fetched one, and he unrolled it across a table still strewn with books and pens in the centre of the room. He planted an index finger on the map. 'It impacted here...' He moved the finger southeast. 'From a first radar track here...' He muttered some more, about miles and speeds, and moved his finger one last time, peering at the map as he did so. 'Which makes a most probable ballistic origin point here!'

Anne looked at the indicated place on the map. 'Just east of... Leipzig.'

'Germany.'

'*East* Germany,' Hamilton said grimly.

The greyness was all that Lethbridge-Stewart could think of or remember. It faded, reducing to white. Edges resolved themselves into walls and ceiling, and a door. Thicker clouds came into focus as trolleys with medical equipment on them. He tried to rise, but something was keeping him down.

He glanced down and saw that he was strapped onto a gurney, and he was in a hospital room. He remembered running through woods, fleeing a fake London, and a fake English village, and then he remembered the gas among the leaves. His eyes were still stinging, and he blinked rapidly to try to clear them.

A man was sitting on a simple wooden chair opposite. He had neatly-parted hair, a hint of a sardonic smile on his thin lips, and was wearing an army uniform with a major's insignia. He looked vaguely familiar. 'Welcome back to the land of the living, er...?'

'Lethbridge-Stewart. Alistair Gordon Lethbridge-Stewart. Colonel, Scots Guards. 642592. You can tell that to your superiors.'

The other man's eyes went cold. 'Really?'

'Yes. Oh, I see, you're checking if I have a concussion? My head aches a bit, yes, but not so much that I'd mistake my own name.'

'Interesting. Perhaps I should introduce myself. Lethbridge-Stewart. Gordon James. Major, Coldstream. 539922. And taking the identity of a dead child is the oldest trick in the cover identity book.' The major leaned forward, and raised an eyebrow in a very familiar way. 'You'd think a serious professional would have been more original about arranging a cover. Not very clever is it, stealing my little brother's name?'

# — CHAPTER EIGHT —

# *Only Children*

Major James Lethbridge-Stewart was greeted by Captain Kyle when he arrived. 'What happened?' he asked immediately. 'Has the programme been completed, or failed?'

'Interrupted would be a better way of putting it, I think, sir.'

'Interrupted, eh?' He barked a laugh. 'Well, let's see. Where is he now?'

'In the infirmary. He was subdued by Fentanyl-Delta, but we're expecting a full recovery.'

'And he still calls himself Lethbridge-Stewart?'

Kyle nodded. 'It's the old trick; take a dead child's identity, that way there's no chance of running into the person who you're claiming to be. I should have said it was more usual to try that trick with infant mortalities than older children, but I'm sure his handlers had a reason.'

'Then who is he?'

'Individually, in terms of his own personal identity?' Kyle shrugged. 'It doesn't really matter, does it? It's his nationality and political affiliation that matters. There are two questions, as I see it, which must be answered urgently: What is he doing here, and where does he come from?'

James nodded. 'Yes...'

She looked downward for a moment, sadly. 'I'm not sure any of his true identity still exists, even subconsciously. Whoever sent him, they did an astonishing job in building his cover personality.'

'Just their bad luck that it was caught and flagged?'

'Exactly.'

'Marianne... You've read the reports, read his file, observed him... Where do you think he comes from?'

She thought for several moments, then shrugged. 'I don't know. Really, I can't tell.'

James sat opposite the gurney to which 'Colonel Lethbridge-Stewart' – Subject Zero – had been strapped. He was half tempted to step across and give the moustachioed man a good slap for persisting in taking his dead brother's name, but what good would it do? James was angry, but he doubted that it had been Subject Zero's idea. The anger really ought to be directed at some nameless and faceless spymaster who-knows-where, but Subject Zero was a face that was here, within arm's reach. That was what made a violent response tempting.

Tempting, but not professional.

'Look,' James said at last, 'I believe that you... Well, that you believe what you're saying, and that you honestly believe you are who you claim to be.'

'Oh, thank you,' Subject Zero said dryly.

'But I also know for a fact that you can't be who or what you claim.'

'And yet you believe me in spite of your facts?'

'If your psychological programming—'

'Brainwashing?'

'Brainwashing, yes. Oh, you mustn't hold it against yourself. Clearly you're a victim in this too, and it would make sense for us to help each other set things right.'

'Ah, good cop bad cop, eh? You know I have seen this tactic before, and Geoje was quite a place—'

James wouldn't be put off. 'You can see our problem, I'm sure. A man in a colonel's uniform is parachuted in from who-knows-where, bearing an obviously false identity...'

'My identity is far from false.'

'Whoever you were originally has obviously been completely broken out of you. I wish I knew who trained your unconscious to reach that stage; they must be a genius. I'd have the government pay ten times whatever he or she earns wherever you came from. But, that said, whoever your superiors are, they've had the most damnable luck with your identity. You see, Alistair was my younger brother. He died as a child.'

'You took the words out of my mouth,' the prisoner said coldly. 'Except that James was older than I when he died.'

James thought for a moment. It made sense that the prisoner's handlers would have also gone with a dead brother story, but there was something about the tone of the man's voice that sent a chill down James' back. Something in his eyes, perhaps. Maybe it was a hint of familiarity, a familiarity from long ago, but he couldn't shake the sensation that someone had just walked over his grave. He told himself not to be daft. Presumably Subject Zero's mystery handlers had picked a man whose brother had died, to get the right unconscious effect.

'Really?' James said. 'How did he die?'

'Lethbridge-Stewart, Alistair Gordon, Colonel, Scots

153

Guards, 642592.'

James sighed. 'It's hardly a military secret.' He stood. 'Still, I can always ask later, when I'm guaranteed the truth.'

'You'll get nothing out of me.'

James waggled a finger at him. 'Oh please, don't. You and I both know that everyone talks eventually; we're trained to delay it as long as possible, not to prevent it entirely. Oh, true, people can withstand beatings or other types of physical torture, but once psychoactives are applied...'

'So-called truth drugs.'

'The best ones are more than that. Intravenous hypnotic narcosynthesis is, I believe, the proper medical term. Henrietta Beswick could tell you for sure; she's our expert.'

'Scopolamine? Sodium Pentothal?'

'Too many counterproductive side effects. Oh, they have their uses when a single piece of information is required from a low-value asset or prisoner, but not from someone we find useful. Doctor Beswick swears by SB-117.'

'Everything has side effects.'

'Quite so, quite so. But, as it happens, the side effects to this are beneficial to our purposes, in that they affect the memory. As a matter of fact it can be used to wipe out the memory of having been affected by it. Ironically, its psychoactive properties were discovered by accident – side effects of what was developed with the intention of being a nerve gas for battlefield use.'

'You've used it on me.' It wasn't a question.

'Several times. Reliably, when you break out of our bounds, and with no permanent harm to yourself.'

'Then you must already have what information you

154

want,' Subject Zero said pointedly. 'Or at the very least the truth.'

James didn't answer. The prisoner had a point.

James took his lunch, and then returned to observe Beswick and Kyle interrogating Subject Zero, this time under the influence of SB-117. They asked all the things he would have expected – his name, his background, his career, what his duties were. Every answer insisted he was Alistair Lethbridge-Stewart of the Scots Guards. There were, however, lots of gaps in his memory, especially with regard to how he arrived at the Establishment.

During a break, James led Beswick out of the room. 'These gaps in his memory… Are they a product of your programming, to keep him from getting too nosey, or were they there when he originally arrived?'

'The latter. We – I mean Captain Kyle and I – suspect he may have been infiltrated to the vicinity while unconscious, to create exactly that effect.'

'So he can't betray whatever pipeline they have?'

'Exactly.'

'When we resume the session, I want to ask some questions.'

'You're senior officer present; he's all yours.'

'What's the last thing you remember before first waking up at the Establishment?' James asked. He, Beswick, and Kyle sat around Subject Zero's gurney, which was now in a sort of darkened operating theatre. A slightly starry effect was projected on the ceiling, helping to put the prisoner's unconscious mind at ease.

'I was setting off for Tibet.'

'In an aeroplane?'

'I don't remember, but that would seem the most appropriate. I certainly didn't intend to drive there in a jeep.'

'Do you remember being in flight? Or just heading to the airport or airfield?'

'No. I was... Dreaming. In the dark.'

Kyle cleared her throat. 'Do you remember a parachute, or being in a metal capsule?'

'A parachute... maybe. I'm not certain, I'm afraid.'

'How did you know you weren't in England?' Kyle asked.

'*The Radio Times*. All the same issue, ten years out of date. And the times of sunrise and sunset. Too early for England at this time of year. Simple orienteering skills, really.'

'Where do you think you actually are?' James asked.

'Not quite sure, but a couple of hours east. East Germany or Poland probably.'

So it went on, for over an hour. James knew – they all knew – that the SB-117 had unlocked their prisoner's mind completely. Their problem was that the contents were clearly still jumbled. Finally, the interrogation was almost over, but James wasn't finished. As far as he was concerned, the most important question was the one he would ask alone.

He ordered Kyle and Beswick to wait outside, but didn't switch off the recording devices in the room. He wasn't really sure he wanted to ask this question, but knew he had to.

'How did your brother die?'

'I don't remember, but Ray told me that there was... a

picnic. It was to be a teddy bear's picnic near Golitha Falls.'

Chilled, James remembered it well. There had been a teddy-bears' picnic of sorts to celebrate his upcoming twelfth birthday. His younger brother Alistair, and their friends Raymond, Henry, and Jemima had been playing hide and seek in the woods.

'We found James standing on the edge of the Falls, looking down into the waterfall. Ray and I stopped there – we couldn't believe the look on James' face. He said things, about how it was supposed to be me...' Subject Zero's voice cracked a little, but he couldn't not go on. 'He talked about someone called Maha... his imaginary friend. Or so we all thought at the time, but I've since learned that...' He stopped for a moment. 'James jumped off the waterfall.' Subject Zero's voice became distant. 'Ray and I went down – he didn't want to let me – and found James' body, but I couldn't reach him.'

James shivered. He remembered that about Alistair – teasing him over his short arms, that their mother insisted would grow when they were ready. 'Forget that question, and its answer,' he said quietly, falling into deeper thought. He remembered that day well, but he remembered it differently. There had been no imaginary friend, for one thing. He'd not resented having to watch out for Alistair, but would have rather not have had the responsibility. He took it seriously, though, and had been immediately concerned when Alistair had disappeared from the group.

There had been a sudden chilly shower of rain, and they had all taken shelter under leafy canopies or tree branches. Then Jemima had noticed Alistair's absence, and they milled around looking for him. They had found him soon enough, in a clearing at the edge of the falls, where he had found a rocky overhang under which to shelter from the rain.

'Get over here,' James had snapped. 'You nearly gave me a bloody heart attack.'

Alistair's face had fallen, but he came. 'I'm sorry, James. I'm coming.' In his urge to take the shortest route back, he had cut across the curve of the edge of the falls, but hadn't taken into account that the mossy rocks were now slick from the rain. He slipped sideways, and in terrible slow motion had toppled. Ray and James both leapt forward, but too late.

James could still hear Alistair's scream. Almost twenty years ago, but still he heard it. The voice was not totally dissimilar to that of the prisoner, he realised, taking into account that he last heard Alistair speak before his voice had broken.

At Golitha Falls, back in the day, Ray and James had scrambled down the side of the gorge, shouting for Alistair. Ray had stopped halfway, and James shouted at him to go and get their parents, and anyone else who could help. James had kept going, all the way down to where the tributary from the falls joined the River Fowey. The water was wild and roiling, surging through and over tree roots and rocky formations. There was no sign of Alistair's body, but there was blood on some of the highest rocks.

Alistair's body had been found a mile downstream in the Fowey the next morning.

James exited the room, and found Kyle waiting. 'Doctor Beswick had to attend to a patient,' she explained. James nodded, and walked only a few feet before stopping, and turned to look back, as if he could watch Colonel Lethbridge-Stewart through the wall. Kyle halted as well.

'You've spent more time working with him; you know him better than I do... Do you believe him?'

'I don't know what to believe,' she admitted. 'I believe in the efficacy of the treatments and interrogation techniques, and what we get from them fits with much of his conscious memories – and certainly his personality – but it all conflicts with the reality of the world... I don't know.' She hesitated. 'There is something of a resemblance. But they'd have picked someone for that, to go with the name. Or chosen the name to go with a resemblance.' She shook her head. 'You can tell he's a good liar. Or at least well trained.'

James nodded. 'I know it sounds unlikely, but... I don't believe he's lying. He honestly believes he is who he says he is.'

'His handlers have done an excellent job, yes. You're right about that, sir. And yet... He says he's your younger brother, who died as a child! Doesn't that... offend you? It must have some effect, surely.'

James waved his fingers slightly, dismissively. 'I pride myself a good judge of character, and of honesty. Or lack thereof.'

'We all pride ourselves on that.'

'True, but I have the professional track record to back up my pride. And the training, for that matter. After all, it's my job.'

'Then what do you see in his story? That he's your baby brother returned from the dead?'

159

'Of course not!' James closed his eyes for a moment, then abruptly marched off. Kyle followed, all the way to the infirmary. He was unbuttoning his jacket as he entered, and shrugged it off, flicking it neatly on to the nearest chair. 'Henrietta!'

Doctor Beswick appeared at an interior door. 'I'm treating an injury—'

'Good. When you're done,' James said, rolling up his shirt sleeve, 'you can take a blood sample from me.'

'All right. Why?'

'You still have samples of Colonel Lethbridge-Stewart's blood?'

'Of course.'

'I want you to compare them with mine, by any and all means available to you. I want to know if there's any chance of there being a genetic or family link between us.'

She gave him a sidelong look. 'I can do that, but I don't see a point to it.'

'That doesn't matter. Call it curiosity.'

Major Lethbridge-Stewart's next duty, he felt, was to look at the wreckage of the bombers that had been recovered by the RAF. They were nothing like as technologically advanced as the capsule, of course – which he intended to consult Mackay about next. Mostly they were made of wood, with metal framing underneath.

'Do you recognise the type?'

Kyle shook her head. 'Colonel Lethbridge-Stewart – I mean, Subject Zero – does though. He called them Wellingtons.'

'Could they be some experimental prototypes?'

'With radial engines and propellers?' she scoffed. 'No... They're something else. They look like something from the 1920s or '30s. We recovered what's left of the bodies, and some personal effects. All the paperwork on them is dated 1939.'

'Twenty years ago,' James murmured.

'And Subject Zero—'

'We may as well keep calling him Colonel Lethbridge-Stewart. It doesn't sound as pretentious.'

She smiled faintly. 'Colonel Lethbridge-Stewart said some things recently about it being ten years ago... I mean, that he thinks 1959 is ten years ago, for him.'

'So, aircraft twenty years out of date, and a man who thinks he's ten years out of his time. Could that be a side effect of his treatments?'

'I have no idea.'

The next day, James, Kyle, Beswick, and Lieutenant Knight convened for a conference in what had been Colonel Lethbridge-Stewart's office. James had taken up residence there, and was now waiting for an incoming call from London. When the phone buzzed, he answered it with a 'yes, sir'.

After a moment, he covered the mouthpiece, and reached for a small grey box on the desk, on which he threw a switch. 'You're on speakerphone, sir.' He hung up the telephone handset, and introduced the three people in the office. 'This,' he told them in return, 'is the Director of External Security at the War Ministry.'

'I've read your report on Subject Zero,' the director's crisp voice said. 'Most interesting, and bears some thinking about. We still need to know who sent him. The Americans? Russia?'

James started pacing around the room.

'He won't tell us,' Knight said. 'To be honest, considering the levels and efficacy of his treatment, I don't believe he knows himself. He's not faking, or resisting; if he knew, on any level, he would have told us.'

James stopped pacing, span around and snapped the fingers of his raised had. 'Yes! He would, and perhaps he has.'

'Major?' The director asked.

'He used a word, when I spoke to him... He said he could resist because of... Goeje.' He crossed the room in two lanky steps, and ran his fingers along a row of encyclopaedic directory folders.

Beswick looked baffled. 'Koji? What?'

'That's what I thought he said at first. Koji is a common Japanese name, but he was referring to "at" whatever it was.' James pulled a folder from the shelf and opened it with a flourish. 'Goeje...' he spelled it out for them '...is an island, in Korea.'

'The Co-Prosperity Sphere...?' the director's voice said, in a tone suggesting he was mulling it over.

'It makes logical sense,' Beswick admitted. 'Chinese specialists are the best in the field. Who could have more effectively removed our prisoner's own persona and memories so completely? Who could have performed such exquisite programming if not our cousins in Manchuria?'

'And yet he remembered to mention it?' Knight said sceptically. 'How convenient.'

'Most programming of this type is very context-sensitive.

If there's a context they couldn't predict, or that pre-exists in his mind but they didn't know about, then...'

'Then it's to our advantage,' Kyle suggested. 'If we can deduce who sent him, the next question remains, why? General ongoing information gathering, a sleeper in case of potential future need, or does he have a specific objective to fulfil?'

'Could be any or all of those,' Beswick said. 'And he probably doesn't consciously know.'

'In which case,' Knight said firmly, 'it may be safer just to eliminate him. Take no chances.'

Kyle shook her head. 'Then they'd just send someone else that we don't know about, who we don't know to keep an eye on.'

'And observing him would give us clues to their long-term military and intelligence goals,' James added.

'That was our original thinking also,' the director said, 'in the hope we could identify his origins through his activities. That project seems to have reached, at best, a natural crossroads.'

'Then we should continue with that strategy now that we can relate his activities to a source government,' Kyle said. James couldn't help wondering if she was a little biased in the matter of Subject Zero. 'The intelligence advantages will be far greater.'

The director cleared his throat. 'Another question springs to mind. Does this mean the capsule also originated from the Co-Prosperity Sphere, given that it contained a man with whom Colonel Lethbridge-Stewart admitted to being familiar, and who could have been a contact?'

'Doctor Mackay thinks that's unlikely,' James said,

'given the European origins of the capsule. But we probably shouldn't rule anything out at this stage.'

The director was silent for a minute, then said, 'I would so love to gain more out of this project, but Lieutenant Knight is correct; it's reached the stage where the risks outweigh the rewards. Complete the interrogation of Subject Zero for any miscellaneous information he may yet have, and then liquidate him.'

'Yes, sir,' James heard himself say. He saw Knight's small smile of triumph, and Kyle grit her teeth. He switched off the speakerphone, and waved everyone to the door. 'We'll carry on with the interrogation tomorrow. I want everyone at their most alert.' He ushered them out, and then walked along to the infirmary.

Subject Zero had been allowed – and to some degree chemically encouraged – to sleep in a normal hospital bed in a locked private room, and James stood watching him through an observation window. In profile, there was something very familiar about the man, and James could almost see the boy that his younger brother had been somewhere in the face. It was stupid, and he cursed himself for being an idiot for being suckered into entertaining the thought for the merest second, but he just *knew*.

'Major!'

He turned, and saw Doctor Beswick approaching, with a handful of papers. 'Yes?'

'I made those tests you asked about, looking for genetic similarities between Subject Zero – Colonel Lethbridge-Stewart – and yourself. As you can imagine, it was pretty inconclusive – there are only so many blood types, and so on – but then I thought I'd give it a go with Wilkins, Watson and Crick's recent techniques, which are much more specific and detailed.'

'And?'

'His cellular makeup as well as blood type shows a first-generation relationship to yours.' The room seemed to tilt around James, and he let himself drop into a seat as she continued. 'Without a sample of Alistair's blood, I can't compare the two. He may or may not be your younger brother Alistair, but there's a better than eighty percent chance that he is *a* brother of yours.' She spread her hands helplessly. 'I'm not sure what else to say. Do you need anything? A bowl, an anti-emetic?'

He shook his head, pretending he didn't regret it. 'I'll be fine.'

She shook her head. 'Don't lie to me, Major. You're going to be bloody miles from fine when you have to kill that man tomorrow.'

# CHAPTER NINE

# *Disunity*

It was a damp and grey morning in Wiltshire, and the world outside the Joint Warfare Establishment's canteen windows was as monochrome and grey as anything Anne had seen on BBC1 over the years. Even the sturdy Land Rover that she saw drive up to the door seemed dark grey rather than dark green, but she perked up when Colonel Douglas emerged and hurried inside.

Leaving the remains of her breakfast on the table, Anne hurried out to meet Douglas in the entrance hall. His face was somewhat grim. 'Walter,' she said, much to the surprise of the various guards and personnel around. 'What—?'

'Is the professor around, Miss Travers?'

'He's still asleep. Apparently he only went to bed at three in the morning.'

'Well, I hate to wake him, but…' Douglas stalked across to the adjutant on desk duty, and had him send a runner off to find Travers.

Her bleary-eyed father appeared, shambling along, a couple of minutes later. 'All right, all right,' Travers grumbled, 'I've proved I'm not dead. Either tell me what couldn't wait, or let me catch up on some sleep.'

'It's happened again, Professor.'

'It? It? You're not in a *Carry On* film, Colonel, are you?

Eh?'

'Another capsule has fallen. This time it was caught on radar, appearing at eight thousand feet over Brittany, and coming down somewhere in the vicinity of Mont Saint-Michel.'

Travers was awake and alert immediately. 'I should hope someone is looking for the landing site?'

'The French army and gendarmerie, yes.'

'Excellent! Now, have there been any reports of anomalous men or vehicles in the area?'

'Not so far.'

'Well, that's as maybe, but warn the French authorities to be on the lookout for such things. I should expect some, if I were them.'

'Why?'

'Because so far there have been temporal anomalous events in the immediate vicinity of all these capsule landings, so it's pretty damned likely that there'll be something similar at this one.'

That was that, then, Larry Greene realised when he finally returned home from Germany. Chucked out like a pair of old boots, the Official Secrets Act slapped on him.

He was still tired when he walked in the front door, but he headed straight for the phone in the living room, ignoring the questions from his wife. He dialled a familiar number, one he hoped he would never need to use again, and waited for the smug voice on the other end.

'Hi, Harry, it's me.'

Greene waited for Harold Chorley to stop talking, moaning, complaining about the way Greene had dumped him a couple of months ago.

'Yes, Harry, I know, you're right and I'm sorry. But listen, I have a story for you… Well, to share with you. How are you fixed for a pint?'

Larry Greene smiled, knowing how easy it was to reel Chorley in. Greene wasn't going to take this lying down. He'd been tasked by Hamilton to get to the bottom of things, and he was going to do just that. Official Secrets Act or not!

James opened the door to Building Four, expecting to see the familiar sight of Doctor Mackay and his subordinates working among the disassembled capsule pieces, and to some degree he was not disappointed. He was startled, however, to only catch glimpses of them behind Captain Kyle, who was standing in the doorway with her arms folded. For such a petite woman, she filled the door quite effectively.

'Good morning, Major.'

'Captain.'

'When is Colonel Lethbridge-Stewart's execution set for?'

James didn't try to step past her, not yet. 'It isn't.'

'Is this because of some connection you think you've been lured into?'

'*You're* saying that? You were as keen to swing the director's decision away from a death sentence.'

'The difference is I can set aside my personal feelings, and live with doing my duty.'

James resisted the urge to ask if her opinion would be the same before hearing that she might have a rival. 'Is it your duty, though?'

'It's a direct order—'

'From an officer of what rank?'

'Well... he's your—'

James moved her gently aside with one hand, and stepped through. 'He's a civil servant, not an officer, not military, and not in the chain of command. He can probably give a direct order to the civil police, or Special Branch, or members of his own department, but we are not bound to follow his orders.'

'We have done before.'

James looked around the room, trying to spot anything different, and work out for himself how the analysis of the pieces was going. 'They've been sensible before. And, yes, to be fair it's generally accepted that the military will co-operate with security, but... This is one of those cases where we don't just go ahead.'

'That'll still be seen as insubordination.'

'Not in the slightest. We do this by what our American cousins call *The Book*. Specifically, we refer the order up the Army chain of command.'

Kyle sighed. 'And they'll say to obey the order. You know that.'

'Yes they will. But it'll give us some time to think.'

She stepped back and they regarded each other coolly. 'What is there to think about?' Kyle asked at last.

'What's best for the project, and for the country.'

'And for us?'

'I suppose. But, Captain, if you didn't think there were considerations to be made, you wouldn't be standing here talking to me.'

'I'm sure there's a lot we could learn from him, and his

being sent by the Chinese is one thing, but... You believe he's somehow your brother? Don't bother to deny it; I can see it in your eyes.' She shook her head. 'If your brother's body had never been found, then I could understand. But it's not as if you even have that possibility.' She gave James a surprisingly coquettish look. 'Or perhaps you're thinking he's some kind of... reincarnation? Which would be odd, given that he must have been born well before your brother died.'

'I don't know. It's just... Body language, tone, I don't know how or why, I just...'

'You just feel it.' Kyle looked around at the sound of approaching footsteps. James saw Mackay appear behind her. 'Just... *think* about what you feel, sir,' she said.

'It's fascinating,' Mackay said. 'I hope you don't mind my venturing an opinion, because I think it might explain a few things about this.' He waved a hand, indicating the pieces of capsule. 'And I couldn't help overhearing. Lovely echo in this building.'

'You're the science expert,' James said, 'or so I'm led to believe. If science can help, who am I to dismiss it?'

Mackay nodded. 'Let me see if I have this correct. It's you and Colonel Lethbridge-Stewart, yes? Each of you believes the other to be an impostor who has adopted the identity of a brother who died in childhood. Interesting. That's a new one on me.'

'It must cast doubts on the major's loyalty,' Kyle said

'If you're a paranoiac in government, probably. Too many politicians are.'

'Think about it logically,' Kyle insisted. 'They cannot both be telling the truth. They can, however, both be lying.

At least one of them must be.'

'Not,' Mackay said firmly, 'necessarily.'

'Please, do explain,' Kyle said coldly.

'Colonel Lethbridge-Stewart identified the aircraft as "Wellingtons". Named after the old duke, I presume.'

'I've never heard of a plane by that name,' James pointed out.

'Nor have I. Which is interesting in its implications, isn't it? Either it's a fiction or a delusion, something only in his head. Or else it's knowledge not available to us. There were logbooks found with the bodies of the crews, and those logbooks were dated only up to 1939.'

'Twenty years ago,' Kyle said. 'Or thirty, according to Colonel Lethbridge-Stewart.'

Mackay nodded, and pointed at her. 'Exactly. Twenty years out of date. A temporal anomaly.'

'Time travel?' Kyle asked sceptically.

'I wouldn't rule it out.'

'But the bombers may have time travelled, not Colonel Lethbridge-Stewart.'

'Well, I never said it was a solution. Just an example of how timelines can be changed; somewhere there's a timeline where those bombers simply completed their mission.'

Colonel Douglas had spread out a number of aerial and satellite photos across a table in the air traffic control centre. Travers, Anne, and le Cheminant leaned on the edges of the table, poring over them. They showed a small typical European village, wooded on one side, and with fields on the other.

'What are we looking at?' le Cheminant asked.

Douglas tapped a picture. 'According to Miss Travers' calculations, the launch point of the capsules.'

'If there's some sort of launch site for lifting bodies there, it's well hidden,' le Cheminant said.

'It isn't you know,' Travers said smugly.

'Isn't what? Well hidden, or there?'

'Both, I suppose. At least I didn't expect to see anything there.'

'Why not?'

Anne snapped her fingers. 'The temporal anomalies.'

'First Class, Anne! The men from 1914, the ship from 1939, and so on.'

'What have they to do with it?' Douglas asked.

'Everything! Each of those capsule landings has been accompanied by a temporal anomaly, and none of the capsules have engines, which means they're launched by some external power source, yet they cause a temporal distortion...'

'They're being launched from a different time,' Anne summarised.

'And the temporal energy – don't ask me to elaborate further, I'm no expert,' Travers grumbled, 'is somehow causing a... displacement, like a splash, upon landing. And that's where your out-of-time people are coming from.'

Le Cheminant frowned. 'So, are these things coming from the past or future, in your estimation?'

'How the hell should I know? The technology is neither very much ahead or behind our own. Perhaps they're even coming from... Sideways in time?'

'Sideways?' le Cheminant echoed.

'If someone changed the past, they could change the

172

present, according to some theories I've heard.' Travers shrugged. 'Perhaps they come from one of those changed presents?'

Lethbridge-Stewart was under no illusions that things had changed, and not for the better. Not for him, anyway. He could see it in the eyes and postures of the people working in the infirmary, every time their gaze slid his way surreptitiously. It was the way people acted around a dying man.

He remembered that he had been questioned again, though he didn't remember all the details. And, as the major who called himself James had said, he knew that everybody talked eventually. He just wondered what it was they had been after, and whether they had got it.

He could feel that he was being watched, and went to the door to the private room. It was locked, of course, and James was on the other side, watching him through the glass panel. 'I take it my execution has been ordered,' Lethbridge-Stewart said. 'I hope you're going to grant a last request.' He wasn't going to let them see how unnerving being in a condemned cell was.

'I'm sure a hearty breakfast will be along.'

'I'd like to speak to Captain Kyle as well, at some point before... Well, before.'

'That can be arranged.' James looked thoughtful, as he turned to go.

'Let me ask you something, Major.' James hesitated, then nodded. Lethbridge-Stewart continued, 'You said before that I was parachuted in. Was that simply an assumption as to how I arrived in the area, or a definite fact?'

'That's a fact,' James said. He turned back, and unlocked the door, keeping Lethbridge-Stewart covered with a pistol. There was a military provost waiting discreetly to one side, and James had him cuff Lethbridge-Stewart's hands in front of him, before holstering his gun. 'Come with me,' he said. 'You can consider this part of your last request.' The laugh he barked was totally mirthless, and seemed more for the provost's benefit, as he followed the pair through the corridors.

James led Lethbridge-Stewart to a vault adjacent to the armoury; a sterile and cool room filled with vertical cabinets that slid silently out of the walls with the turn of a capstan wheel. James went to a particular slot, and turned the wheel. The grey cabinet slid out, revealing shreds of silk and nylon rope. They were hanging from a hook on the inside of the door, above an open parachute pack and harness. There was also a uniform identical to his own, and a duplicate set of identity papers in a wallet. A clipboard was also mounted on the door, and he handed it to Lethbridge-Stewart, who took it in his cuffed hands.

The top sheet had a load of serial numbers and reference codes which Lethbridge-Stewart didn't recognise. Underneath was a brief recap, which summarised the material: 'Documentation assigned: Lethbridge-Stewart, Alistair Gordon. Rank: Colonel, British Army (Scots Guards). Identity: Unknown. D.O.B.: Unknown. Nationality: Unknown.' The documentation continued in that vein. At the bottom of the page was an authorization: 'Kyle, M., Captain, Intelligence Corps.'

Lethbridge-Stewart leafed through the other attached

pages. There were pictures of himself, asleep or comatose in a hospital bed, and draped in the branches of a tree. There he was half-covered in parachute silk over a torn uniform. Two maps were attached as well, one rough and hand-drawn, the other a Photostat of the equivalent section of a proper map.

'And that was when I was found?'

'Still wearing the parachute harness, having come off worst in a fight with a tree.' James put everything away, and led him and the provost back out of the vault.

Lethbridge-Stewart glanced at the locked steel door to the armoury, then relaxed. There was no chance of getting through it, and tensing himself to try would be foolish. Better to save his strength for any future opportunity.

'Perhaps we should go and talk to Marianne,' James said. 'While you're making your farewell tour.'

Ten minutes later, Lethbridge-Stewart was looking at Marianne Kyle across the desk of his – what used to be his – office. Her expression was carefully impassive, but he could sense the tension in her poise. James and the provost had stepped outside, but he knew they were both waiting there, doubtless with hands on their weapons.

'You wanted to see me... Colonel?'

'I wanted to know... How long have we really known each other? If at all.'

'About four months,' she said at last.

'And how much of our... good terms, are real?'

'Where they don't conflict with my duty...? All of them.'

'Did you know there was... someone else, back home?'

'I knew your cover said so, but I also knew it was a

fiction.'

'Except it's not a fiction. Not a cover.'

'Then who is she?'

'I've no idea.'

Silence, then Kyle spoke again. 'Sometimes, no matter what stage of… processing you'd been through, you'd talk in your sleep – I could play you recordings – sometimes you say a name: Sally.'

Sally… He recalled a woman in a corporal's uniform. Sally… Wright. His fiancée. He wondered if she was worried about his absence, or whether, if he had already been declared dead, she had been all right at the memorial service. There must have been a memorial service, surely?

He nodded to Kyle. 'Thank you, Captain. That's… all. Carry on.'

She returned his nod, and opened the door, letting James and the provost in as she stepped out. James halted her before she could go. 'Captain, I have a job for you.'

'Sir?'

'Take a search party – low key, side-arms only – to these co-ordinates.' He handed her a piece of paper.

'This is where he was found,' Kyle said curiously, indicating Lethbridge-Stewart.

'Yes.'

'What are we searching for?'

'I'm not sure. But if the man in the capsule at Deepdene was a potential contact for Subject Zero, then maybe a similar capsule.'

'Right, sir.' She departed, and James faced Lethbridge-Stewart.

'It's time.'

'And how are you planning to murder me? Firing squad, or just a bullet in the back of the head at the Lubyanka?'

James glanced at his watch. 'I believe the intent is for a lethal injection, since you're already under medical observation, but...'

'But?'

'If there was an element of "shot while trying to escape" then...'

'It's an old tradition.'

James turned to the provost. 'Prepare a firing party for the rifle range. I want them in ten minutes.' The provost saluted and stepped away, but James called him back. 'Oh, and best give me the keys, just in case.' He held out a hand.

The provost gave him a set of keys, including, Lethbridge-Stewart noticed, the keys to the cuffs he was wearing, and then set off at the double.

'Come on,' James said grimly. He led Lethbridge-Stewart out of the building, and turned towards the training areas that included the firing range, which were beyond the raised helipad and hangar for the base's helicopters.

Lethbridge-Stewart had no idea why the man was still maintaining this 'James' identity – keeping a cover was habitual, he supposed – but he had no intention of reaching the firing range. As soon as they passed out of sight of the building's windows – Lethbridge-Stewart was certain that a corner of wall blocked any sight from that direction – he moved.

He barged sideways into James, knocking him aside, and threw his cuffed wrists around the other man's neck.

'What are you doing, you—?' James was cut off as the handcuff chain dug into his windpipe.

He jabbed his elbows backwards, and tried to stamp on Lethbridge-Stewart's feet, but Lethbridge-Stewart was expecting these defences, and turned, forcing James off balance instead. James stumbled to his knees, tearing his head free of the cuffs, but gashing his cheek. Before he could rise, Lethbridge-Stewart gave him a tremendous punch to the side of the head, putting him on the ground.

'That's for stealing my brother's name,' he muttered, as he fished the keys from James' pocket, and took his pistol.

There was a sound next to his ear that was like someone cracking a knuckle, and he realised it was a high velocity bullet narrowly missing his head. A patrolling guard at the far end of an alley between hangars had spotted what was happening, and was shooting at him. Lethbridge-Stewart knelt behind a thick steel junction box, and returned fire. The man dropped, but it was too late; the gunfire had drawn attention, and alarms were beginning to blare.

Lethbridge-Stewart quickly undid the handcuffs and dropped them onto a groaning James, then darted back in the opposite direction. Getting out would be preferable, but he knew he'd never make it across the open ground near the perimeter alive. No, it was better to find a place to hole up, let them think he'd got out, and smuggle himself out in a vehicle later.

He ran for the fire-control training tower. It was used for the base's emergency personnel to train in rescuing people from burning buildings, just as civilian firemen did, and to practice abseiling. It would give him good observation of the whole base and its activity, and it was enclosed, unlike the radio masts which would also have given him a good viewpoint. With any luck he could climb it without being seen.

Luck was not with him. He slipped around a storage building, and came almost eyeball to eyeball with Lieutenant Knight, leading a squad of soldiers. Knight's eyes widened, and Lethbridge-Stewart dove aside as his men opened fire. Bullets chipped brick from the walls as he rolled under a truck and dashed for the cover of an alley nearer the tower.

Boots clattered on the tarmac, and two men followed him into the alley, both with submachine guns. He shot one, and the slide jammed back on his pistol, meaning it was empty. He ducked behind a shed as the other man fired, and squinted against the splinters that flew around his eyes. The soldier must have thought he had kept running, as he now dashed past the side of the shed, and halted in surprise at seeing neither a fleeing nor dead man. Since the soldier's back was to him, Lethbridge-Stewart obligingly cracked him across the back of the skull with his empty pistol, and then pocketed it in favour of the soldier's submachine gun and some spare clips of ammo.

He could hear Knight shouting orders, and, further away, the cough of engines starting up. He took the opportunity to complete his journey to the tower, and slipped inside. Though tired, adrenaline gave him a boost, and he took the steel stairs two at a time, to emerge on to the roof. He was moving so quickly that the rifle butt that would have all but taken his head off missed, and glanced off his shoulder. He cursed himself for not realising that Knight would have put a sniper up there. He kept himself doubled over, and ran his head into the man's belly, his momentum carrying them both to the edge of the roof. The sniper's arms lashed out frantically for a handhold, but to no avail, and he disappeared with a scream.

'Stretcher party!' he heard Knight shout, and then bullets were pinging off the edge of the roof. He withdrew out of the enemy's sight, and slammed the stairwell door closed, using the sniper's rifle to jam the handle.

Then he slumped. Instead of a hiding place, he had made himself a trap. It wouldn't be long before men came up the stairs and blew the door off its hinges. He wondered whether the firing party would still get their shilling, or whether an over-excited Soviet squaddie would just throw him off the tower. Already he could hear boots clanging on the stairs.

The door shook and rattled, bullets punching through it, and then there was a pause. They'd be fixing a charge now. Well, he wasn't going to give them an easy time of it. He reloaded both the pistol and the submachine gun.

Several things happened at once. Lethbridge-Stewart heard a roaring from behind him – did Valkyries sound like that? – as the door exploded open, pieces of broken rifle flying towards him, a heavy steel piece hitting his forehead with a flash of light and pain. He staggered aside, squeezing short bursts into the murky figures filling the smoky doorway. He was rewarded with screams, and a heavy metal ball that arced out and bounced towards his feet.

With nowhere else to go, he turned, hurling himself forwards at a helicopter that was dropping in to the edge of the roof. The floor of the passenger compartment was almost level with the roof's edge, so he leapt headlong, slamming painfully into the steel floor. Immediately, the chopper lurched upward, and he heard a sharp thud and a shower of metallic pings as the grenade went off on the roof that was already falling away.

Lethbridge-Stewart scrambled forward and into the co-pilot's seat. He looked at James, in the pilot's seat, as he caught his breath, and rested his hand on the butt of his pistol. He wasn't sure whether to draw it on James or not. For the moment he settled for strapping himself into the seat into which he was being pressed as James launched the chopper higher into the air.

'Where are you planning on taking us?' Lethbridge-Stewart asked, once he'd pulled a headset on.

'I don't think I'd planned that far ahead, I'm afraid. This was something of a spur-of-the-moment choice.' James glanced pointedly at Lethbridge-Stewart's pistol. 'I suppose I should mention that if you have a burning desire to visit a specific destination at the expense of my wellbeing, shooting me will just mean a rather painful and almost certainly fatal crash.' He smiled thinly. 'Benefits of altitude.'

'At altitude we'll be visible on radar. How confident are you that we aren't going to be intercepted very soon by a jet fighter?'

'Wasn't thinking that far ahead either, I'm afraid. So we probably will.' James glared at him. 'By the way, allow me to congratulate you on the display of the most idiocy I've seen in my career.'

'Idiocy?'

'Kyle's sent away, the provost's sent away, and you don't think the man who made sure to have the key to your handcuffs did that for a reason?'

'You're saying you were planning to let me go? I find that hard to believe.'

James remained silent for a while. 'I won't pretend to

know exactly what's going on, and I know you don't believe a word of me being *your* dead older brother somehow returned… But I do believe you're *my* dead brother somehow returned.'

Lethbridge-Stewart was stunned. 'How?'

'I've no idea, but since it motivates me to not have you executed, does it matter?'

'It does if you're a madman. Or even just delusional.'

'No offence taken.'

A shadow flashed across the windscreen a second before the chopper shook as it was buffeted by turbulence. Another helicopter swooped around in front of them, and Lethbridge-Stewart realised that it wasn't mere turbulence that had hit them.

'The rotor wash,' James said, confirming his thought. 'They're trying to force us down.'

'At least they're not shooting at us yet.'

'They will eventually.'

Lethbridge-Stewart leaned forward and set the radio to a broad range of frequencies that he knew the military used. 'This is Colonel Lethbridge-Stewart aboard helicopter RW-117. I have taken control of this aircraft and am holding Major Lethbridge-Stewart prisoner. If you have any concerns for his welfare, pull back your helicopter.'

'Colonel Lethbridge-Stewart,' Knight's voice came back after a moment, 'you will allow yourself to be escorted to a safe landing place, and surrender yourself, your vehicle, and your prisoner.'

Hollow pops and clangs rattled behind Lethbridge-Stewart, and he ducked instinctively. 'Can we shoot back?' he asked.

'Sorry, this whirlybird isn't armed.'

'Not even a pintle-mounted LMG back there?'

'Did you see one when you boarded?'

'No,' Lethbridge-Stewart admitted sharply.

'Then I doubt anyone has installed one in the meantime.'

'There's no need for sarcasm, Major.'

'Is there a need for rank, Alistair?'

'Age also has its privileges.'

'Really? But if you are who you claim to be, I'm the older brother, *Old* Man.'

The chopper shook again, buffeted by rotor wash, and then the enemy chopper swung away.

'Can they force us down that way?' Lethbridge-Stewart asked.

'Theoretically possible, if they could interfere with our rotors enough, but very unlikely. After all, choppers do fly in formation.' James shook his head. 'No, they're just trying to frighten us.'

'We need to lose them if we're to get away... somewhere.' There was a triangular window set into the cockpit window next to Lethbridge-Stewart's head and shoulder, but it wouldn't open far enough to allow him to stick his arm outside with a pistol.

He unbuckled himself, and clambered back into the passenger compartment.

'Where are you going?' James asked.

Lethbridge-Stewart brandished the SMG he had left on the floor when he boarded the chopper. 'This is the only real weapon we've got. I'm going to get into a position from which it can be used, if necessary.'

'Make sure you hang on to something – tie yourself to

183

something, ideally. It's a long way down.'

Lethbridge-Stewart glanced around, and saw a couple of straps with carabiner clips hanging from a reinforced bar in the centre of the ceiling, probably for door gunners or perhaps to abseil from. In any case, he grabbed both, and clipped the straps onto his belt.

He hauled the door open, and was assailed by a wall of icy air that almost made him drop the SMG.

'They're coming again,' James called through the headset.

Lethbridge-Stewart looked around, and was rewarded, or punished, with the sight of the enemy chopper above and behind them. He couldn't get an angle on it with the SMG without risking falling out, and knew it was still too far away for such a weapon to do any good anyway.

'Can you get alongside them?'

'I expect they'll provide that service themselves, Old Man.'

Sure enough, the other chopper swooped down like a bird of prey dropping on a hare, blasting air ahead of it. At the last minute, as before, it banked aside to afford the door gunner a clear field of fire, but this time Lethbridge-Stewart was waiting.

Bracing himself with one foot against the inside of the door's edge, and his back against one of the jump seats, he set the SMG's stock to his shoulder, and fired. He tried to keep the bursts short as he didn't know how much ammunition he had to spare, and he was sensible enough to lead the target, but he had never engaged in aerial combat like this before and so wherever his shots went they didn't hit the chopper or gunner as far as he could tell.

The enemy had a larger gun mounted in the door frame, like those he had seen in news footage from the American adventures in Vietnam, and their gunner was clearly more experienced. Lethbridge-Stewart flung himself backwards into the passenger cabin as holes were punched in the side of the fuselage, and sparks flew from ricochets on the steel floor. Then he was flung into the bulkhead separating the cabin from the cockpit as James threw the chopper into a desperate evasive manoeuvre.

'Are you hit?' James called, and Lethbridge-Stewart realised that he'd been shouting every obscenity he knew at the top of his voice.

He cleared his throat, and said, 'No damage so far. Just frustration.' He thought fast, running tactics through his head. There had to be a way of getting the other chopper off their backs so they could land somewhere undetected. 'They've kept coming in from the right side of us,' he said slowly. 'I think perhaps they only have the mounted gun on their left.'

'That sounds reasonable,' James agreed.

'Then we need to get on their other side.'

'They'll know that, but I'll try.' The chopper immediately tilted and pitched again, as another shower of metallic hail peppered the right side of the fuselage. Lethbridge-Stewart could see thin lines of vapour and oil streaming past the open door. He took his mind off the matter by checking his ammunition, but that wasn't reassuring either; one and a half clips, or about forty-odd rounds, which would last only a few seconds on full auto. Plus a few more if he counted his pistol.

His stomach felt as if it was boosted up into his throat as

James dropped the chopper by what felt like a hundred feet. He swayed, forcing himself not to throw up, and now saw trees flashing past. Risking a closer approach to the door, he saw that they were now hustling down a chalky-sided river valley, and the trees jutting out of the cliffs on the right were getting ever closer. Lethbridge-Stewart was momentarily alarmed, but then realised that there wasn't room for the other helicopter to get between them and the foliage. They would have to come from the other side, as he had hoped.

The chopper began to shake under turbulence again, so he pulled open the door on the left of the cabin, and looked out. The other chopper was descending over their rotors, but instead of a mounted machine gun at the door, there was a winch above it on that side. Lethbridge-Stewart smiled grimly, braced himself, and raised the SMG. He squeezed off a couple of short bursts at the cockpit windscreen, and was gratified to see white cracks flash across it. Then the SMG's clip was emptied and the enemy chopper pulled up and away.

'Now we'll really be in trouble,' Lethbridge-Stewart called back.

'They'll send an interceptor,' James agreed. 'We won't even see the plane before the missile hits us.'

'Get as low as possible. We need them to lose us on radar, and then find a place to go aground and work out our next move.'

'Whatever you say, Old Man.'

— CHAPTER TEN —

# *Anachronysium*

The helicopter tilted this way and that, staying low as it headed south. Despite the swooping and lurching, Lethbridge-Stewart found himself relaxing, physically at least. Now that the adrenalin was wearing off, his legs, shoulders and ribs were beginning to sting and burn.

Being out of the base was good, as was not being executed, but he was still on the run, accompanied by a man who could only be a Soviet agent. He certainly couldn't be James, who died so many years ago. Then again, he reflected, perhaps he was really still strapped to the gurney under Henrietta Beswick's ministrations, fighting his way only through a drug-fuelled nightmare. Well, if so, then there was nothing he could do about that.

'Where are we going?' he asked at last.

James, or whoever he really was, thought for a moment. 'Looking for you, Old Man.'

Lethbridge-Stewart raised an eyebrow. 'Really? To see "my" gravestone, you mean?'

'I don't think you want to see that, do you?' Lethbridge-Stewart didn't answer. 'But it might benefit everyone if we can determine where, when, and how you got here.'

'I'd have thought Doctor Beswick had got that kind of thing out of me already; she always seemed quite proficient.'

'She is, but you can only tell us what you know.'

'Then it seems I must apologise for my lack of omniscience.'

'I suppose as the elder brother, omniscience should be my job.'

'You know, there's really no point maintaining this "brother" thing, *Comrade*.'

'*Comrades*, then?' James shrugged. 'I'd like to think the day has shown that it's worth maintaining the "allies" thing.'

'*Detente*, perhaps.'

'It has its uses.' James consulted a map that was open on his leg. 'Where do you think we should go?'

'Well, I for one would like to get back to my unit.'

'You'll never get to England. And if you do it'll be the end of you.' James glanced at the map again, and looked down at the ground below. 'This should be roughly the right area.' He started throwing switches, and took the chopper into a gentle descent. Lethbridge-Stewart saw some rocky hills rise beside him, and a clear patch of rough ground gently meet the chopper's landing gear. The machine settled with a bump, and James unbuckled himself from his seat as the rotors above slowed and halted. 'We'll go on foot from here.'

The helo landed on rough grass, near a rocky outcrop that overlooked a gentle hillside. In the opposite direction, trees – mainly firs and pines – stretched over undulating small hills, with a couple of low, jagged peaks in the distance. James let Lethbridge-Stewart step down to the ground first, and then threw him the submachine gun. 'I can't see you needing that out here, but if giving it to you makes you feel more trusted…?'

Lethbridge-Stewart looked at it, and checked that it was all in good working order. 'I suppose I do feel trusted; I'm just at a loss as to why. From your point of view, I'm still a fugitive enemy spy with an unknown mission, am I not?'

James sat on the edge of the chopper's rear door, and nodded. 'Intellectually, at least, that would be the logical conclusion with the data available. But perhaps I have more intel than you know. Such as the results of blood tests that Henrietta carried out.'

'Which are doubtless supposed to convince me that we're brothers.'

'No, they're meant to convince *me*. In any case, you're the one with incomplete memories; how can you be so sure of anything?' James sighed, sat back, and stretched out his legs, turning the ankles to undo the tensions and incipient cramps in them. 'I suppose not. The logical thing for you to believe is that I'm simply a foreign agent maintaining my cover identity, and/or that I'm still trying to convince you, in the hope that there's still a concentration of SB-117 in your bloodstream. Which, incidentally, there undoubtedly is.'

'So I believe you and tell myself it's the drugs that make me that way?'

'If it helps you feel better. Though I must also point out that, of course, I have not been subject to Henrietta's chemical ministrations – as far as I know, which is always a matter of faith – and so have no such excuse.'

James stood and reached into a compartment in the chopper, pulling out a rucksack, ration packs, water bottles, and a few other bits and pieces of gear suitable for hours of hiking.

'My brother had an imaginary friend,' Lethbridge-Stewart said suddenly.

'Maha,' James said quietly. Lethbridge-Stewart went pale, and James knew he had not been expecting a correct answer.

'How could you know that?'

'How do you think, Old Man?'

James' words followed Lethbridge-Stewart as they walked into the woods. He knew enough basic psychology to understand that some unconscious part would want it to be true, want James to be back, to finally know the brother he had no actual memory of, but he was also pragmatic enough to set that aside.

But how had he known about something from Lethbridge-Stewart's childhood, which he himself had only recently begun coming to terms with the knowledge of?

He also momentarily wondered why he wasn't simply pointing the gun at James, and forcing him to fly west. Maybe it was some effect of Doctor Beswick's psychoactive drugs – they'd doubtless be in his system for days, and it had probably occurred to this man James at some point to plant an order forbidding such an action – or maybe it was because he needed to know himself. How the hell had he got here?

'East Germany seems surprisingly pretty for a nature walk,' he offered.

'How did you work out where you are?'

'A simple matter of having done rather well in orienteering courses during training, I'm afraid. Comparing a view of the stars to the reading of a compass… This town is on the same latitude as the home counties, I'd wager, but too far east.'

'The nearest city's Leipzig, if you were wondering. Nice place if you have an interest in medieval architecture.'

'I'm sure it is.' Lethbridge-Stewart frowned; the area was, he had to admit, strangely familiar. 'This region… Have I been here before?'

'Yes.' James pointed east. 'You were found about half a mile that way, unconscious in a tree.'

Lethbridge-Stewart felt a shiver run down his spine, and thought he heard the wind rushing around him. He stumbled, momentarily dizzy, overwhelmed by a familiar sound and sensation in his head.

'Is something coming back to you?' James asked.

'Perhaps, Major…'

They kept moving, well into late afternoon. They heard the occasional flight of a plane or helicopter overhead, but none swooped down for a closer look, and so neither of them would admit to being sure of whether any of the aircraft were those out looking for them.

Occasionally James would spot something, and guide them slightly left or right; he seemed to know the area relatively well, and Lethbridge-Stewart couldn't help but admire his field-craft, regardless of who he really was, or might be.

As dusk began to fall, and the air between the trees greyed and thickened, Lethbridge-Stewart spotted something metallic. 'What's that?' he asked.

'I don't know, but I could always hope it's what we're

looking for.' James moved ahead, following Lethbridge-Stewart's pointing finger.

The sky seemed to lighten, and Lethbridge-Stewart realised that the leaf canopy was gouged apart here, letting in more of the open sky. Splintered tree trunks were scattered around, mostly angled to point south, and there were more golden glints appearing through what was left of the growth.

Lethbridge-Stewart checked his gun and moved forward, until he saw that the glints of light were gleaming on a misty white background. The shapes were familiar, but the context was not, and the thickening twilight didn't help. He put a hand out to push into the mist, and felt his palm slap on solid, if lightweight, metal. Aluminium, he realised. He saw the golden patches for what they were: the reflection of the setting sun on glass portholes. They were the cabin windows mounted in an aircraft fuselage – a pale grey-white fuselage that was cracked open like an eggshell, and grimy with weeks, or months, worth of exposure to the elements.

'Fascinating,' he heard James murmur beside him.

Lethbridge-Stewart moved forward as if compelled by an unseen voice. He stepped through the wide split in the curving fuselage wall, and, there, Lethbridge-Stewart remembered.

He remembered.

He was slammed against the sides of seats, as a chunk of the fuselage exploded out and away. Emergency lighting flashed, stabbing into the darkness. There was a deafening roar approaching along the aisle, and for a moment Lethbridge-Stewart looked for a weapon, but then he realised *he* was approaching the roar, tumbling towards the gaping wound in the skin of the plane. The wing had been torn away with part of the fuselage skin. It was the wind that roared, screaming out the pain of the dismembered plane.

The cabin spun around Lethbridge-Stewart as the engine on the remaining wing pulled it around in a deadly corkscrew. As he slammed from cabin floor to ceiling, he knew the plane was falling. How high were they, and how much time they had before impact, he had no idea.

The cockpit door fell open, and one of the pilots tumbled through, shoving a parachute towards Lethbridge-Stewart. 'Mike's going to try to stabilise her,' the man shouted over the background roar. 'Get this on.' He braced himself against the seat, to stretch the parachute harness around the colonel. Lethbridge-Stewart struggled to keep still long enough to fix the catches on the harness.

'How high?' he called.

'A couple of thousand feet. Seconds. Don't talk.'

Something else cracked, a sound like a shot but much louder, and the seat wrenched sideways, twisting and crumpling the co-pilot's leg. He screamed, his arms flailing uncontrollably. Lethbridge-Stewart tried to steady him, but one arm slammed into him. He stumbled and fell, and this time there was nothing for him to fall onto. There was just the wind shrieking around him and tearing at his uniform. He was rolling, falling on his back, and he knew he couldn't pull the ripcord in that position, or the parachute would just wrap itself around him like a burial shroud.

Orienting himself was difficult, as he had nothing to leverage himself against. He twitched and flailed, half-certain he would hit the ground in the next second, and wondering whether he would have time to feel the pain. Then he was momentarily face-down into the freezing airstream, and his arm yanked on the ripcord without thinking. There was a slippery cracking noise, and his spine and head jerked painfully upwards. As he caught his breath, the rush of the wind slowed and quietened a little, and he was able to hear the blood rushing in his ears instead.

Lethbridge-Stewart looked around and downwards, in search of the ground. Somewhere in the distance to his left, there was an explosion, telling him that the plane had reached the ground. It was hard to tell in the cloudy night, but he thought he was descending towards trees and hills. There was no sign of an open space or soft landing area, and he tried to remember what he'd been told by Old Spence about making parachute jumps. Night drops, Pemberton had said, were the trickiest.

There was a loop from the canopy to each hand that could supposedly aid him in steering himself, but he couldn't make out anywhere to steer to, and so simply concentrated on trying to keep in a straight line, and more or less the right way up.

All too soon, the treetops were rushing up at him, and he wondered how the hell he was supposed to bend the knees and roll when he landed. Then the question was made moot, when the trees reached up and beat at his legs and back, cracking ribs and making him feel as if he was being torn limb from limb.

Whatever whipped round and hit his head, ending his worries, had done him a favour.

*

'And that's why you were found in the woods to the north,' James said. 'Unconscious on a lucky sort of... hammock of branches that had come down under you. No limbs broken, which is a minor miracle, I suspect.'

'Cracked ribs and bruises,' Lethbridge-Stewart agreed.

'So, since we knew you were parachuted into the area, it's in our interest to know who sent you. But, looking at this, you weren't exactly sent, were you?'

'I wasn't sent. At least, I wasn't sent to be parachuted anywhere. I was on my way to Tibet. Or rather, I was flying to Cyprus, after which I'd catch a connection to Nepal, and then cross over into Tibet. But something hit the aircraft.'

'You were shot down?'

'No, something crashed into us, and took one of the wings off. Whatever it was must have come down as well, and not too far away, I should think. Have you lost any aircraft that could fit?'

James shook his head.

Lethbridge-Stewart surveyed the wreckage quickly. 'This isn't the whole aircraft. There's a wing and engine missing.'

James looked inside the wreckage, shaking his head. There was a skeleton in a tattered uniform against what was left of the rear bulkhead, and when he shone a torch into the now-dark cockpit, he saw a skull grinning back at him. 'Nothing was found near you. That said, depending on the descent path, either plane could have come down miles away.' He reached back into the rucksack on his back, and pulled out a large R/T box. He lifted the handset and squeezed the transmitter switch set into it. 'Lioness, this is Eagle, come in, over.'

'Eagle, this is Lioness,' Kyle's voice crackled over the

airwaves.

'Report your position, over.'

'Eagle, we are one and a half miles southwest of your position, over.'

'Form up on my position.'

'We're on our way, Eagle. Over and out.'

Lethbridge-Stewart aimed his gun at James. 'So you were just pretending.'

'If you believe that, then shoot me.'

'Which means you've rigged the gun. Removed the firing pin, I suppose.'

James nodded towards the crashed plane. 'If you want to be sure, give that a burst.'

Lethbridge-Stewart did, and was so startled by the loudness of the gunfire that peppered the fuselage with holes that he nearly dropped the submachine gun. He looked at James in utter bafflement.

'If my escape was staged for my benefit, then why...? Never mind. Did you get what you wanted from me?'

James barked a laugh. 'Your escape was staged, yes, but not for your benefit; for that of the War Office. I did get what I wanted, though, yes. Specifically, I got the truth of your arrival.' He sat on a tree stump. 'I'm not going to ask you accept the truth of our family relationship; I know you won't be able to. I will ask you to accept that we are at least friends – or allies, if nothing else – working from different ends to undo a Gordian knot, of sorts.'

'Friends and allies? A Soviet training school in East Germany, and a British officer?'

'We're all British officers.' James frowned. 'And the Soviets were defeated by White Russia in the '20s; I can't imagine there are many left.'

Lethbridge-Stewart was lost by that. History wasn't his strong suit, but he couldn't really imagine a Soviet officer saying such a thing.

'Oh,' James went on, 'you're thinking of our faux London? It is a training ground, of course, but for security personnel in the event of an attack on an important location.'

'And Deepdene?'

'A residential village for the families of British soldiers stationed here. And, before you ask, the Joint Warfare Establishment is one of several we use. As I said, I won't ask you to believe the empirical facts, but will you believe, at least, that I believe what I say.'

'People often believe what, on some level, they know isn't true, or simply hope is true, so I suppose...' Lethbridge-Stewart waved a hand at the wreckage around them. 'All right, what if for some reason I did believe you're my elder brother? Even though you're clearly younger. What does it mean? That I died in this crash, and all this is some kind of afterlife? I'm afraid I should find that entirely impossible to believe.'

'Do you think it's any less... odd, for me? Facing a man who, I think, honestly believes he's Alistair, a person I saw die, and who now seems older than me?'

'Then why do you?'

'Because... There is no because, really. Just the difference between what one knows and what one feels. They aren't the same thing, after all.'

'Aren't they?'

James rose. 'Whatever else you are, whoever else you are, you're clearly an Army officer, and a good one, if I'm any judge. Have you lost men under your command?'

Lethbridge-Stewart immediately thought of Ben Knight – the real one – and various other soldiers, cut down by enemy bullets in Korea and Aden, and by vicious claws in the London Event. 'Yes.'

'Have you lost men under your command, and know it wasn't your fault?'

Lethbridge-Stewart turned away. 'Yes.'

'And do you feel it was?'

Lethbridge-Stewart didn't answer. He didn't have to.

By now they could hear rustling, and footsteps, and then Captain Kyle stepped into the clearing made by the plane crash. She used hand signals to direct a couple of her soldiers to take up sentry positions around the site, and another to set up a couple of shaded lamps.

She saluted James, and looked uncertainly at Lethbridge-Stewart. 'Reporting as ordered, sir.'

The remaining three men of her unit stood where they could keep an eye on Lethbridge-Stewart. They fingered their SMGs, clearly unsure whether to keep him covered or not. Lethbridge-Stewart himself didn't particularly care. It had been a long day, and he had taken a lot of knocks as well as walking for what felt like miles. Now that it was dark, he'd happily be locked in a gulag, if it meant he could lie down and sleep.

As it was, however, James waved the guards away. 'I don't think Colonel Lethbridge-Stewart is capable of running away at the moment.' He pursed his lips in thought. 'At this juncture, I should say the best thing to do is: somebody get a brew-up going.'

The soldiers around grinned.

*

Kyle stepped up beside Major Lethbridge-Stewart, and gave him a quizzical look and a twitch of the head. 'Shall we discuss it in private?' he asked. They walked out of range of the light cast by the lamps.

'Have you lost your mind, sir?' she asked sharply. She regretted the strength of her tone instantly, but didn't apologise; she had worked with the major long enough to know he wouldn't take it personally. Probably. 'The ruse to get him to explain his arrival, fine... But how many good men did he kill today?'

'Only ones who were trying to kill him. Knight has the potential to be a good officer, but he needs to rein in his instincts.'

'Oh, Knight's a fool, yes, but the director likes him. And he won't like this.'

'The director likes results,' Major Lethbridge-Stewart said with a bitter edge, 'and he's got them now.' He looked at Kyle. 'So, what now?'

She looked out into the darkness, and she could feel that this was one of those times in which she held a balance of power, of some kind. That feeling was one of the reasons she had worked to join the Intelligence Corps, rather than another branch of the military – not so much that she liked it, as she didn't like leaving it to others. 'Do you remember that sergeant major, Arnold, and his son? The day I found you trying to straighten your nose in a grenade pit on the range at Salisbury.'

'I remember.'

'Did you know the director sent them?'

'No...'

'It was just for practice, I gather, more so than any message to you.'

'Well, you did fix the nose.' Kyle remembered he had screamed. It didn't bother her. Sergeant Major Arnold had screamed later too, and from such small cuts. 'How do you know he sent them?'

She chuckled. 'Intelligence Corps, remember. It's what we do.'

'What shall we do with our colonel, Captain? That is what you really want to ask, isn't it?'

It was, of course. 'Since killing him is clearly not going to be an option for you, the only logical thing is make use of him. Somehow.'

'My thought exactly. First, report in to the Establishment, and let Lieutenant Knight know that Colonel Lethbridge-Stewart is in custody. Make sure that's also passed up the chain of command, and across to the dear old director.'

Suddenly, one of the soldiers called out. 'Major, Captain!' They ran to the source of the sound, Kyle sure that Colonel Lethbridge-Stewart had made a break for freedom. She was surprised to see, however, that he had gathered up several of the troops around himself, and was directing them to shine lights down off the edge of a set of rocks a few hundred yards from the plane crash.

'What is it?' Major Lethbridge-Stewart asked.

'One of your sentries has found something rather interesting,' Colonel Lethbridge-Stewart said. He and a sergeant carefully descended the rocks, keeping their torches trained on something below. The major and Kyle followed, and the sergeant passed her torch to Kyle so that the officers could have a better look.

Smashed upon the rocks, hidden from the air by overhanging trees, was a familiar shape – a capsule just like the one from Deepdene. The major looked across the wreckage at the colonel. 'It looks like we found what hit your plane.'

'There's something else out there,' Kyle said. 'Across the valley.' She squinted. It was hard to tell at night, but she had excellent night vision and she could just make out a thin stream or string of light. It stretched out from a cliff face a couple of miles away, which meant that whatever that line was, it must be something of an impressive scale. Everything in her training said it was time to take Colonel Lethbridge-Stewart back to base and prepare a proper investigation. She knew that, but she didn't feel it.

She felt that it was important. She could almost see it in her head: the capsules, the line of light, Colonel Lethbridge-Stewart...

'Form up,' the major said, looking in the same direction. 'Tonight seems to be a night for answers; let's not miss any.'

They gathered their gear, and descended on foot to cross the valley. Kyle didn't like the idea of letting their sometime-prisoner keep a weapon, but she wasn't going to disobey the major. Not unless he did something stupid enough to threaten her or her troops, anyway. She was perfectly capable of keeping an eye on Colonel Lethbridge-Stewart herself.

The weather was beginning to turn as they walked, too. The air became cloying and heavy, as if there was going to be thunder. There was a strange sound, a buzzing, like the

201

sound of an electrical generator, except that the sound was coming from the sky. Above, clouds were gathering, dark and with a strange greenish tint to them. They were coalescing above the line of light, as if somehow drawn to it.

'What the hell is going on?' Kyle breathed.

'I'm sure I have no idea,' Major Lethbridge-Stewart said, 'but I don't like it in the slightest.'

The line resolved itself into a wide metal rail, which curved upwards at the end farthest from the cliff. Colonel Lethbridge-Stewart looked along the rail, watching the glow of St Elmo's fire spread along the polished metal. 'In this instance I most certainly agree with you. It looks too much like a Doodlebug launch rail for comfort.'

'A what?' the major asked. Kyle filed the word away for future reference, sure there was some significance to the malapropisms of the colonel's. 'Never mind, you can explain later, Old Man. But I don't like us being so close to a giant lightning rod, with these clouds.'

'I wonder if that's what it's for...'

'A lightning rod?'

'Well, something to do with attracting electricity. It's certainly working well on the cloud.' There was a distant whine of hydraulic power from somewhere far along the rail, and a set of floodlights snapped on, their bright white glare drowning out the blue coruscation that had already been building. A strange alarm began sounding, and the major and colonel exchanged glances.

'They've spotted us,' Major Lethbridge-Stewart said.

'No,' Kyle answered. 'It came on with the lights and some sort of mechanism. It's an alarm; a clear the range kind of thing. I'm certain of it.'

'I agree,' Colonel Lethbridge-Stewart said quietly. 'We aren't about to stumble across one of your facilities?'

'Not that I know of.'

The colonel turned to Kyle. 'Speaking of what the Intelligence Corps does... Captain?'

She shook her head. This was as baffling to her as to anyone else in the group. 'There's no military or contractor facility here that I know of. Though obviously I'd say that even if I did know, if I was ordered to.'

'Thank you for that convincing pearl of wisdom, Captain,' Colonel Lethbridge-Stewart said acidly.

The major glared at him, and said, 'Captain, take your unit and establish a perimeter two hundred yards to either side of the rail.'

'Yes, sir.' She slipped away into the undergrowth,

Lethbridge-Stewart approached the strange rail. Energy crackled over its surface. He reached out a hand to touch it, but then thought better of it; it felt just a little too much like the third rail in the Underground, and this one didn't look switched off.

'Listen,' James said, and Lethbridge-Stewart did, concentrating hard. There was a barely audible vibration emanating from the metal. 'Something's coming—'

'A Doodlebug—'

A dully gleaming object hurtled along the rail towards them, speeding at the limit of what the human eye could see.

'I don't believe it,' James said.

It was a capsule identical to the one from Deepdene, and

suddenly it swung upwards, guided by the rail. Sparks coruscated around it, and lightning flashed.

A glowing nimbus surrounded it as it flashed past James and Lethbridge-Stewart, and a sudden wall of pressure smashed both of them to the ground. The air was hauled from Lethbridge-Stewart's lungs until he didn't have enough to call out, or to try pulling himself further away from the blazing rail. He looked for James, and saw him a few feet away. Then everything went black for a moment.

The air came back with a vengeance and a chill, the cold of it burning his lungs. Everything was still dark, but as his eyes adjusted he realised that he could still see James, at least. What he couldn't see was the capsule, the floodlights, or the rail.

Kyle winced and looked away as the capsule flashed upwards into the lightning, and just in time, as the next flash was as bright as daylight even through closed eyelids. There was a loud boom, and everything went dark again.

When her eyes adjusted, she saw that the glow around the rail had faded, and the clouds were dissipating. In the distance, that whine of a servo started again, ending with a noticeable clunk before the floodlights switched off.

The capsule, however, had gone and, when she looked through her night-glasses to where the major and colonel had been, she saw that so were they.

# CHAPTER ELEVEN

# *Nowhen*

There was a distant rumble from somewhere far off. His brain was sluggish, so Lethbridge-Stewart wasn't sure whether it was thunder or artillery. He rolled painfully onto his back, and found himself staring up at a hazy cloud cover. Maybe it was smoke rather than cloud, if the sound was artillery.

Under his back, the earth was lumpy. He pushed himself up to a sitting position, then stood, very unsteadily. What the hell had just happened? He remembered a plane crash, and a parachute, and soldiers shooting at him, and then... Of course, the capsule on its rail, shooting into the air in a cloud of lightning. He and James had been a little too close.

James. His comrade in arms, or captor, or... brother. Filled with a sudden certainty that James had died, Lethbridge-Stewart looked around frantically for him

There was a groaning figure about twenty yards away, wearing the same uniform as he. Of course it was James; Lethbridge-Stewart recognised him immediately, surprised by the relief he felt. He ran over and helped James up. James coughed and looked around. 'Thanks, Alistair.' He looked upwards at the clouds, then spun to look behind him. 'What the hell is going on? It sounds like someone has started a shooting war.'

'Not over me, I hope.'

'Not personally, I shouldn't think so. Knight is rather overeager, and probably in vengeful mood, but the scale of this goes far beyond the search for a fugitive. The capsule, on the other hand, well...'

Lethbridge-Stewart wished he could get the cotton wool out of his head. The conversation was going a little fast for him, with all those names to try and put faces to. The military concept he could understand, however. 'One of those capsules coming down could easily be interpreted by an air defence operator as an aircraft breaching restricted airspace, or even an incoming missile.'

'Spot on, Old Man.' James frowned, looking back up at the muddy sky. 'I wonder where it went.'

'I wonder where that launch rail went.' Lethbridge-Stewart pointed all around. 'Look, it's gone.'

James walked a few paces, looking in all directions, then kicked at a couple of clumps of mossy earth. 'No, it's not the rail that's gone – it's us! I wonder where we went.'

Lethbridge-Stewart turned to seek out a memorable fixed point that he recognised from before being flattened. The cliff was still there, but the trees opposite had vanished. A few smaller, weaker trunks were dotted around, and there were ruined walls all across the valley floor. The walls hadn't been there before he was knocked down.

'You're right; someone has moved us, probably a couple of miles. We must have been unconscious longer than I thought. We were definitely both out.'

'It felt as if we were hit by some sort of pressure wave.'

'Like from a blast bomb.' Lethbridge-Stewart agreed. 'Except there was no explosion. Just that... thing being flung into the air.'

'Into the storm, you mean. Perhaps we were hit by lightning? Or at least some kind of electrical discharge.'

'Well, whatever it was, we're probably pretty lucky to be able to stand around and talk about it afterwards.'

It suddenly occurred to Lethbridge-Stewart that they were missing someone. 'Where's Marianne? I mean, Captain Kyle?'

'I don't know. But if someone has moved us, she won't rest until she finds out where we were taken.'

'She does have a tenaciousness to her,' Lethbridge-Stewart admitted.

'An admirable trait. There is one thing though. If we were unconscious, and someone found us… Why not take us either into custody, or into a hospital, or something like that? Why just leave us free out in a different area of open countryside?'

'Perhaps we can ask them if we find some of them.'

There was a long silence, before James asked, 'What now then, Old Man?'

'You know the terrain better than I do. Would we be wiser to make our way back to the helicopter, or head for the end of the launch rail?'

'My preference would be to find who launched that capsule, but with the rail gone we might not be able to find them. My every instinct, therefore, says return to the helicopter and use it to conduct an aerial search.' That was exactly Lethbridge-Stewart's instinct also, and he nodded. 'We landed on that slope,' James said, pointing. 'It can't be more than a couple of miles.'

'Then we'd best get going.'

*

They had only been walking for a few minutes when they came across a battered military green vehicle parked between two tumbledown walls. It wasn't a regular jeep, although similar. It was covered in a thin layer of dust and spotted with rust; clearly it been there for a considerable time.

'That could be useful if it still works,' Lethbridge-Stewart said thoughtfully. He leaned in to examine the dash, and sat in the driver's seat to try and start it up. The engine coughed and spluttered, but fired up after a couple of attempts. 'I'll drive.'

James stood in front of the vehicle. 'No, I'll drive. I'm the elder brother, after all.'

'Except I'm older,' Lethbridge-Stewart said pointedly.

'You're also a better shot, if we run into trouble.'

'That's very kind of you, I suppose.'

James shrugged. 'I have nothing to prove, so there's no shame in assigning a man by his most useful skill.' He pointed to the side, and Lethbridge-Stewart slid across into the passenger seat. He checked the weapons as James turned the vehicle in the direction of where they had left the helicopter.

Marianne Kyle had the platoon form up on her position, and took a head count. Only the Lethbridge-Stewarts were missing, which at least was something. She led her platoon back to their truck; only a few hundred yards from the helicopter that Major Lethbridge-Stewart had landed.

'Sergeant?' A red-headed woman appeared with a salute. 'You're trained to fly one of these things, aren't you?'

'Yes, ma'am.'

'Good. Check whether it has enough fuel for a quick recce to the other side of the valley, and then to return to the Establishment. If there's enough fuel, we'll fly back via the top of that cliff.'

'And the search platoon?' Sergeant Leigh asked.

'Corporal Vincent can take charge. They're to drive directly back and make their report to Lieutenant Knight, if we don't get there first.'

'Right you are, ma'am.' The sergeant ducked into the chopper for only a few brief moments, then nodded to a pleased Kyle, and went to pass on the instructions to Corporal Vincent.

Vincent immediately rounded up the rest of the soldiers, and they boarded the truck. Kyle could hear it drive off as Sergeant Leigh conducted some pre-flight checks. She climbed into the co-pilot's seat and buckled herself in. The engine whined, and the rotors began to noisily cut at the air.

The chopper lifted off and tilted forward, arcing across the valley.

'Be careful, Leigh,' Kyle said. 'If there is something there, they may not appreciate nosey visitors. I wouldn't, if I was them.'

'Understood.'

Kyle looked down through the plexi-glass panel surrounding her feet, and focussed on watching for a glint of metal. The rail must still be down there at least. She guided Sergeant Leigh slightly northwards, and was rewarded with the briefest glimpse of reflected light. Now that she knew what to look for she recognised more of the rail, following it back to a low cliff. There was no sign of floodlights, but she assumed they were hidden, along with a tunnel entrance from which a capsule could emerge.

A short way beyond the top of the cliff edge was a long, low and wide building, which could be either a warehouse or a factory of some kind. Despite her warning to Leigh, there was no sign of hostile activity. Just a few cars in the works' car park, and a couple of people in overalls walking around. There was a set of lettering mounted on the top of one edge of the roof, but she couldn't make the name out at this angle.

'Can you get an angle on that sign?' she asked Leigh.

'I think so.'

The chopper tilted and swung a little nauseatingly. She could see the lettering through the port at her feet: *Hardt Farben*. She'd never heard of it, but that was something that was about to change.

'Let's return to base.'

Henrietta Beswick laid out the sheets with the spectrographic and chemical analysis results of Colonel Lethbridge-Stewart's blood test on her desk. She hadn't been asked to do such comprehensive tests, but one never knew when such information would come in handy. And it wasn't as if there was a law against it, plus it could, potentially, save lives. If she had had such equipment a decade ago, she... She stopped herself, not wanting to go down that road. Not without wine, or something stronger.

Lethbridge-Stewart was certainly in the best of health, with no underlying conditions that she could see, but then something caught her eye. Was such a level of background radiation and carbon normal? The increase wasn't much, a fraction of a percent, but it was there.

She went to a filing cabinet and drew out the major's results for comparison. They were definitely normal, but now she saw even more minor chemical differences. She thought for a moment, and then lifted her desk phone.

'Switchboard, this is Doctor Beswick. Put me through to Doctor Mackay.'

After a moment, Mackay came on the line. 'What can I do for you, lass?'

'Not call me lass, for a start. I wonder if you could take a look at some spectrographic results I have. I just need a fresh pair of eyes on them.'

'Bring them down.'

Doctor John Mackay had also been looking at records, but of a very different kind. He had long since telexed out a request for records from the Republic Archives on various company names that he had noted down from components of the disassembled capsule, and one had struck what he hoped was gold.

When the door to Building Four opened, he expected Doctor Beswick to walk in, but instead it was a slightly dishevelled Marianne Kyle.

'You said that thing was metallurgically local,' she began, before he could issue a welcome. 'Just how local?'

'Within a hundred miles, certainly,' he said, wondering where she was going with this.

'You also said there were some company names on some of the components, but none that still existed.'

'Yes...?'

'Was one of them, by any chance, Hardt Farben?'

He felt a chill at the base of his spine. 'Yes, yes it was. You've heard of it? Don't tell me it still exists? Companies House said they went out of business decades ago.'

'Well, at least one building with their name on it still exists, and last night I saw a capsule just like this one launched from there.'

'You're joking?'

'Do I look like the sort of person who jokes much?'

'What's the joke?' Doctor Beswick asked, coming in to the cavernous room just in time to hear Kyle's comment.

'Whatever it is, it might be on us,' Mackay said.

'You could well be right.' Beswick handed him a sheaf of papers. 'This is a comparison between Major Lethbridge-Stewart's blood, and Colonel Lethbridge-Stewart's blood. The same comparison that indicates they are brothers.'

'And?' Kyle snapped. 'You didn't come in just to repeat that.'

'*And* some of the chemical markers and contaminants in the blood, and in hair samples, are not found in our world.'

Kyle glanced at Mackay, then asked wearily, 'What do you mean in our world?'

'I mean exactly what I say. That's why I came down to ask Doctor Mackay to look at these markers. I wonder if they also show up in the capsules, or Colonel Lethbridge-Stewart's clothing, or the bomber remains? They certainly do in the remains of their crews.'

Mackay took the papers, his expression becoming immediately excited. 'Yes! This is exactly what I was hoping to see!'

Kyle sidled round him, looking past his shoulder at the papers. It was all Greek to her. 'What does it mean?'

'These chemical signatures are not found in the capsules, but there are some variations from our atmospheric norms. They are, however, present in the materials of the bombers.' He paced around, waggling a finger at the pieces of capsule on the floor, and his accent grew slightly stronger as he got more excited. 'These samples, whether from blood or clothing or construction materials, betray an origin in a slightly different atmosphere – a different world – than our own. One that's a little more advanced in polluting the atmosphere. A stage we haven't reached yet.'

'Yet?' The Scotsman nodded in answer to Kyle's question. 'Are you seriously of the opinion that Colonel Lethbridge-Stewart is from the future?'

'That was my original thought, yes. He certainly believes that the year is 1969, but... Too many of the details, the things he mentions, don't match modern history.'

'Well, they wouldn't, if he's made up a fictional decade to come.'

'Yet his version does bear internal consistency. There is a logical explanation for the discrepancies that actually allows him to be telling the truth, though.' Mackay shook his head slightly. 'You'll think it's crazy, but it would explain a lot of things.'

'And what is that? Assuming you're going to tell me he's not simply from the future, or delusional, or a well-trained liar.'

'That he's from a parallel space-time continuum.' Kyle and Beswick looked at him blankly, so he continued. 'An alternate world to ours, sideways in time, rather than forwards or backwards.'

'Alternate...? A sort of mirror universe?' Kyle asked.

'Exactly.' Mackay went across to a forklift truck in the corner, not needed at the moment. He tapped the mirror above the driver's seat. 'A reflection of ours.'

Kyle reached out a hand to the mirror, letting her fingertips brush its surface like a lover's skin. 'Have you ever thought about the reflection in a mirror? Where it comes from, or where it goes?'

'Can't say that I have, really,' Mackay said. 'It's just an optical effect.'

'Of course it is. But I always liked to imagine something else. Like the mirror was a window, and I was looking through it to another me on the other side.'

'Where the grass is greener, Alice?'

'Something like that. But here's a thought. If I'm here, and she's there, what's in between?"

'The glass,' Beswick said, rather obviously Mackay thought.

'Exactly. The reflective surface itself.' Kyle nodded, looking from Beswick to Mackay, and back to the mirror. 'Which leads me to wonder – what are these… alternatives, if you like, being reflected *from*?'

The jeep squeaked to a halt on the slope. The chopper was gone. If Lethbridge-Stewart was any judge, it had never been there – the terrain was much rougher than he remembered from yesterday, and there were no indentations from the chopper's landing gear.

'Something's wrong here,' James muttered uncertainly.

'I think we might have moved more than we thought.'

James nodded, and Lethbridge-Stewart himself began to feel a certain unease. It wasn't just fear or nervousness, but a physical issue, like being under a looming thundercloud.

In fact, he realised, something dark was above them. They couldn't see it through the clouds and smoke, but they could feel its mass oppressing the air, and hear the faint hiss of rain drumming against it. After several long moments, the sky lightened a little, and the dust and smoke among the clouds swirled like stirred paint.

'Something was up there,' Lethbridge-Stewart said.

James nodded. 'That's putting it mildly. And whatever it was didn't have either jets or propellers.'

'We should find a road. Try to make our way back to either the Establishment or the nearest town. At least there we can get our bearings.'

'Good thinking, Alistair. Good thinking.'


'What were you about to tell me before Henrietta came in?' Kyle asked Mackay.

'Aye, the thing about this company, Hardt Farben.' He trotted to his desk, sweeping a pile of papers off it, and handing her a manila folder with a Republic Archives stamp. She opened it curiously. 'Those are *Deutsches Heer* records from the World War,' he said. He flipped a couple of pages for her. 'You'll probably find this part interesting.'

She read the report aloud, translating as she spoke. 'A vehicle, thought to be an observation compartment lifted aloft by hot air balloon, crashed to earth in the vicinity of Hauptmann Koerner's artillery company. The compartment was sent to the Hardt Farben facility near Leipzig for investigation, while two dead men found within were buried locally.' She paused and looked at the beaming Mackay. 'You're saying this was the same type of capsule as we found at Deepdene?'

'Exactly.'

'But this was forty-five years ago. Before the creation of the Republic.'

'Aye, it is. And it gets a little stranger. Look: an artillery unit from Koerner's company vanished on the same date, though they were not engaged in action at the time.'

'Units get lost in combat, and in wartime generally, even when they're not actually in a fight at the time.'

'And yet doesn't it remind you of something? You yourself have lost the major and the colonel in the vicinity of one of these capsules. I don't think that's a coincidence. I also don't think it's a coincidence that two anachronistic aircraft appeared over Deepdene so soon after that capsule fell there.'

'What correlation could there be?'

'A splash. No, hear me out. When you throw a stone into water, it displaces some of that water upwards and outwards – a splash. Most of it falls back where it belongs, but if it's close enough to the shore, some ground gets wet. If it's close enough to you, you get wet.'

'So if someone or something's too close to a capsule when it hits whatever passes for water, they get... displaced?'

'That's what seems to be implied here. It's what I think.'

Kyle nodded, taking it in, and finding herself believing it. 'Is there a way to work out where the colonel and the major have been displaced to? If that's what happened.'

'Perhaps. It's not as simple or straightforward as a where, or even when, though. One capsule arrived here in 1914, and displaced a group of soldiers somewhere. The bombers came from 1939, but were engaged in a war that never happened – and they're built to a design that never existed. That tells me they didn't come from quite this Earth.'

'And not another planet, but another Earth?' Kyle merely raised an eyebrow. 'Those bombers were certainly never built for travel in outer space.'

'No, of course not. I think they were displaced from a parallel space-time continuum, from a world where another war started in 1939. That means a capsule must have landed there, and displaced the bombers. The artillery crew, I think, went the other way; they were displaced to a parallel continuum – whether the same one or another – by the arrival of the capsule.'

'And now the Lethbridge-Stewarts have been displaced in the same way, but to somewhere else?' Kyle nodded to herself. 'They may be gone for good, but at least we've now got some intelligence on where these capsules come from, and what they are, albeit not their definite purpose. And now we have an idea of where to look for confirmation of that. Someone page Lieutenant Knight for me.'

One of the artificers moved to an intercom phone and put out the call. Kyle could hear a buzzy and echoing version of the call outside the building.

Knight appeared five minutes later. His features were a lot more grim and drawn than Kyle remembered from the previous day.

'Where's Subject Zero?' he demanded.

Kyle didn't like what she heard in his tone. It wasn't the anger that she was concerned about, but the bitterness. She had been caught up on what had happened during Colonel Lethbridge-Stewart's escape.

'In the custody of the major,' she said sharply. 'As for

217

their geographical location, we were just discussing that.'

She had Mackay quickly fill him in on the details.

'Well, Captain,' Knight began once Mackay had finished. 'The colonel was always your project. If he's really – what did Mackay call it? Displaced? – then all the work that has been done is based upon a false premise, and—'

'And yet has also been valuable experience for our staff in deprogramming deep cover operatives.'

'Always looking at the silver lining?' Knight asked.

Kyle sighed, and nodded. 'At least it is a bright side.'

Knight hesitated. 'That he's not a foreign agent surely is a silver lining too? Less need to be worried about his true motivations.' He snorted. 'He still killed several of our men.'

'That's what soldiers do, Lieutenant. They kill and they die, sometimes. Not all of them, but it's an accepted risk of being in the business. And if you think I like what happened any more than you do, then...' Kyle gritted her teeth. 'There'll be an inquiry, that's what they're for. But first, we have things to do.'

Knight glowered, but straightened to attention. 'Before our reports are made. *Both* of our reports. Yes, ma'am.'

'Our first order of business is to investigate the Hardt Farben facility to the south. Activity related to these capsules takes place there, as we confirmed on a recon last night. It's possible that the major and the colonel are there, if they're still in our world at all.'

'I thought Doctor Mackay said the company no longer exists?'

'He did. But their building does. Which means either that someone has taken it over – in which case we need to know who and why – or else the report of the company's

218

demise is deliberate disinformation for covert purposes. So, we still need to know.'

'I see.'

'To that end, we'll take a platoon each, and secure the Hardt building—' She broke off as he looked around.

'No,' Knight said.

'What?'

'I'm not going to let you do that, Captain.' He drew his pistol.

Kyle couldn't believe her eyes. Was he so angry at Colonel Lethbridge-Stewart that he was going to go completely off the rails? This was why she didn't trust others to have authority. 'Let me? Have you heard of a little thing called the chain of command, Lieutenant?'

'I have a better grasp of it than Major Lethbridge-Stewart. The War Office determines what the armed forces need to do, and the director *is* a superior with a right to give orders. And I have orders from the Director of External Security that that building, among others—' Kyle's ears pricked up, wondering which others. '—are not to be subject to such visits.'

Kyle took a step back. 'And don't you wonder why the director has given this particular order? Why he doesn't want Hardt Farben investigated, or raided?'

Knight sneered. 'No. It's ours not to reason why.'

Kyle shook her head in mock sadness. 'Stationed in Germany and you haven't learned the most important lesson that the old Prussian General Staff ever taught: the best officer is the one who knows when to disobey orders. Or at least when to reason them, as Kipling might have put it.'

'And do you know why?'

She gave him her sweetest smile. 'Not a clue,' she said, 'but I intend to find out.'

'I'm afraid you won't have the chance—'

A shot cut him off, and two more silenced his thrashing and yelping. Kyle slid the safety on her pistol back to its 'safe' position and looked sidelong at the men on either side.

'If you're going to kill somebody, talking isn't shooting.' She looked around at the scientists and artificers – plus a few soldiers on guard duty – in the room. 'Does anyone else here take orders from the Director of External Security instead of their superior officers?'

# — CHAPTER TWELVE —

# *Grass No Greener*

The light that stabbed down onto James and Lethbridge-Stewart's vehicle did so completely without warning, from a totally silent sky. The engine of the jeep stalled, and both men instinctively threw themselves aside from it, each rolling into a ditch on opposite sides of the pitted narrow road.

Lethbridge-Stewart cocked his submachine gun, while James, opposite, drew his pistol, and aimed upwards. The light remained on the jeep as it coasted to a halt at the roadside, but no gunfire, or any hostile activity, followed. Instead, the light switched off, and a boat of sorts descended from the clouds. It was the size, Lethbridge-Stewart judged, of a Second World War motor torpedo boat, but with over-scale helicopter type landing skids. The whole thing was suspended from a large cigar-shaped balloon, perhaps a little larger than the famous Goodyear Balloon that Lethbridge-Stewart was used to seeing on TV.

The boat part settled on the road ahead, and several figures scrambled out, pointing rifles and SMGs in all directions. Lethbridge-Stewart took aim at the nearest, just in case, but he could see that they were simply covering the area in general, and not aiming specifically at James or himself. He held his fire, and hoped James would do the same.

One of the figures on the boat shouted, 'Over here, quick!' Lethbridge-Stewart looked for any sign of who the man was calling to. 'You two idiots from the jeep! Come on, they'll have tracked the engine by now!'

James and Lethbridge-Stewart exchanged uncertain glances, then rose to their feet. They were outgunned either way, so it was as well to co-operate, especially if these people weren't hostile. Nevertheless, Lethbridge-Stewart kept his SMG ready; not aimed at the figures, but at the ready.

'Hurry!' They picked up their pace, and a couple of the occupants of the boat held out hands to help them aboard. Nobody made any move to take their weapons from them, which was a surprise.

As soon as they were aboard the airship's gondola, the one who had called to them waved to a woman at the helm. 'Take off, now.'

He turned back to James and Lethbridge-Stewart. He was a fit but tired looking man, with sleepy hooded eyes, and blonde stubble. Like everyone aboard, he wore a grey uniform that looked to Lethbridge-Stewart like something out of an old Sherlock Holmes film.

'British officers?' the man asked rhetorically. 'Excellent. We can always use more experienced military hands.' Before either of them could ask any questions, there was a flash and a loud crack from below. Looking down through a viewport, they could see orange flames dotted around where the jeep had been.

'I told you,' their rescuer said. He turned to the helmswoman. 'Set course for the *Phoenix*, Irene.'

\*

Anne Travers was beginning to think that half of NASA, the British Rocket Group, and heavens alone knew what other scientific institutions, were packed into the hangar she and her father had been put in charge of in darkest Wiltshire. Although, she noted, she didn't recognise anybody from the Vault. She guessed, on some level, she represented them, and wasn't too sure how she felt about that.

The place looked like the props storehouse for a huge Technicolor sci-fi epic. Humming computers were everywhere, along with electron microscopes, spectral analysers, gas chromatographs, monitor screens linked to Jodrell Bank and Downphilly, and some bits and pieces that even she didn't recognise or understand. Thick cables snaked all over the floor, and she was in a permanent state of nerves that induction between some of them would cause either interference with the equipment, or a fire.

Her father was prowling through it all with glee, like a child in *Hamleys*, and she suspected that, if he wasn't careful, he would end up devoting more time to enjoying experimenting with these toys than actually solving the problem at hand: how to backtrack the capsules to their source, and, perhaps, even return the favour.

She sidled up to him, and asked, 'How goes the search?'

'Search? Oh, yes, see what you mean there. I don't know,' he sighed. 'Without knowing how they were powered, all we can do is establish that they were from a parallel space-time continuum, and we already know that.' He slumped, losing the air of an excited child, and Anne suddenly felt terribly guilty for having brought his mood down. 'If I'm honest, I doubt we'll be able to really do anything, besides try to collect these things when they arrive.

And they've been coming for a long time.'

'Perhaps,' a Russian voice said, 'I can be of some assistance.' It was a rather stocky man, with a short dark beard that was peppered with grey. He offered a hand and a smile. 'Obviously the, er, agency for which I work cannot make any official contribution, but... Well, let us say we have a mutual friend, and so I have taken some vacation time, yes?'

'Mutual friend?' Travers asked.

'Colonel Lethbridge-Stewart. We met some years ago. To be perfectly frank with you, Professor, I'm somewhat surprised he isn't here.'

'The colonel is... missing,' Travers said sadly. 'A plane crash.'

'Oh. That is... most unfortunate.' The Russian frowned. He hesitated. 'Nevertheless, my offer of help with this problem still stands.'

'Thank you, Doctor...?'

'Kashchei Stravinksy. No relation, I'm afraid.' He looked downwards momentarily at the floor, and stepped to one side. 'Perhaps a study of the charge of the particles making up the structure of the capsule pieces will be a good place to start?'

The airship had been travelling for at least a full day when the man in charge announced that they were about to dock with the *Phoenix*. He had said his name was Jürgen, and claimed to be a lieutenant in the *Preisses Heer*, the Prussian Army.

Lethbridge-Stewart joined James at the gondola's window, expecting to see an aircraft carrier on the ocean waves. Instead, to his amazement, he saw a circular complex like a giant tyre, three or four storeys high, covered in portholes, supported by a veritable fleet of enormous Zeppelin-style gas envelopes.

'Bloody hell,' James muttered, 'maybe Beswick has been dosing me with something.' He recovered himself momentarily. 'If ever I had cause to doubt either my sanity or my senses...'

'You may find it runs in the family,' Lethbridge-Stewart said drily.

Lethbridge-Stewart wondered how the airship would actually dock with the larger floating citadel, as there didn't seem room for both gondola and envelope in any of the openings he could see. His curiosity was satisfied when the airship rose slightly, above the upper surface of the circular citadel, and lowered itself into a sunken berth. This way, the gas envelope probably added to the support for the construction as a whole, he supposed.

Jürgen opened a ramp that descended between the gondola's landing skids, and invited James and Lethbridge-Stewart to descend. This they did, into a curved anteroom of steel grid floors, and girders with holes cut from them to lighten them. The walls were metal, and seemed to Lethbridge-Stewart to be aluminium, and therefore light. He supposed they'd have to be, if this contraption was to stay afloat in the clouds.

Several people were there to meet them. Most were in the same grey uniforms as Jürgen, and seemed to be waiting to take their shift aboard the smaller craft. There were civilians also; a woman carrying a toolbox, and men in workers' overalls, fiddling with tubes and pipes on the walls.

There was also a man with thick black hair in a neat parting, and firm black moustache, but with lines of pain etched prematurely into his face, and in his eyes. 'Good evening, sirs,' he said, in a mellifluous Eastern European accent. 'Are you both all right, after being caught out on the surface like that?'

James nodded. 'As well as can be expected under the circumstances, I suppose.'

'Good. I was concerned that you'd been harmed.'

'That makes a pleasant change.' Lethbridge-Stewart eyed the man's hairstyle and moustache. 'Are you going to tell me you're a Lethbridge-Stewart too?'

'A what? No, I'm a scientist, and seeker of truth.'

'I meant your name.'

'Oh, I see. My apologies; of course I should have introduced myself.' He held out a hand. 'Nikola Tesla.'

Lethbridge-Stewart glanced at James, and was gratified to see that he looked as doubtful as Lethbridge-Stewart felt. 'Of course you are,' he said, deadpan. He was accompanied by his dead brother after all, why not a man who had died over twenty years earlier, too?

The man who thought himself Tesla continued, 'And there is only one person called Lethbridge-Stewart aboard.'

Kyle looked at her hands. They weren't shaking too much; not yet, anyway. Control was slipping away from her, and that would never do. She had summoned an RAF lieutenant to the Officer's Mess, so that she could give orders while convincing herself that she was simply dealing with a blood sugar problem. Sergeant Leigh was there too, awaiting her next orders. Leigh had kept a clear head, Kyle felt, during

226

the past twenty-four hours, and Kyle liked that. Leigh seemed reliable.

Kyle addressed Lieutenant Nolan first. 'Get me all the aerial photos we have of the Hardt Farben facility south of Leipzig. I want all intel on the company, especially on any military contracts it has had with either our government, or anyone else's.'

'What do we do when we get there?' Leigh asked.

'That depends upon how co-operative they are in answering our questions.' Kyle could guess, though; whoever occupied the building would not be in the slightest bit co-operative.

'Why wouldn't they be?'

'Lots of reasons. They could be a front for a foreign power, they could be a front for internal dissidents, they could be just idiots... Do you have a counterargument as to why they might?' She was genuinely curious, and it made an interesting test of Leigh's thinking. After all, Knight's demise had left a vacancy for a new lieutenant.

'They might not be doing anything wrong. They might be working on a government project from another department.'

'Optimism? How quaint.'

'It's not against regulations, last time I checked, ma'am.'

'You're right, Sergeant. It's not. Now let's hope you're right to be optimistic, because we move out in one hour.'

Tesla led Lethbridge-Stewart and James through the central thoroughfare of the *Phoenix*. There were plenty of people around, both in uniform and civvies, and Lethbridge-Stewart couldn't believe the scale of the thing.

Neither man had mentioned the capsules on their walk, but both were curious as to which Lethbridge-Stewart Tesla had meant when he spoke of there being a member of their family on board. After all, the Lethbridge-Stewarts had a distinguished and well-storied military history going back hundreds of years, and it wasn't like he knew *all* their names.

They emerged from the wide thoroughfare corridor onto a gantry overlooking what must have been the inner surface of the hull. A number of tunnel-like circular openings were cut into the walls, and a group of workers were manoeuvring an object into position before the nearest.

Lethbridge-Stewart's eyes widened and, when he glanced at James, he saw that his expression was just as shocked and surprised.

'That capsule,' James breathed. 'It's identical—'

'To the one Captain Kyle and I recovered from Deepdene. Do you think Kyle knows about this?'

'If she did, I would,' James said. 'Something else entirely is going on here.'

Tesla turned, his expression curious and astounded. 'Gentlemen, I don't mean to eavesdrop, but are you implying that you have seen one of these vehicles before?'

'More than one,' James said. Tesla opened and closed his mouth, looks of joy and worry chasing each other across his features. 'In fact, we came here in one.'

Tesla paled. 'But how—? No, the how is less important than the where, and the when.'

'Leipzig, 1959,' James said.

'Apparently,' Lethbridge-Stewart added.

'That's impossible!' Tesla exclaimed. 'It cannot be! The system was never designed for travel into the future.'

Captain Kyle crouched with Sergeant Leigh and several other NCOs behind a hedge a couple of hundred yards from the target building. They were all wearing dark battle fatigues, with deep brown and green makeup on their hands and faces. The building loomed against the night, with only a few yellow interior lights visible. The sign reading Hardt Farben was clearly meant to be illuminated, but remained darkened through visibly broken bulbs. That suggested to Kyle that someone had simply taken over the building as a cover, and that the company wasn't an ongoing concern.

'Our primary objective is to secure the main factory complex. If they have been reverse engineering the capsules like the Deepdene one, then we want their equipment and records intact.'

'What's their security like?' one of the NCOs asked.

'Earlier recce suggested only a handful of actual guards, but make your approaches carefully. Use bayonets to check for mines and tripwires, and be aware there may be pressure sensors and electric eyes. Also, be wary of potential snipers. All that said, the evidence so far suggests that deception and camouflage is the backbone of their security.'

'You mean they're more reliant on just not being noticed?

'Exactly. And heavy security would attract attention to what's supposed to be an out of business factory. But let's take no chances. I want success first, not glory.'

Over the next few minutes, Kyle's forces approached the building slowly, from a variety of angles. There were no shots from hidden snipers, and no mines went off. If there were electric eye alarms, nobody was willing to give away the building's true occupied status by responding to them outside.

The first guards they encountered were patrolling a perimeter corridor just inside the door to the building. A gas grenade took care of them silently, but Kyle discovered that there was no apparent access to the interior of the building. There was, in fact, no factory floor, though it took the soldiers half an hour to work that out. Whoever was using the building had constructed a literal maze of breeze-block corridors to hide guards and alarm beams.

Fortunately the soldiers were moving in slowly, taking their time, and gassing the armed guards – men in anonymous black coveralls with no labels – into unconsciousness as they went. They used dental mirrors to detect and deactivate several electric eye beams along the way. Yet still they found no factory, and no capsules.

'They have to be below us,' Kyle said to her troops, after the last guard had been put out of action. 'Perhaps in the cliff. Form search parties, and find a lift or stairs. There must be some.'

The process took another half hour, with Leigh eventually stumbling across a cage in an outbuilding attached to the main factory, which turned out to be the cage of a service lift.

'Clever,' Kyle said to Leigh. 'The interior of the main building was simply a diversion.'

'Like everything else with... whoever they are,' Leigh agreed.

Kyle posted her own guards at strategic points within the ground floor maze, and outside the building, and then led the rest of the troop into a cavernous expanse below.

The space under the factory was huge, stretching for hundreds of yards, and portioned off into workshops, control rooms, a cafeteria, and so forth. Armed guards patrolled throughout, while white-coated scientists busied themselves at the controls of huge electrical generators, with ceramic insulators the size of helicopter tail rotors.

As they watched, two scientists in shiny protective coveralls escorted an elegant, tall and slightly androgynous looking man to the capsule. The man wore a flight suit covered in hoses, tubes, and other paraphernalia.

'That's Ebbing,' Kyle said quietly to Leigh. 'Our most renowned test pilot. But this can't be a test aircraft, not without engines.'

'FP1 transition trigger in ten minutes,' a tannoy voice announced. 'Repeat: ten minutes. Medical teams to emergency stations. Degaussing technicians report to standby positions.'

In front of the capsule's nose was a sloping steel rail that gleamed like a sword's edge in the evening sunlight. At regular intervals along the rail, circles of metal and ceramic electrical gubbins looped around. Kyle wondered if they were going to be set alight for the capsule to shoot through.

At first Kyle thought her eyes were blurring, but everything else she looked at was in perfect focus – it was the capsule itself that was somehow quivering and fading. Suddenly it sprang forward, more smoothly than any vehicle acceleration she had ever seen, and sped through all the loops of electrical equipment.

Just at the instant when she thought the capsule would sail into the air, it just somehow wasn't *there* anymore. She tried to tell herself that it had accelerated beyond the speed at which the eye could see, and been shot off the end of the ramp, but somehow she knew it hadn't. It had disappeared before it reached the end – probably vaporised by all that lightning.

'Transition plus three seconds,' the tannoy announced. 'Ballistic trajectory stable. Calendar trajectory within projected limits.'

'Displacement projected. Repeat: Displacement projected.'

'Begin emergency degaussing!'

And that was when one of the guards looked up and saw Leigh on the maintenance gantry.

'Intruders!'

He raised his rifle, but Leigh fired first. The guard fell sprawling, and an alarm began to blare.

'Focus your fire,' Kyle shouted, as all hell broke loose. 'We want the scientists and equipment undamaged!'

Gunfire erupted throughout the cavern, and Kyle hoped she could practice what she preached.

'I'm not certain I should be introducing you, gentlemen,' Tesla said. 'And yet... I feel something is happening of great importance.' He beckoned to one of the people working to move the capsule. 'Alastair!'

Lethbridge-Stewart steeled himself, but it didn't prepare him for the face of the boy who came over. He was only about fifteen years of age, and had shaggy shoulder-length hair and no moustache. Lethbridge-Stewart remembered seeing that face in the mirror every day; harder perhaps, distant even, but it was definitely him as a teenager. Lethbridge-Stewart shivered, couldn't speak, but he didn't really have to, as the boy's jaw dropped. Alastair could clearly see the resemblance too.

The boy dragged his eyes from Lethbridge-Stewart and looked at James, who was looking from Alistair to Alastair with an expression of pure emotional overload. It could have been joy or sorrow, probably both; the expression of a man experiencing too much.

'James?' Alastair asked. And burst into tears.

Lethbridge-Stewart needed to sit down. No, he needed to lie down. It was all too much. Bad enough to be confronted with the brother he didn't remember, a brother who had died so long ago, but to be confronted with this... reflection of himself. His heart was palpitating, his eyes stinging; he couldn't breathe properly. He started to take a step forward, but never completed it.

The battle had lasted only a few minutes, and thankfully Kyle's troops were good shots. A few pieces of equipment had taken hits, and one or two of the scientists had decided to join in by shooting at the intruders, resulting in them having to be pacified by force, but for the most part, she felt she had attained her objective: captured equipment and records, dead guards, live scientists.

While her troops cleaned away the bodies, and put the scientists under guard, Kyle walked over to examine the rail. It was the same one as she had seen previously, but this time she was able to make out more detail. She also mulled over some of the phrases she had heard during the process; in particular, the one about incoming displacement. It was probably too much to hope that might mean the return of the major and the colonel.

She was surprised to see one of the scientists approach her. It was a man with glasses and a thick black beard. 'You, Captain, is it? You're not by any chance Captain Kyle?'

'I am, yes.'

'Colonel and Major Lethbridge-Stewart said if I... well, if I lived, I should contact you.'

Kyle felt as if her head was spinning, worse than the vertigo attacks she occasionally had as a child. 'You've met them? Where are they?'

'Aboard the *Phoenix*.'

'The what?' Things were running away from her again, too fast. She hated it, and tried not to let it show in her voice, or take it out on this man who clearly had something important to say.

'Oh, you don't have one, of course. I wasn't sure they really understood that, despite my best efforts, but that's the military mind for you. No offence.'

'I'm confused, not offended.'

'Of course, of course. Well, to cut a long story short, the colonel and the major are in my world – a space-time continuum parallel to this one. I imagine they got there through interaction with the Phoenix Project, and the capsules.'

The face was familiar, but she had to think about it for several seconds before realising where she had seen those breaded features before. 'You... You were in the capsule at Deepdene.'

'I suppose I was, yes. Not the most comfortable way to travel.'

'But you were dead. I saw your body fall from the capsule. Hell, I even ordered your autopsy, and signed off

234

on the report that was written...' Kyle stopped and shook her head. 'How, exactly, did you get here?

Travers shrugged. 'I wish I knew. I entered the capsule, of course, and then... Well, it wasn't a very comfortable arrival. No, not in the slightest. Anyway, then I know I was in a truck, and I vaguely remember something like a hospital ward. And then I woke up in a bunk here. Most confusing, I have to say.'

'You were in a hospital room?' Kyle began to suspect where this story was leading.

'I remember that kind of environment.'

Kyle beckoned Leigh over. She was nursing a bloodied hand. 'Sergeant. Contact base and have Doctor Beswick bring a medical team over.'

'Yes, ma'am.'

'And, Sergeant? Make sure she comes in person.'

'There's some work for you and your staff, Henrietta,' Kyle said an hour later, when Doctor Beswick led half a dozen medical orderlies into the cavern. Beswick wrinkled her nose at the scene of blood and cordite, and directed her orderlies to the few wounded scientists, and a couple of Kyle's soldiers. They started work efficiently and without any awkward questions, Kyle was glad to see. She was also glad to see they were unarmed. She led Beswick into a small control room that was partitioned off from the main cavern. 'I want to ask you something, and I will not respond well to evasion or disinformation.'

'What do you mean not respond well?' By way of an answer, Kyle drew her pistol, slipped off the safety catch, and laid it on the table with a solid clunk. She kept her hand resting on it. Doctor Beswick looked at it, shocked, her eyes wide. 'Captain Kyle…'

'Look over there.' Kyle jerked her head to the side, towards Travers. 'Do you recognise him?' Doctor Beswick didn't heed to say anything; Kyle could tell by her pallor that Beswick recognised him. 'I'll take that as a yes. Now, Doctor Beswick…' She smiled as pleasantly as she could, which was very pleasant. 'Henrietta. You conducted an autopsy on him, which Colonel Lethbridge-Stewart and I signed off on. So why is he standing there instead of having been buried?'

'He wasn't dead.'

'That much is obvious. Why is he still walking and talking?'

Beswick looked behind her, as if afraid of being overhead. 'He was deeply comatose, but the orderlies who escorted his body back from Deepdene to the Establishment noticed en route that he was actually still breathing – though so little that it barely justified the word.'

'And they didn't report it?'

'Of course they reported it! It was a medical matter, so they reported it to me.'

Kyle's fingertips tapped lightly on the pistol. 'And why didn't you report his survival to Colonel Lethbridge-Stewart, the major, or myself?'

'Because I was ordered not to.'

'Ordered? By whom—?' She shook her head. 'Never mind. The Director of External Security?'

'He was quite insistent.' Beswick looked at the pistol again.

'He's not in the military chain of command, as Major

236

Lethbridge-Stewart reminded us.'

'Well, this was before the major made that point, and, as I said, he was very insistent. Very.'

'Define insistent.'

'There were threats made.' Beswick looked away. 'I already failed to save one of my sisters. I can't lose the other.'

'All right.' Kyle reset the safety catch and holstered her pistol. She rose, and paced around the room. 'Well, you did what you thought was your duty, which we may all regret at some point, and now you're making your report to me.'

'Off the record?'

'That remains to be seen. How did Travers manage to leave the infirmary, and the base?'

'External Security collected him. I didn't know where they might have taken him. I've never even heard of this place.'

Given how secret and below-the-radar the facility was, Kyle was pretty sure that, at least, was true. 'Was he awake or still comatose?'

'Still comatose at the time, but one of the people who collected him was a doctor, so I imagine that there was or is some plan to revive him.'

'They'd be wasting their time otherwise. Who replaced him in the morgue?'

'A civilian, victim of a road traffic accident. He was put in place just in case Colonel Lethbridge-Stewart should want to attend the funeral, and lest any other potential contacts try to access the body to check his pockets and personal effects...' Beswick tailed off, and spread her hands. 'I wondered why he was taken.'

'If we take the connection to the capsule as being the

major factor involved, then you can probably guess. If you'd been studying the capsules for forty years, and suddenly along came a man who'd travelled in one as intended, from the source, wouldn't you want to talk to him?'

'Too bloody right I would. But, wait... You do realise what you're implying, don't you? A covert link between Hardt Farben and External Security – or at least the director thereof.'

Kyle nodded. 'I know exactly what I'm implying.' The question she asked herself now was simple: Was that connection good or bad, both for her and the country?

'Then why are you going on with this? Why not just accept that External Security knows what it's doing – that the director knows what he's doing – and let it alone?'

'For two reasons. Firstly, because their actions have clearly reduced security and increased threats to the British Republic, and I don't believe they're stupid enough to have achieved that through incompetence. Secondly, because I really do not like being hobbled by the treasonous actions of those who ought to be on our side.'

'Treasonous?

'What else do you call acting against the Republic's security, and causing threats to it?'

'And do two treasons make an act of loyalty?'

'Only in retrospect, I should think, but yes.'

Kyle left the control room, and walked across to another partition which was fronted with a far wider door. With the help of Travers, she hauled the doors open, revealing two more capsules. She wished she could have been surprised to see them.

'Get Mackay here,' she told Beswick.

# CHAPTER THIRTEEN

# *Everland*

The *Phoenix*'s sickbay was a mix of hospital and circus tent, with thick canvas bulging out slightly from the steel ribs and aluminium walls that it hid. James, a pensive Tesla, and the boy who was obviously Alastair, had all followed the orderlies who had rushed to carry the older Alistair – Colonel Lethbridge-Stewart – down here.

James balled his fists to keep his hands from shaking. Finding an alternative version of his kid brother who had survived past eight years old was disturbing and unbelievable enough, but two of them? Neither the brain nor the heart were built for something like that. And to lose one of them again? That would be worse. That would be to be cheated in the worst possible way.

He watched the medics checking over the recumbent Lethbridge-Stewart on a sickbay cot, and felt utterly sick at the thought that this must be how he had been feeling for most of his time under Beswick's care. Confused, never sure what to believe, unable to trust his own mind or his own senses... James found himself hoping that he was actually lying comatose in Beswick's infirmary himself. Unfortunately he knew better.

'What's wrong with him?' he asked the doctor at last. Perhaps there was some side effect to flipping between worlds? Maybe the air was too different, or the magnetic field of the planet, or something.

'Exhaustion, mainly. His system's been shot to hell by some weird chemical cocktails as well. Aside from knocking his body and brain chemistry all over the place, and buggering up his memory, I wouldn't be at all surprised if he was getting to a stage of being addicted to the psychoactives that have soaked into him.'

'Do what you can,' Tesla said briskly. 'Both he and his brother here could prove very useful as we approach the end point of Project Phoenix.' With that, he stepped back a little, giving the brothers some privacy.

'Is he me?' the boy asked. 'I mean, me from the future?'

'You from *a* future,' James said absently.

'You look older,' the boy Alastair said. 'Where have you been? After you left for the battle at Helsinki, nobody would tell me anything. I thought...' He fought back tears, gulping them down. 'Bloody foreigners. Hiding with their planes and their saboteurs so the army never quite knows where to go.' James didn't know exactly what to say, but he felt the tingle of what people called someone walking over their grave. He'd never felt it so literally before, but he knew – just knew for an absolute certainty – that this other, younger, James had fallen at the battle he had gone to. 'Since mum and dad died in one of the bombing raids... I thought I was alone,' Alastair concluded, obviously not sure of how he should be feeling, but being equally overawed by everything as James was.

'No,' James said at last. 'You came aboard here with me, didn't you?' It was a guess, but a reasonable one to make. Alastair nodded. 'Well... I've been posted to a few different places. Doing secret work, some of the time. But I managed to get back for a visit, so you wouldn't worry.'

'How come there's a me from the future? I thought that the project didn't work that way.'

'Honestly, that's something I can't really answer,' James said carefully. 'But both of us are hoping to discuss it with Mr Tesla here. He's the real expert, I believe.'

'Does this mean they're coming soon?'

'Who are coming?'

'The enemy.'

'And who are they? Who are you fighting?'

'Foreigners. I reckon it's the Russians, but some say it's the Chinese.'

'How can you not know?'

'Cos they're good at keeping secrets.' Alastair said this as if it was the most obvious thing in the world.

'Maybe I'll ask Mr Tesla about that as well.'

At the sound of his name, Tesla had come forward again, with a thin, but genuine smile. 'Yes, Major, I should most definitely like to have a chat over tea with you about that. And with your older-younger brother.'

'What is the meaning of this, lass?' Mackay looked positively twitchy as he wandered around the cavern. Like the proverbial flea on a griddle, Kyle thought.

'It's Captain, not lass, and I'd have thought my meaning was clear and plain. Your presence is required to analyse scientific records and equipment now that the Hardt Farben complex is secured.'

'Really?' Now he was interested. 'Well, if you put it that way, Captain.'

'I do. And I should like your analysis to include at least one working capsule and launch system.'

Mackay froze. 'One what?'

'The capsule from 1914, and/or others that have fallen since. I saw one launched the night before last, and another this morning. And as you see, there are still two left.'

'Aye... I see. I wish we knew how many capsules there were altogether. And how long they'll be used.' Mackay went to the nearest capsule, and opened the hatch, shining a torch inside. He scraped at the glass on some dials with his fingernail, and then squinted at something on the door itself. Then he repeated the inspection on the second capsule. 'Wait, this serial number is the same as the one...'

Kyle looked in over his shoulder, and... 'So is this, and this. This is impossible. It must just be copies of the same part, hence the same number.'

Mackay's accent became a sort of low growl, as he thought aloud. 'Oh no, I don't think they are.'

'Well, there's only one other logical inference you can make.'

'Yes.' He stepped back from the capsule, regarding it with an expression that suggested it had pulled a gun on him.

'And it's an impossible one,' Kyle said.

Mackay grimaced. 'Not impossible, just somewhat unthinkable, I should say.'

'That these two capsules are the same capsule? That's insane! It's...'

'Terrifying, Captain? The same capsule, reused. It's been sent through time at least twice.'

\*

'The capsules won't work properly without the converter to harness and guide the necessary power,' Tesla was saying.

Some food and rest had brought Lethbridge-Stewart back to his feet, and now he and James sat in Tesla's private study, looking out at a glowing, shimmering device suspended at the hub of the floating citadel. The younger Alastair had been sent to assist a technician working on preparing one of the capsules.

'It was found during the first months of the war, about... Oh, five years ago? Yes, 1940.'

'Which war?' Lethbridge-Stewart asked.

Tesla grunted. 'The war against... Actually if I am to be precise, I should say simply that we do not know against whom the war is fought. The war against the sky, if you like.'

'How can you fight the sky? Come to think of it, how can it fight you?'

'It fought us with gravity. Much more difficult to fight back against.' Tesla sighed. 'Something was up there, high in space. We don't know who or what they were, only that they clearly had some form of dislike for our planet, ourselves, or both. Several observatories, such as Mount Palomar, detected something back in the spring of '40.'

'Spaceships, you mean?' Lethbridge-Stewart said.

'Yes. At first science was excited – we wanted to know who were they, what did they want, how had they travelled? But they never landed. They stayed high in orbit.'

'Watching?'

'Bombing. With meteorites. That's what I mean by fighting us with gravity. They don't need to manufacture rockets or explosives; they simply tow meteors into

243

position—' Tesla raised a hand with its fingers pinched together, then opened it with a turn of the wrist. '—and let them fall.'

'Here's an odd thing,' James said to the room in general. 'These people are at war, but they don't know who with.'

'Maybe an EMP blast stopped their communications. Those clouds look like something from the aftermath of a nuclear blast,' Lethbridge-Stewart said.

Tesla was silent for a while. 'The surviving governments decided it was best not to inform the public of the truth, because the panic that could arise would hamper resistance efforts.'

'So you told them they were fighting.'

'An unknown foreign power, yes. Humanity has fought enough wars to be, as a species, used to the idea of countries being a war with one another. Tell the public they at war with another country, and they will bear it, they will pull together, they will resort to patriotism if it helps. But tell them they are at war with the great unknown, with something far beyond any human ability or intelligence...'

Lethbridge-Stewart saw what he meant. 'They'll become disheartened.'

'They will give up,' Tesla said gravely. 'They'll accept that their fate is in the hands of the gods, and that the gods are ones who have come to kill them.'

'And this is... What?' James asked. 'A base for resistance?'

'The *Phoenix*?' Tesla laughed. 'Oh, no, gentlemen, it's much more than that. As the name implies, it is intended to restore humanity!'

'With those capsules? They're not armed, so they don't

make much of a secret weapon.'

'Oh, they're not a weapon. At least not exactly, not in the conventional sense.'

'We theorised that the capsules were some kind of aircraft escape vessel,' James said.

'That's basically correct, though not how I'd describe it, of course. But, yes, twenty capsules were built for launch from the *Phoenix*, not to escape from the vessel, but to be launched from the correct altitude as a lifeboat for... for the future of humanity in my world.' Tesla stood, pointing to the openings along the inside surface of the tyre-shaped hull of the *Phoenix*. 'The idea is to accelerate the capsules from those launch bays. We estimate that eight thousand feet is the lower limit of altitude from which the temporal transference can be made, driven by the Converter.'

'Then they're not launched from the ground?'

'Of course not. The capsule would then be fighting against gravity in order to reach the correct altitude. The power requirements would be increased by several orders of magnitude, and the temporal and geographical ranges both limited in turn.'

'You said temporal,' Lethbridge-Stewart said, interrupting. 'Do you mean to say you've invented some kind of time machine?' he asked, feeling a familiar headache forming.

'Once again,' Tesla replied, 'not in the conventional sense. The Converter found five years ago was, we believe, part of the invaders' gravitational drive from one of their spaceships. I studied it, and reverse-engineered it with the intention of using its power to send those capsules back in time with a warning. They will prepare humanity for the

245

attack, so that our planet's and people's survival will be assured.'

James cleared his throat. 'Well, then, it looks as though you should be thanking us for bearing the best of news for your project. It works. At least partly. Your capsules have been landing across Britain and northern Europe for... years.'

Tesla sat back in his chair. 'That's... good to know, if a little confusing.'

'Confusing in what way? You built something to send these objects back in time, and that's exactly what's happened. So, next time—'

'You don't understand, Major. We have never launched any capsules.'

James looked at Lethbridge-Stewart then back to Tesla. 'What?'

'Perhaps it would be more accurate to say we haven't launched any capsules *yet*.'

'But several of them have... Oh, I see. Since they're designed to be shot back in time anyway...?'

'The energy requirements to push the capsules back in time – even using what we can make of the aliens' own power source – are so intensive that it's, shall we say, unlikely that we can reliably generate the required power multiple times for separate launches. Tomorrow morning, twenty capsules will be pushed back through time by the power of the entire planetary atmosphere's electrokinetic storm system transformed through the Converter.'

James held up a hand. 'But it doesn't quite work that way, does it? Your capsules – from our point of view – didn't go back in time.'

'They must do. I am never wrong about such things,'

Tesla assured them. 'The problem which you seem to be describing is that they didn't – won't – all arrive in the same timeline. There must be some kind of an offset in what I like to call the space-time continuum, so that the Phoenix capsules arrive not in our past – this timeline's past – but in one of two other timeless at equal...' Tesla gave a peculiarly Gallic shrug. 'Distance is the wrong word, but the correct one hasn't been coined yet. Suffice it to say they must arrive with an equal offset to either side.'

'Some in my world... and some in Alistair's?'

'Exactly. I know it's hard for either of you to believe, but...'

'There are reasons why it's harder for Alistair to believe,' James said, and once again looked at his older-younger brother. The man was listening, his brows creased in concentration. He stood up and began pacing the room.

'Yes, the psychoactives,' Tesla said. He leaned forward. 'Are the worlds so different? One where he died, one where you died.'

'No, he's not stupid, but...' James watched Lethbridge-Stewart, but the man was no longer paying any attention. 'He's undergone some treatments. He has memory loss, that kind of thing. It's a long story, which you can probably deduce for yourself, if you have any experience with how a government might handle an unexpected army officer.'

Tesla sighed sadly, looking away. 'Yes, I think I can guess how the security-minded or military-minded might act.'

Lethbridge-Stewart looked down at James and glared. He tried to steer the conversation back in a more practical direction. 'Is it possible to work out where and when they

247

go, and plan a more accurate launch?'

'I don't know. We're in completely uncharted territory here,' Tesla admitted. 'You know, on maps they used to write "here be dragons" on the blank spaces, where they didn't know anything, because nobody had explored the area. Or at least nobody had come back alive.'

'And this is a scientific here be dragons.'

'Nobody's asking you to go out with sword and shield and explore a desolate heath,' James added.

'No,' Tesla said. 'But nobody else has made a study of this unanticipated issue, and I'm not sure how to begin.'

Professor Travers, Anne, and Stravinsky regarded the still-intact capsule in their crowded hangar. Stravinsky walked around it, absently tapping the surface. 'Would it be possible to reverse engineer these capsules?' he asked, sounding as if he was simply wondering aloud.

Travers grunted. 'It would, yes, but why would we want to? We have perfectly good lifting bodies as it is.'

Stravinsky chuckled slightly. 'No, you misunderstand me, Professor. I'm thinking of the ability to send them through time. There must be something within the design or structure of the capsules that includes something of how it was powered.'

'There could be something to that,' Anne said thoughtfully. 'If the power that drives it through time is any kind of electromagnetic force, it probably does leave a charge in the metal, which we can measure. You mentioned that before.'

'But if we could, oh, just for the sake of argument, of course, send a capsule back?'

'To where it came from?' Travers exclaimed in disbelief.

'Yes,' Stravinsky said with a curt nod.

'If they come from a parallel continuum, that wouldn't be the best option. And besides, the power requirements would be astronomical to a degree that, well... If only we had more time to plan.'

'Then what if we went small-scale?' Anne suggested.

Travers stroked his beard. 'In what way?'

She waved around, indicating the many technicians and scientists in the room. 'We have artificers who work on scale models for use in wind tunnel tests, and radar refraction tests.'

Stravinsky snapped his fingers. 'An excellent suggestion, Miss Travers. If we used a small scale analogue for a capsule, we could launch it with the appropriate temporal deflection gleaned from analysing the change in subatomic charge.'

'What good would that do?' Travers grumbled.

'It could carry a message,' Anne said eagerly. 'In fact it would send a message as is.'

'That we know we're being targeted?'

'That we can reassure them that their technology works, and that we know how, too.'

Lethbridge-Stewart couldn't really believe he was actually asking such a question of Nikola Tesla, but he gritted his teeth and spoke the words anyway. 'Is it possible to send us back to our original worlds?'

Tesla paced for a moment, watching the coruscations around the Converter. 'Yesterday I'd have said no at once, but... If we had a proper analysis of the deflection away from our timeline, we could compensate by reversing that.'

'How would we get such data?' James asked.

'Clearly someone in your world has reverse engineered the system enough to be able to launch you here. We can probably use data on how your bodies' electrical charge can send you back to your world. The colonel... is a different matter. We could send him to your world by the same means, but not to his own. Unless... Is there also a reverse engineering project on your Earth?'

Lethbridge-Stewart shook his head. 'I'd never even heard of these blasted things until a couple of days ago.'

'Perhaps a secret group?' James suggested.

'Not to my knowledge.'

At that moment, a man ran in. 'Maestro Tesla! Maestro Tesla!'

Lethbridge-Stewart recognised him at once, from the black beard, the glasses, and the voice. 'Travers? Edward Travers?'

'Er, yes...' Travers stepped right over to Tesla. 'There has been... Another arrival.'

'A capsule?' James asked.

'Not exactly. A model of one. Exactly one tenth scale.'

'It must be a test launch from a timeline which has received one of our capsules,' Tesla said.

'It must be from your world,' James pointed out to Lethbridge-Stewart.

'My world? Well, if you say so.'

'We know mine uses full size capsules. That leaves yours as the option.'

That seemed logical enough to Lethbridge-Stewart, though he didn't want to jinx the idea by consciously hoping it was the case.

'Excellent!' Tesla exclaimed. 'There is only one problem. The Phoenix Project was designed to send a warning back into the past. It was never meant to send anything into the future.'

'It wasn't technically designed to send anything into parallel universes either,' James said drily.

'As you say. We know that there was a deviation from the course into the past, and that it can be reversed now that we have a record of the exact vector.'

'If you have a sideways vector,' James said. 'Doesn't that also mean you have a vector backwards in time?'

'Yes.'

'Then isn't it possible to reverse that as well?'

'Not specifically, but a reversal of the complete energy programming for the launch should have the effect of creating a deflection forward as well as to whichever was the source timeline.'

James smiled thinly. 'Is that deduction based upon a solid scientific basis, or are you just making up technological chatter for the practice?'

'A little of both,' Tesla replied with a slight smile. 'A logical inference that I sincerely hope will prove correct. The question is whether it's a risk worth taking.'

'I'm willing to take the risk.'

'As am I,' Lethbridge-Stewart agreed.

'The question is whether we can risk sparing the capsules,' Tesla said.

'Yes you can,' James said flatly.

'We only have twenty,' Travers said, with a warning tone. 'And people for each.'

'Yes, and we know that enough of them make it,' Lethbridge-Stewart pointed out. 'We also know that none of them do you any good, that I can tell.'

'Really?' Travers asked.

'We've come from a time when your warning capsules have landed, but carrying dead passengers, in the wrong worlds,' Lethbridge-Stewart said, and James nodded.

'More importantly,' he added, 'if some of those did make it in one piece to the past of this world, wouldn't your history have already been changed?'

Travers and Tesla exchanged a glance and a chuckle. 'No,' Tesla said, not unkindly. 'Remember that here we haven't actually launched those capsules yet, so no change can have occurred.'

Lethbridge-Stewart gave them a sceptical look, but didn't say any more. They, after all, were supposed to be the experts.

Lethbridge-Stewart had dozed off while waiting for the capsules to be programmed, and was awakened by the shrill scream of an alarm. He could hear it echoed and replicated throughout the *Phoenix*.

'Attention, attention,' a tannoy voice buzzed. 'Radar tracking reports incoming aircraft. Airspeed Mach two.' Lethbridge-Stewart knew that was much faster than anything any terrestrial air force had in 1945, and he doubted this 1945 was any different in that regard to his own.

'It's them,' Travers said hollowly. 'They found us.'

All of them ran out of the room, following Tesla to the *Phoenix*'s bridge, a huge multifaceted glass dome that offered a 360 degree view of the roiling clouds. Something silver flashed past in the distance.

'Activate defences,' Jürgen ordered, from a chair in the centre of the room.

The boy Alastair was working at a control panel, as were several other people in and out of uniform.

At various points around the circumference of the *Phoenix*, gleaming steel and copper pylons with a slight resemblance to metal Christmas trees moved into position on gimbals. Something metallic and circular swooped out of the clouds, and immediately one of the defensive pylons flashed a bolt of actinic lighting at it, gouging a deep black scar through its near-iridescent skin. An explosion illuminated the clouds around.

James grabbed Tesla by the shoulders. 'You need to launch the capsules, now!'

The Serbian scientist looked flustered for the first time; almost panicked, in fact. 'We can't! Not yet – they're too valuable, and the message recorders haven't been fitted.'

'You designed them as escape vessels, didn't you? If this isn't a time to be escaping, then I don't know what is.'

'But the message—'

Lethbridge-Stewart spun Tesla around. 'You have people who can tell the story, if they survive. Travers… Pick others. Get as many as you can into those lifeboats, because that's what—'

The shockwave from an explosion slammed into Lethbridge-Stewart, knocking the breath from him, and stinging his eardrums. Off-balance, he stumbled, but James caught his arm, holding him upright. Tesla was sprawled lifelessly a couple of feet away.

'Do they use hydrogen in the envelope?' Lethbridge-Stewart said. 'If those blasts reach it—'

'How should I know what they use?' James asked.

Jürgen looked round from his seat. 'No hydrogen, but there are enough flammable and volatile materials on board to cause trouble. Get as many people into the capsules as you can, at gunpoint if necessary.'

James and Lethbridge-Stewart both nodded and saluted, before James grabbed the younger Alastair's arm and ran out of the bridge.

On the level with the capsule launchers, people already had the idea, but Lethbridge-Stewart could see a problem. 'Which ones are ours?'

'Those two at the far end,' James said. 'Left for you, right for me. You should have known better than to sleep on duty, Old Man.'

Lethbridge-Stewart felt his hackles rise, but kept quiet. Another explosion rocked the *Phoenix*, and the clouds visible above the Converter at the hub were beginning to pour aside and upwards, in the most bizarre way. It was like watching sand flow upwards over some vast object, like a giant sword of Damocles descending from the heavens. Bolts of lightning shot up from the defensive pylons but simply crackled along the edges without effect. Another silver disc swept past and exploded.

They ran past several capsules into which people were squeezing themselves, and Lethbridge-Stewart noticed Travers climbing into a capsule.

'One of us should take the lad,' James shouted over the explosions and screeching of protesting metal. 'We can at least save him.'

254

Lethbridge-Stewart nodded, understanding why James wanted that. If Lethbridge-Stewart could have brought his brother back to life… He pointed to Travers. 'I have a better idea. He should go with Travers.'

'Why?'

'Because we know that capsule makes it.'

James's eyes brightened. 'You had a search made. You weren't sure if there was just Travers in it or not.'

Lethbridge-Stewart nodded. 'But something had moved in the cellar where the capsule was. We weren't sure whether it was something that had come in the capsule, or a…' He blinked, as the memory of the boy running in the woods flashed into his mind. 'It was him!'

Together they hurried the boy towards Travers' capsule. 'Travers!' The bearded man looked up from his struggle with the door. Lethbridge-Stewart grabbed the edge, and held it open. 'Take the boy with you.' It wasn't a request, and Travers' expression showed that he knew that. 'How are the capsules launched?'

'Automatically when all twenty doors are sealed.'

'No,' Alastair shouted. 'I want to go with James!'

In response, with a pained look, James shook his head and pushed him back towards the capsule door. 'I'm sorry, but we know you'll survive in this one.' Together, the brothers shoved boy and man into the capsule, and pushed the door shut. Then they ran for their respective capsules.

Lethbridge-Stewart paused by the door. 'Look after him if you make it. He'll miss you if you don't.'

James nodded. 'Don't waste time talking to me.' He stepped across and bundled Lethbridge-Stewart into his capsule, then darted back to his own. 'Wake up at home, and forget the nightmares Beswick gave you, all right, Old Man?' James pulled the door shut after him, and Lethbridge-Stewart could only strap himself into his seat.

For a long moment he thought the launch would never happen, and that the *Phoenix* would disintegrate beforehand. Already the hull was buckling, and debris was being blasted across his field of vision.

Then the world lurched, leaving his stomach somewhere far behind, or so it felt, and his capsule was falling and fading. He caught a glimpse through the thick window of the *Phoenix* listing in flames. Then there was only a flash.

Something exploded in the side of Alastair's head, and he woke up next to a dead man in total darkness. Shaking, biting back a scream, he flailed frantically around for the door, but only found a sharp corner slick with blood. The left side of his face burned with heat and wetness, and somehow that sensation gave him the strength to find the door lever so that he could get out. He just wanted to get away from the dead man, and the pain, and the darkness.

The door fell open and he stumbled through it, punching it shut behind him so that the dead man couldn't follow.

He was in a cellar, as far as he could tell, filled with papers and cardboard boxes. Dust and light showered him from above, through a hole in the ceiling. He hadn't seen proper sunlight in such a long time.

Soldiers had come later, but Alastair didn't know whose side they were on, so he hid in the darkest corner when some of them – including a man and a woman who found the dead man – came into the cellar.

He had skulked around the village for a couple of days after that, and then set off to find James. He was nearly hit by a jeep when crossing the road, but he knew James was out there somewhere, and that he would find him, and things would be happy again.

# — CHAPTER FOURTEEN —

# *Rule Nothing Out*

'Signal from radar control, sir,' an RAF technician said, turning from his switchboard in the Joint Warfare Establishment's traffic control centre to face Colonel Douglas. Professor and Doctor Travers both looked up expectantly. 'An object at eight thousand feet, descending towards Salisbury Plain.'

'Now?' Professor Travers asked.

'Yes, sir.'

'Get a chopper ready,' Douglas ordered. He picked up the nearest phone. 'Get me the Artillery duty officer at Larkhill. I need a search party prepared.'

Lethbridge-Stewart twisted and turned, trying to escape from the choking heat. Something was pressing in on him from every direction, and he desperately tried to push against it. His limbs felt tied and weighted down, and he realised that the weight that felt as though it were on his chest was actually *in* his chest, the dead and used air that could neither escape nor be replaced by fresh air.

He flopped round, kicking out with his feet at the lever on the inside of the door. It wouldn't move, but he could see black earth through it. He was buried, literally, inside a steel coffin, and had no idea how deep in the earth he was.

He kept kicking, sure that his efforts were weakening, and that in fact he'd just asphyxiate himself more quickly by trying. Then, to his astonishment, there was a small miracle.

The lever shifted, and the door buckled open by just an inch or two. A trickle of damp earth fell in, like crumbling chocolate cake, but there was a foot-high column of clear blue sky at the top of the door. Cool fresh air flooded into the capsule.

Lethbridge-Stewart relaxed. He didn't feel himself pass out, but he wouldn't have minded either; there was a difference between blacking out through lack of oxygen, and passing out from the relief after a successful effort.

The air was cleaner and smelled better when he woke again. Lethbridge-Stewart was able to take the time to unbuckle himself from his seat, and prop himself against the door in order to dig himself out. Instead of trying to push the door open – there was far too great a mass of earth pressing against the outside for that – he pulled handfuls of earth into the capsule, shoving it into the space behind the seats.

As he widened a cavity in the earth behind the door, it began to move more freely, and open a little further. In a couple of hours, he had excavated sufficient dirt with his hands to push the door open far enough that he could squeeze through.

He pulled himself up out of the fresh crater, and saw that he was in the middle of a farmer's field. His limbs burned inside, and he knew that he had pushed himself beyond sensible limits over the past days. As the warmth of the sun hit him, the field began to spin out from under his feet and he passed out again.

Major Lethbridge-Stewart and Kyle looked at each other across the helicopter's passenger compartment. 'Colonel Lethbridge-Stewart?' she asked at last. In truth, she wasn't sure what she wanted to hear; that he was out of the way, an enemy agent dealt with, that the major had released him, or that he would be joining them shortly.

The major opened and closed his mouth a couple of times, clearly unsure what to say. 'He... As far as I know he's safe.'

'Where?'

'In his own world.'

'But how?'

'The science is beyond me, Captain, but somehow they got me here, in our world at the right time, and so I have to trust that they managed the same with Alistair.'

'Trust?'

'What's the alternative? That I should feel I got my kid brother back for a short time, and lost him again?' He rested his head on his elbows and let his head droop. 'No. I won't let myself feel that.'

Kyle understood. Maybe it was better to trust that the colonel was back with his comrades, and his job, and his Sally, than to think of him as a dead foreign spy. 'How are we going to describe this in our after-action reports?'

Major Lethbridge-Stewart barked a laugh.

'That would have the advantage of concise brevity,' she said drily. 'But they'll want more than that.'

'Yes... And I have a thought about that. As a matter of fact, one about which I'd like to pick your brains.'

'Of course, sir.'

'These recent events have been well outside the remit of either the Army, Navy, or the Republic Air Force, at least as is. I wonder if, as we approach a new decade, it might be wise to form a special unit to deal with this kind of... anomalous event.'

'A specialist unit?' It seemed like a logical idea to Kyle.

'Yes. A specialist security force, with a remit to protect the Republic from unusual scientific threats. Something separate from the regular army, with a separate rank structure.'

'And you're going to suggest this in your report to Whitehall?'

'Wouldn't you?'

Kyle thought about it. There could be opportunities there that she liked. 'I just might.' After all, who else could be trusted with such a unit?

Private Harris saw it first, mainly because he was bored. While the rest of the artillery platoon had formed up a loose line that stretched across a couple of hundred yards of Salisbury Plain, and started a walking search, he had decided to fetch his best field glasses from the lorry. He was, after all, an artillery spotter, so it felt more natural to him to look for targets through binoculars than to walk around like police constables looking for a body. Sergeant Craig, who had recently transferred in from the BAOR in Germany, had actually agreed with him

The binoculars also meant he could watch out for interesting birds without anybody knowing the difference. If he was lucky he might spot something rare today.

It wasn't long before he had noticed a red kite – common, but always a joy to watch as it swooped and dove and...

He saw it, just off the edge of the military zone: a dark crater in a farmer's field, with metal glinting in the centre. He was bored, but not lazy, and immediately ran towards the rest of the men, who were walking in the wrong direction. 'Sarge! Sarge! I've spotted it!'

'Where, lad?'

Harris pointed, and handed Craig the field glasses. 'Outside the range.' He noticed the sergeant go pale. 'Is something wrong, Sarge?'

'Bloody hell,' Craig muttered, 'another one of them...' He pulled himself together. 'Right, let's go take a look, eh? At the double!'

Craig gathered the platoon around him, and jogged down to the wire fence that separated the firing range from normal rural fields. There Harris led them to the crater.

'Well, it's not an unexploded bomb,' Craig told them. 'I've seen one of these buggers before, so I can promise you that.'

Harris walked around the strange impact site, and almost tripped over the unconscious body that was lying canted against the side of the crater. 'There's a man in here!'

'Ours or theirs?' Craig asked.

'Looks like ours. But what would one of ours be doing here?'

'That's a point, lad, right enough. All right, cuff him before he wakes up, and let's report back to Larkhill.'

Hamilton considered the report he'd received from both Anne Travers and her father. There was a lot in here he

262

didn't like, things that didn't add up. He hoped Lethbridge-Stewart's report would add some clarity, once he'd been fully debriefed.

And then there was Larry Greene. It seemed he had teamed up once again with Harold Chorley – Harry and Larry, the old team – which could be very bad for all of them. Using Greene had been a gamble, one that had paid off, until now. Phone calls would need to be made.

Major Lethbridge-Stewart remained on board the helicopter when it took off, citing a need to report in person to the War Office. That left Kyle in charge of the Establishment, and she was glad to have the chance to get a shower and some hot food, after she checked in at the commandant's office – now her office, for the moment – for any important signals.

She expected a record of some missed phone calls, or telegrams, but not a visitor.

The man in the office was tall and burly, with a somewhat saggy face. His high forehead led to thin wavy hair in a side parting. He knocked out the ashes from his pipe, and walked around Kyle.

'Director,' she said.

'We need to talk, Captain.'

'Do we, indeed? Shall we start with the Phoenix Project and the concept of treason?'

'We could, but we'd both be wasting our breath,' the director said sharply. 'You're not stupid enough to think that you'll ever manage to do my career or me any real harm, or to think that you'd survive trying.'

Kyle fingered her pistol-butt unconsciously, then smiled as sweetly as she could when she realised the fact. 'I don't respond well to bullies or to threats.'

'And I'm not stupid enough to discard valuable assets willy-nilly. Or to make an enemy of the army.'

'So we're talking about something?'

The director made a waving-away gesture. 'Hardt's researches into the capsules is over, whichever way you slice it. There aren't going to be any more arrivals, and the research is—'

'Don't say destroyed, or gone. I'm not stupid enough for that either. I'm sure that plenty of data was archived off-site, where you can access it if need be.'

The director smiled. It wasn't one that invited a similar response. 'Well, let's say the research is de-prioritised in all practical terms. There are other things that are more important in today's world.'

'Such as?'

'We'll get to that when we're in agreement with each other. The War Office will approve your promotion to major, today. You did good work at the Hardt Complex, even if it was inconvenient to some of us.'

'What about Major Lethbridge-Stewart?'

'What about him?'

'He did better work.'

'And I should make him a colonel?' The director barked a laugh, not too dissimilar to the major's. 'Just because he's my son, doesn't mean I'm going to indulge in nepotism or favouritism.'

'Director—'

The director shook his head, and gave her one of his predatory smiles. 'Call me Gordon.'

*

It had been a long week of medical examinations, and thorough debriefings (which mostly involved others talking *to* him), and Lethbridge-Stewart was just beginning to feel that he could trust his senses again. He was surprised how much of a difference that made to his mind-set; he still couldn't trust his memories, thanks to the psychoactive drugs that had been pumped into him during his time in East Germany, but he was able to trust the present. At least he thought he could.

Not for the first time, he found himself wondering how much of his past was actually true. 'The story of my life,' he told himself as he shaved, ready to report to General Hamilton for the first time since his return.

'What was that?' Sally asked, from outside the bathroom of his Pimlico flat.

'Nothing,' he said. 'Just talking to myself.'

'That's a bad habit.'

'Probably, though—' He broke off, realising that he had been about to give Marianne's opinion on the matter. Why should her opinion matter, when he wasn't even sure she had really existed? Sally's was the one that mattered, surely.

He left the bathroom and joined Sally in the kitchen where she was preparing two cups of tea. He placed his arms around her waist. 'Did you miss me?' he asked.

She turned around so she was looking up at him, her nose inches from his mouth. 'Of course I did. I worried. A lot. But you're back now,' she said, and tip-toed up to kiss him. 'That's what matters.'

Gordon Lethbridge-Stewart, Director of External Security, had one last call to make before returning home. The

London Bounds location near Deepdene had a holding facility, and there he watched through a one-way mirror as a teenage boy of maybe fifteen years bounced a tennis ball off the floor and wall of an interrogation room.

Bounce, bounce, catch, over and over. Good reflexes, Gordon thought. As if he heard, the boy turned his head, glaring through the mirror with his one remaining eye. 'I don't know who you are, but I know you're there,' he said aloud, without missing a beat of his solitary game.

Gordon looked down at the faded photograph in his hand. It showed three boys outside Redrose Cottage, taken over twenty years ago. One of the boys was James, the other his childhood friend Ray Phillips, but it was the youngest of the three that Gordon looked at. The face, although a good seven years younger, matched the face of the boy in the holding room. The face of his dead son, Alistair.

Gordon pressed a button next to the mirror window, so that the boy could hear him. 'Tell me, son, have you ever considered joining the Army? I see a great future for you there.'

General Hamilton shook Lethbridge-Stewart's hand firmly when he entered Hamilton's office at Strategic Command in Fugglestone. 'Colonel! Welcome back.'

'It's good to be back, sir.'

And it was. He had begun to wonder if he'd ever see Strategic Command again. Although he had never been stationed there, he'd spent so much time in Hamilton's office over the years it was almost like a second home. And that's what it felt like now; coming home.

'I'll bet it is,' Hamilton said. 'Considering where you've

been. I'm given to understand East Germany isn't a fun place.'

'I wish I could tell you, really.'

Hamilton held up Lethbridge-Stewart's report. Which was more than a little empty. Lethbridge-Stewart knew he'd have to make a fuller report at some point, but right now was not the time. He had too much to sift through mentally, to determine the fact from the fiction which had been forced on him by the drugs.

'You mean they kept you unconscious, or...?' Hamilton asked.

'Well, I was somewhere east and south of Leipzig; that much I know. But beyond that...'

'Was it bad?'

Lethbridge-Stewart hesitated, and shrugged. Hamilton wanted answers, but Lethbridge-Stewart had none to give. Not yet at least. 'The question I have to ask myself isn't whether it was bad, or crossed a line from interrogation to torture. The question that preys on me, sir, is how much of it was real. Or, indeed, whether any of it was real.'

Hamilton frowned. 'How do you mean?'

'I have memories of doing things that simply can't have happened. Meeting my brother James, a major in the Coldstream even though he died as a child. I was apparently there for four months, though I've only been gone from here for three weeks,' Lethbridge-Stewart said, glancing at the daily calendar on Hamilton's desk. Saturday 3rd May, it read. He had left for Cyprus on Monday 14th April. He cleared his throat. 'And I even met a younger version of me...'

Hamilton glanced down at the report, a look of

understanding crossing his face. 'I wish I knew what to say.'

'I wish I knew what to know.'

'Right.'

'I mean... I wish I could be sure which of my memories were real, and which were put there by Soviet interrogators.'

'Well, I think we can rule out that the man you mentioned was your brother.'

'Yes,' Lethbridge-Stewart said, although he knew his tone betrayed his doubt. It was still a jumble, and considering all that had happened to him since taking over from Pemberton in London... Was it any wonder that he had hallucinated his brother and time travel?

Hamilton picked up another report, somewhat more substantial than that which Lethbridge-Stewart had written. 'Well, the capsules were certainly real enough, but I imagine that getting you involved with them was just an opportunistic thing. They probably thought we'd been investigating them since before your flight left.'

'I don't think I can really rule anything out, sir.' Logically Lethbridge-Stewart knew Hamilton was probably right, but a voice in his head kept reminding him of a phrase he'd heard somewhere: *knowing isn't the same as feeling*.

Hamilton put the report down. 'Well, the next order of business is to get you back in the saddle. The best thing to do when you fall off a bicycle is to get right back on it, isn't it?' Lethbridge-Stewart nodded his agreement. 'Well, it strikes me that you've had enough R&R for one year, and since the doctors are of the opinion that being grounded by a return to work will be good therapy for you...'

'I should still make that trip to Tibet—'

'All things considered, we probably should ease you in

with a more local matter. Well, there is a potential connection to Tibet.'

'Local matter?'

'Kathmandu.'

'You're not going to tell me the little idol is really some kind of alien?'

'Not Kipling, Colonel. This Kathmandu is a musical act; a pop group. Their lead singer, Ed Hill, is making a comeback.'

'I'm rather afraid music isn't my speciality,' Lethbridge-Stewart admitted.

Hamilton grunted. 'Doesn't have to be. Do you remember the Revolution Man?'

It struck a distant memory. He'd read about it in the papers a couple of years ago. Some anarchist and his followers causing trouble. 'Vaguely, sir.'

'Well, it seems that was Ed Hill, and he's doing some kind of concert in Wembley soon.' Hamilton handed him the file. 'It's all here. Right up your ally.'

'Not sure I see how, sir.'

Hamilton nodded to the file. 'Read it,' he said. 'This fellow Hill's making a comeback from the dead.'

Thank You

This book could never have happened without the (long-suffering) support of Andy and Shaun at Candy Jar, and I'm very grateful to them – and to you, the patient reader – for their patience and understanding in what has been an unusual process for me, punctuated by illness and bereavement. It's also the first time I've written a book without an outline first.

*David A McIntee, Wetherby, England, September 2015*

The editors would like to thank Marcus R Gilman for German translations.

# Beast Of Fang Rock

On Fang Rock Jennie Rudge was also making progress. She was a great believer in ghosts – had been all her life. So when the opportunity came to spend a night at Fang Rock she'd jumped at it. Her mum thought her mad, but then she always did. The lamp room, although not out of bounds to them, was supervised, with the principal-assistant light keeper, Ivan Heggessey, stationed at the gate at the top of the steep steps.

Jennie smiled at him, and with a few muttered words of caution, the light keeper opened the small gate and allowed Jennie to enter the lamp room. She walked around the lamp, or the optic as the light keepers liked to call it, careful not to look directly into the light as it flashed every ten seconds. She always imagined the walk-space around the optic would be wider, but it would have been a squeeze to pass another while walking around. According to what she had read, the old lamp room, prior to the fire, had been a lot larger, and the lamp itself much smaller.

She looked out of the window at the gallery beyond. Entry onto the gallery was strictly prohibited, but she had to admit that's where she wanted to be. She knew the stories of Fang Rock well enough, knew that if you stood on the gallery long enough, facing east, you would hear the voice of Lord Palmerdale, his tortured screams as he was attacked and thrown over the gallery railings to meet his painful death on the rocks below.

She looked back. The light keeper was still standing there, but he was looking away, facing the ladder. Jennie turned to the small brass plaques screwed to the iron wall beneath the windows. There were four such plaques, each of them indicating which way you were facing on the compass. She walked around the lamp room until she was facing east. Beside her was the hatch that led to the gallery.

'I imagine it's lonely up here, eh?'

Jennie turned around at the voice, expecting to see the light keeper approaching her. But she was alone. Another voice responded, this one younger, his accent more befitting someone from Hampshire.

'You make do, sir.'

'I don't suppose the wage is very good, either.'

Jennie stood still, listening intently. The two voices continued, drawing closer to her.

'Oh, it could be worse,' said the younger voice. 'They keep you in steady work.'

'I daresay a bit of extra for the pot wouldn't go amiss, though, eh? Fifty pounds, perhaps?'

Jennie smiled. She had read about this. It was Lord Palmerdale, trying to bribe the expectant light keeper, Vince Hawkins. A shiver passed through Jennie.

'It is important I get a message to London. You are familiar with the apparatus downstairs?'

Jennie mouthed the words along with Vince. 'It's the Trinity House telegraph, sir. Not for civilian use.'

'Fifty pounds is all I have about my person, but I can

give you another fifty pounds when I return to London.'

Jennie closed her eyes, imagining Palmerdale showing Vince the money. She'd seen daguerreotypes of the two men, Palmerdale looking smug and all entitled with his stupid moustache, while Vince always looked to Jennie like a man who was just a little too trusting... but definitely cute with it.

'That's a... I don't want to be caught up in anything illegal.'

Jennie took a deep breath and opened her eyes. It was exactly as she had heard. With one last glance at the light keeper by the ladder, Jennie crouched down and opened the hatch.

'Illegal! Don't be so daft, Hawkins,' the voice of Lord Palmerdale said.

Outside it was cold. Jennie wrapped her arms around herself, wishing she had dressed a little more appropriately, and peered over the guardrail. Inside the lamp room it was hard to truly get a sense of height. Even though she knew the lighthouse was 132 feet high, looking out through the window with the English coast a vague shape in the distance, there was no tangible feeling of being high up. But now, standing on the narrow gallery with only the guardrail stopping her from toppling over, Jennie felt the height. Luckily any chance of her actually falling was curtailed by the scaffold-like cage that surrounded the gallery: the support struts for the helipad that now sat atop the lamp tower. She looked up. There was a ladder that led to the helipad, but she didn't want to risk climbing it in this wind. She was pushing her luck as it was.

'Gear!' she said, trying her best to hold back the smile

on her cold lips, the light air almost taking the word from her.

She looked down, placing her hands firmly on the railing, and couldn't help but feel the urge to jump. Just at the thought of it, her heart was in her throat. She'd never do it, of course, but she knew she wanted to.

'...if the Beast has come back, well, we all know the legend. Two keepers dead, one driven mad by fear.'

Jennie looked around slowly and almost slipped in surprise. Through the window, inside the lamp room, she could see Vince Hawkins. The young man, looking not much older than Jennie, was dressed in a white polo-neck jumper and a thick woolly hat. He stood there with his arms folded, looking both perplexed and worried. He was talking to another man, a little taller than Vince, dressed in a grey frock coat, with a head of dark unruly curls.

'Reuben is out of his mind, Ben's dead. I'm the only one left.'

'That's superstitious rot,' the other man said, his voice deep.

'It's not! Look at Ben.'

'Eight of us, Vince, against one of it. When it attacks, we'll be ready.'

Jennie frowned. She had read transcripts of many of the conversations overheard from the ghosts, and they were always the same. Replayed over and over again like an 8-track on repeat. But she had never read anything about nine people being in the lighthouse in 1902, or that an unknown something was attacking them. The transcripts made it clear what had happened, and it was a conclusion many people across England had drawn. Reuben had killed them.

So who was the man talking to Vince? Jennie had spent many hours, days, months even, researching the haunting of Fang Rock and she knew the faces of all seven people involved. But the man in the lamp room – he was new!

And just what was this 'it' the man referred to?

Movement dragged her eyes and mind back to the gallery. Beside her, looking much like his photograph, dressed as he was in his Edwardian dinner suit, stood Lord Henry Palmerdale, a somewhat unscrupulous financier from London at the turn of the century. Jennie had tried to look him up, but there was scant information on him. Had he lived, perhaps Palmerdale would have amounted to something, but he was cut off before his prime and, even then, he had a reputation for cheating his way into his money.

For a brief moment Jennie was eye to eye with Palmerdale and, despite his mode of dress, it was clear that before her was a man with something to hide. Palmerdale looked out across the English Channel, peering through the night, looking for... Jennie wasn't sure. Probably the fortune in London to which he had been trying to return before his yacht came afoul of Fang Rock. For many years it was believed to be Palmerdale who had killed the other six people; so much of the recorded ghostly conversations and arguments were concerned with his aggressive need to return to London, talk of bribes and blackmail. But more recent observations had revealed the truth about Reuben.

Jennie knew that ghosts were often considered malevolent, but she believed they were simply echoes of the past. Not lost souls tormented in their isolation. And so she stood there watching, keyed but not fearful.

Then it happened.

A strange green glow emanated from below the guardrail. Jennie looked over, careful to maintain her balance, and saw what looked to her like a large green jellyfish complete with tendrils that writhed around it. But it was no jellyfish, Jennie knew that. It was... alien somehow. Palmerdale was also glancing over the edge, his upper torso passing through the cage – it hadn't existed back in 1902, of course, there had been just a simple guardrail – but before he had time to consider what he was seeing, a tendril lashed out and wrapped itself around his neck.

Electricity arched all over Palmerdale's body and he let out a piercing scream. Jennie knew she'd never forget the sound. It was full of so much pain and horror. The sound of a man who knew his life was about to be painfully torn from him. Just like his body, which was violently torn from the gallery and flung over the railing.

Jennie couldn't watch any more. She knew she could do nothing, that Palmerdale had died almost seventy years ago, but nonetheless it seemed so real – like it was really happening now!

It was exactly *why* she had insisted to her friend that they took up the offer for a visit.

132 feet below, Jim repositioned his camera for a better shot of the lamp room, a task not made simple by the uneven craggy ground that made up Fang Rock.

He looked through the camera. ''Ere, ain't that one of your lot up there?'

He was accompanied by one of the students, a teenager

from Cornwall called Owain, who seemed more interested in walking about the rock than drinking with the rest of his lot inside the lighthouse. Even now they could just about hear the distant sounds of *The Dawntreader* coming from the lighthouse. Jim wasn't too sure if he liked Joni Mitchell's music or not, a fact he and Owain had been discussing before Jim spotted the figure outside the lamp room. Owain did; he especially liked *The Fiddle and the Drum* from her new LP, an anti-war song aimed at America and its war in Vietnam, and had recommended that Jim listen to it. Jim liked peace as much as the next person, but he was old enough to remember that sometimes you just had to say no, and that war was not always as avoidable as so many young people liked to believe.

Owain shielded his eyes from the wind and rain and looked up. 'Could be,' he said in his soft Cornish accent. Jim let him look through the camera. Owain laughed. 'Yeah, that's Jennie Rudge. Good chick, really great on the guitar. She's teaching me how to play. All the way here she's been going on about visiting the gallery, though. Looks like they let her in after all.' He wiped his long wet fringe out of his eyes.

Jim pointed at Owain's earring, the silver semaphore symbol used by the followers of the Campaign for Nuclear Disarmament. 'Ain't that cold out here?'

'Yeah, man, but you know that's how it goes when you're on a rocky isle in the English Channel, right? Which bit of you isn't cold? Stung a bit at first, but getting used to it.'

Jim laughed. He liked Owain; he seemed to have his head more screwed on than most of the students he'd been introduced to since arriving on Fang Rock. Mostly the event seemed to attract the hippies, with their bright glasses and clothes not even slightly suited to being on a rock like this one. Obviously Owain was as much one for peace and one-love as the rest of the beautiful people, but he at least had the good sense to dress in a manner suitable for a rock lighthouse. Owain handed Jim the blunt they had been sharing, but Jim shook his head. There was only so much of that he could stomach. Owain shrugged and returned it to his mouth.

'You believe in ghosts?' Jim asked.

Owain considered this, his eyes distant. 'Kind of, yeah. But not in the way some people do. I think ghosts are more echoes of people that once existed, than any kind of supernatural creatures. There's a scientific reason for them. You've heard of the stone tape theory?'

Jim had to admit he hadn't.

'It's the idea that emotional or traumatic events are stored in rock and can be played back in certain circumstances, which is why you get haunted houses... or *light*houses.' Owain smiled. 'Not my first haunted gig,' he said.

Jim pursed his lips. He wasn't convinced, but it was clear Owain was. Well, Jim had travelled enough to know that people usually had good reasons for what they believed, and it wasn't up to him to judge them on that.

He turned back to his camera.

He blinked.

'What the hell!' He pointed. 'Look!'

They both watched as a flash appeared in the dark sky. It was an odd reddish colour, and it stretched out, leaving behind it a red trail of light.

'A shooting star?' Jim wondered out loud.

'A red one?' Owain shook his head and looked through the camera lens. 'Can you zoom in?'

'I can, yeah.' Jim barely got a chance to before Owain stepped away from the camera with a huge grin on his face.

'That is no shooting star. Look,' he said, and Jim looked at it through his camera. He swallowed. There was a shape inside the light.

'It's a bleedin' UFO!' he exclaimed, and wondered at the strength of the blunt.

'Mint,' Owain said still smiling. 'Knew something like this would happen eventually. My uncle's going to dig it.'

'Your uncle?'

'Yeah.' Owain pointed at the light as it dropped closer to the English Channel. 'Keep filming,' he said, 'the colonel needs as much proof as he can get.'

Jim kept filming. Suddenly the assignment had got interesting.

*Available from Candy Jar Books*

## LETHBRIDGE-STEWART: THE FORGOTTEN SON
by Andy Frankham-Allen

For Colonel Alistair Lethbridge-Stewart his life in the Scots Guards was straightforward enough; rising in the ranks through nineteen years of military service. But then his regiment was assigned to help combat the Yeti incursion in London, the robotic soldiers of an alien entity known as the Great Intelligence. For Lethbridge-Stewart, life would never be the same again.

Meanwhile in the small Cornish village of Bledoe a man is haunted by the memory of an accident thirty years old. The Hollow Man of Remington Manor seems to have woken once more. And in Coleshill, Buckinghamshire, Mary Gore is plagued by the voice of a small boy, calling her home.

What connects these strange events to the recent Yeti incursion, and just what has it all to do with Lethbridge-Stewart?

A brand-new series of novels set just after the *Doctor Who* serial *The Web of Fear*, featuring the characters and concepts created by Mervyn Haisman & Henry Lincoln.

ISBN: 978-0-9931191-5-6

*Also available from Candy Jar Books*

# Tommy Parker: Destiny Will Find You
by Anthony Ormond

When Tommy Parker packs his bag and goes to his grandpa's house for the summer he has no idea that his life is about to change forever.

But that's exactly what happens when his grandpa lets him in on a fantastic secret. He has a pen that lets him travel through his own memories and alter the past. Imagine that! Being able to travel into your own past and re-write your future.

*Tommy Parker: Destiny Will Find You!* is an exhilarating adventure that redefines the time travel genre.

You'll never look at your memories in quite the same way again...

ISBN: 978-0-9928607-1-4